GUARDIAN OF THE PINES

THE WINDSOME SERIES

GUARDIAN OF THE PINES

THE WINDBORNE SERIES

LAUREL WANROW

Sprouting Star Press

Copy Edit by Joyce Lamb
Cover Design by Deranged Doctor Design
Created with Vellum

Wanrow, Laurel

  Guardian of the Pines/ Laurel Wanrow. ~ 1st ed.
  ISBN 978-1-943469-15-4

First Edition: April 2019

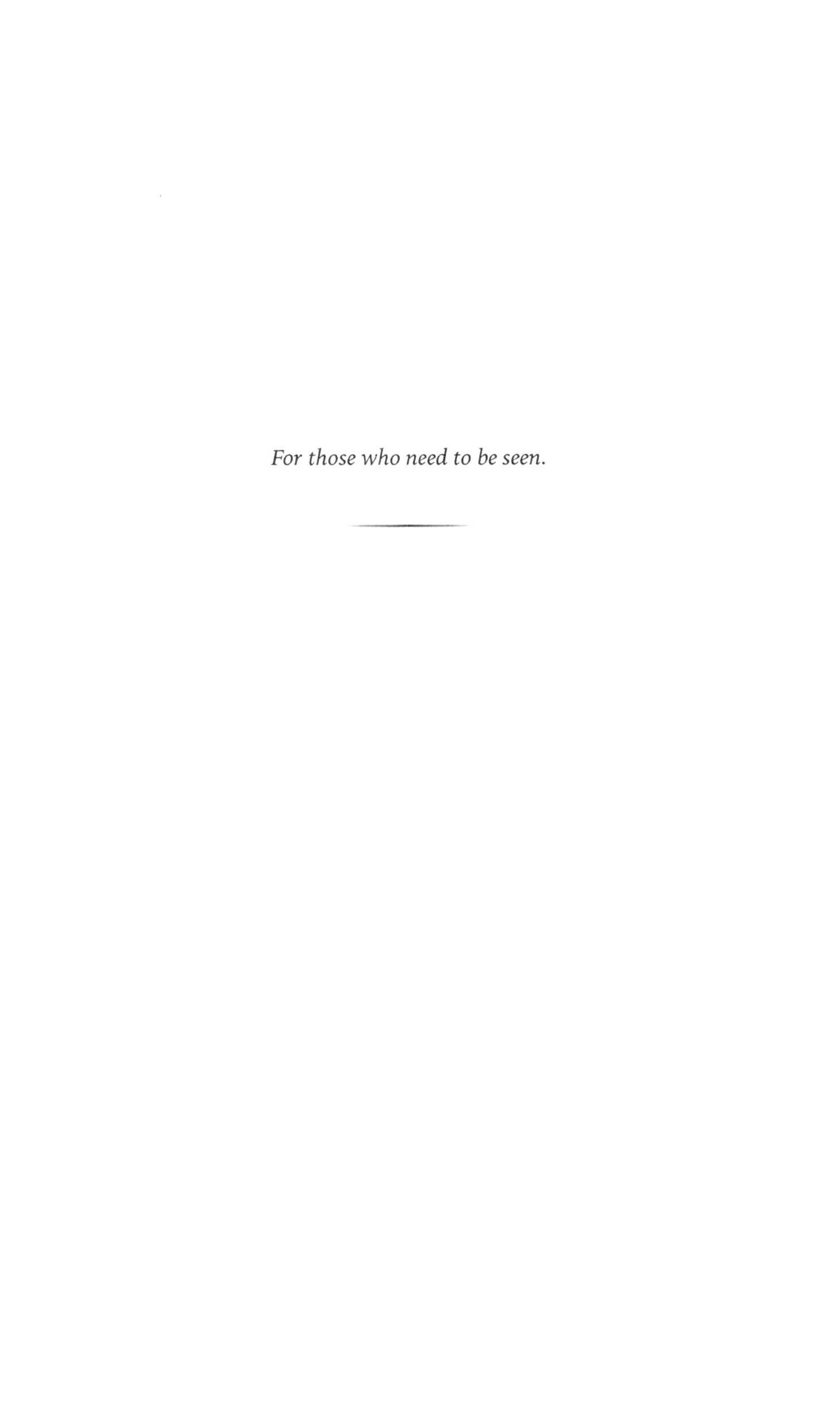

For those who need to be seen.

1

METHODS OF ESCAPE

Well past midnight, Cor glided in a serpentine motion down dark, tree-lined streets. His longboard's wheels made a rhythmic *thump* crossing the concrete's seams, and he pumped his wings every five thumps to keep up his speed. As the houses, dressed up with flowers and guarded by fences, spread farther apart, he slowed and turned a corner. Ancient rowans arched overhead, making the passage feel like a cathedral. Tonight, he'd timed his entrance perfectly with the crescendo mounting in his earbuds.

With a flourish of swinging arms, he pointed left, then right. Gold magic sailed from his fingertips and filled the gaps between branches. Some shone like soap bubbles, others caught webs and left glowing lines in lacy patterns. The best trapped leaves. His magic lit their tissue from within and left the veins as dark skeletons.

At the block's end, Cor swung a wide arc in the intersection to face his creation and halted with a stomp of his foot,

Dvorák's violin concerto racing to its crashing peak. Every tree was aglow with his stained-glass windows, the farthest fading ones enhancing the impression that this natural wonder extended forever.

The music ended. With his thumb, he clicked off his mobile phone, savoring the last notes and flickers of light until his magical forest fell dark again.

If he could get to a truly wild version of these old trees, he'd never leave.

Cor pulled a pair of leather gloves from his pockets, tugged them on and picked up the longboard. To earn an internship at a Windborne forest took *being* in one place long enough to build complex tree spells. These rowans contained his best shot from the summer. Not the light show. That was the icing on the cake. The underlying magic he'd sparked came from weeks of developing a defensive spell against boring insects, a project he could show wizard foresters at the Windborne Arboriculture Conference.

If he managed to get into the exclusive meeting.

He walked across the intersection, checked to verify no one else was about, then flapped his dark brown wings to rise above the high stone wall surrounding the Gruen Estate. Spruce boughs reached from the inside, giving the illusion of an open, friendly place—only an illusion. Still, the branches were useful for marking his entry point, and their shadows camouflaged his brown skin and black clothing while he hovered between them and searched the top of the wall... *Red stone, red stone...*

He spotted it and lowered to inches above the wall's magical shield before he shrank his wings to nothing but pure energy and drew it in. That, and the rest of his magic, he shut into his storage cores. The estate's security would detect a magical-aided entry—and a physical one if he wasn't careful.

Excitement surged through him, as it always did at this point of sneaking back in. With his sister gone at art camp, he'd had to find his own fun. Some of this she would have tattled, but he missed having her to confide in about his problems with freakin' Marty—or his plan to pretend to be an attendee at a conference of adults.

The ball of one booted foot tapped down on the red stone, and he moved the other to a flecked stone two over, both of which he'd removed the warding from. With his free hand, Cor reached up and found the ropes with carabiners knotted to the ends. He clipped one to a ring welded to the longboard and let it swing first. By the time it stilled, he'd screw-locked a second rope to the climbing harness he wore. He grasped the rope in gloved hands, folded his body into a crouch—damn, he needed to lay off the doughnuts Master Harold so willingly shared— then aimed for the trunk of an old pine set back from the wall.

The aim was what had taken practice. Hours at the climbing center of holding his elbows in and feet together, weight balanced. Any bit of him sticking beyond the two-foot slot of the exclusion tunnel he'd spelled into the barrier and he'd set off the alarm.

He sprang off the wall. In a rush of wind, the swing carried him ten, fifteen, then twenty feet and past the inner edge of the zone designed to detect people jumping the wall. The swing stayed true to the target. He kicked up his feet as stoppers against the pine's trunk and bent his knees to absorb the impact while throwing an arm over the nearest branch.

Safely inside the barrier, he waited, listening. Only the breeze whistling through the treetops. And an exchange of hoots.

He stowed his equipment, collected his longboard and climbed down. Slate paths for visitors wound over the grounds, but he took the most direct route to the manor house through the trees.

A shadow dove at him. He dodged—and smacked his head on a branch. "Ouch!"

Kee, came a soft but insistent hoot, and an owlet landed on a branch in front of him, ducking her head and fluttering her wings, her baby calls still croaky *kee-wiks.*

Cor laughed. "You brilliant beggar. No, go hunt your own food."

Rubbing his head, he offered his leather-clad arm. When the tawny owl hopped on, he petted her crown, removing a few baby-down feathers she'd missed preening. He hadn't fed her in weeks, but bringing her mice that had invaded the greenhouse had probably saved this youngest hatchling. Her larger, older brothers usually nabbed the prey dropped off by the parent birds. Still, she begged. *She's not a pet…* That was hard to remember with all her cuteness. She was as close to a pet he'd ever had, since their family traveled so much.

"You're a beauty, Toots." He rubbed his knuckles over her open beak.

Squeaking, Toots walked up his arm, sat on his shoulder and nuzzled his neck. He smoothed her wings to her back, hugging her light body to his. For all of thirty seconds. She nibbled at his earring and, when he brushed her off, yanked a curl of his hair.

"Hey, bugger off." She fluttered to the nearest branch, then hop-flew along as he walked and tried to pretend she wasn't there.

Everyone wanted something from him tonight. Aunt Syl haranguing him about chores, the nursery saying they needed twice the inventory if he wanted them to carry his seedlings for sale and, an hour ago, Marty demanding payment for the *privilege* of walking the streets over near the falls. Bloody arrogant boss of his bloody neighborhood.

If the only beeches in Bonterra didn't grow on that hillside above the river, he'd never go there. But those seedlings sold the best. Despite the ache from an energy shockball to his thigh, Cor was glad he'd refused to bend to the gang's demands. For the first time, he was carving out a place in the wizard city he'd been born in.

When the owlet landed on him again, he grasped her around the middle and tossed her into the air. "Go hunt. That's what you do." With a thought, he activated his energy cores and released magic to form up his wings and arched them to deter her. As much as he liked Toots, he couldn't let her waste her hunting time following him. She had to find her own territory. He knew little about birds, but figured the parents hunted the estate, and it wasn't hard to spot other tawny owls in the city. His birds needed a permanent home, someplace they wouldn't need to leave, in wilder country.

So did he. In September—three weeks from now—his parents would return from their summer's travel for the Gruen Foundation, and their family would be off again. Autumn in the States. The winter in Costa Rica. Spring somewhere else he'd forgotten after hearing they'd have only a week between in Bonterra. He had presented several internship possibilities—all shot down. Rooting out a winning option during the conference would be his final hope before he was dragged off.

He hit a path and kept to certain slates that weren't warded. The trees became smaller and more ornamental closer to the manor house. A few lights lit the inside, but the conservatory to the side was dark, as were the windows of the old cook's cottage, both the main floor and his aunt's bedroom window upstairs.

"Nice evening for a walk," said a deep voice.

Cor stumbled. A frantic flap of wings lifted him, and at the last second, he landed on the wrong stone—

Lights flared to life, freezing him like a deer.

Beyond them, in the dark, someone sighed. "My mistake," the man said. "Cancel the alert."

"Got it, Master Harold," came the guard's voice over the radio.

The lights cut off, but their damage was done; Cor was now night blind. *And caught, blast it!* In his personal scoring system, he had to make it to his room across from Aunt Syl's or the success of sneaking out and in again wasn't credited. He blinked and raked up the curls over his head, checking they weren't flattened or had stuck leaves to reveal his activities.

"And a nice night for riding, I suppose," Master Harold added with an amber-lit gesture to Cor's board.

"True," he agreed warily. The head gardener had hired him to water in the greenhouses and garden beds. For someone so old, Harold kept terrible hours.

"Have something for you, if you have a minute." Master Harold pivoted through the open conservatory door, casting a dim light around his large frame. His bald head glinted like richly polished chestnuts, and he wore his usual evening attire, a monklike robe that he said was most comfortable after a day of dirty work in the gardens and greenhouse. Master Harold wasn't frowning, or even remotely angry, but his full cheeks were lifted in an annoying, knowing smile within his neat, sycamore-bark-silver beard.

Cor sucked his teeth, a sound the old man had told him came across as bad as back talk and recommended he not do it. Cor couldn't seem to break the habit. "I do," he said quickly to try to smooth things over—Master Harold hadn't reported him—and picked his way across the path on the correct stones.

"Still would like to know how you learned so quickly which to use," Master Harold said.

Cor doubted the truth would be accepted—the tree roots had shown him. Harold preferred the botanical rather than the magical side of plant growth, ironically, since the Gruen Foundation focused on increasing tree energy. Instead, Cor dug a handful of beechnuts from his pocket that he'd scavenged from the leaf litter. "More to start tomorrow. Copper beech."

Master Harold dipped his bald head approvingly before

taking the main walkway through the conservatory. Cor closed the door behind them—the moisture still felt correct, so Master Harold hadn't had it open long—and propped his board against it, then followed. The air was scented with orchids, the rich humus of the soil and something new tonight.

"Delivery?"

Master Harold cast him another glance. "After you left. The dozen juniper bonsai starts we ordered."

"You want me to pot them up?"

"I said I had something for you, not a chore. Which reminds me." The older man paused at the bed where Cor had been working that afternoon and pointed. "Forget something?"

No...he'd finished transplanting the orchids and put away the pots. To be certain, he stepped closer. Something twinkled green in the dark.

Leafbringer.

Cor groaned. He reached, flowing gold magic to his fingers, and the broadsword wiggled in the ground where he'd stuck it after using it to take yew cuttings and plant them. The sword rose and sailed lazily to him, not as promptly as it would for his sister, Hazel, but it came. And hilt first.

Harold handed him a rag. "Make sure the soil is out of the engraving and get it back to the armory. Tonight, so I have no questions to answer during the morning's tours."

At least Harold didn't rail at him about getting permission. Leafbringer's magic invigorated his plants the same as it did for Hazel, so why not use it? With him wiping the weapon, they left the conservatory and approached a door just inside the main house. Master Harold put a hand to it, letting his magic flow unlock it.

The old gas lamp flared as they entered, a combination of a motion detector and magic. Stirring the rich, moist scent, Master Harold waded among dropped tools, gloves and plants on every surface. Some he'd forgotten he was carrying when he returned to his office. Other pots on the broad stone windowsills he was nursing along. Harold plucked an envelope from the fronds of a fern and handed it to him.

Cor glanced at him before tucking Leafbringer under one arm. He broke the seal and lifted the flap. The cream card matched, and above the printing was—

He stuffed it back and shoved the lot at his boss. "No, thanks." Cor strode from the office before he could snatch back the envelope, because an *invitation* to the Windborne Arboriculture Conference meant everything. Listening to the latest research, meeting the forest wizards and finding one who needed a worker to do anything that would get him someplace green where he could stay for a year or two. He pushed the conservatory door, before remembering the sword and backtracking down the hall.

Footsteps sounded behind him. "You didn't even read it."

"Can't take a handout." His aunt would be furious. She'd certainly tell his dad. His parents' rules were he and his sister had to earn stuff, not be handed it because of who they were.

"It's a job, as a volunteer gofer for the conference. You'll be running your legs off, which certainly isn't a handout."

Cor stopped. A…job? "Not as an attendee?"

Master Harold barked a laugh. "That would take more pull than I've got. One of the coordinators asked if I had any academy students who could fill tomorrow's last-minute vacancy. I recommended you."

Cor turned. "Me?" The question spilled out before he had a chance to think of how bloody desperate he sounded. "I'm not in academy and likely can't swing it next year."

"You. The chap who won't study for the entrance exams because he'd rather visit the ailing elms across town and ward them against infection. Who steals my catalogs and orders exotic bare root stock with his own pocket money and hides the saplings in the optimal beds. Who will have those bonsai planted before my first cup of coffee is even made."

So the old man had noticed.

Master Harold held out the envelope.

He shouldn't, but…a job Aunt Syl would agree to. He took it and pulled out the card, lighting his own fingers this time. He scanned where and when to report, attire to wear and duties. "Field trips?"

"Likely you'll just have to fill in for what the sick gal was supposed to cover." His boss shrugged.

Cor pretended to read it over again, but his mind rolled with the possibilities. He'd already researched the speakers, their home enclave tree species, their pet research projects. He'd have to prioritize who he'd most like to ask about internships. *If only I don't blow it.*

"I might not get to those bonsai."

"I will. Do me the honor of being on time and sticking to the duties they assign, not disappearing like you are wont to do. If I might suggest…"

Cor stuffed the card and envelope in his jacket pocket. "What?" He brushed a hand over the black leather. "I should color my clothes into something pretty?"

"Leave your leather armor at home for once."

"You've been listening to Aunt Syl. I don't wear it to put people off." But it did. People looked at him, a black guy in black, and zipped their gazes away in disdain, rejecting him before even finding out anything about him. Cor glanced at his hand, the warm red-brown of sessile oak leaves in autumn compared to the sleeve's true black. At least the jacket let him fade into the background when alone in a crowd, because when he was beside his dad, he was never overlooked.

"First impressions matter. Your docent uniform will be suitable. Consider toning down the jewelry. And try to smile. Like you're happy to be there."

No one needed to know if he was happy or not. Now that he had a legitimate way in, he simply had to say enough without being a show-off or bloody sappy. Too much was riding on his chance to get a real internship to mess it up by blurting how keen he was about trees.

2

IT'S ALL ABOUT THE CONTROL

Boulder, Colorado

"You gonna wait for Mr. Magic?"

The calculus text fell from Fern's hand. The commotion following the school dismissal bell drowned out its thud at the bottom of her locker, but not her friend Amanda's laugh. *No!* There was no way Amanda knew. Fern wanted to jump in after the book.

"Don't try and kid me, Fern Fields." Amanda leaned closer to Fern's locker. "I see the way your eyes light up when he comes into advanced biology. Beri Moors has you under his spell." She stretched his name into a howl of *Mooooors* that echoed within the metal locker.

Fern steeled herself against the tingle rising in her arms. *Please, not now.* Not when she'd convinced Mom her control of her magic could be trusted, even with her human friends, at their human school, Boulder High. If so much as a green spark slipped out, Amanda would see it in the shadowed locker.

"Cute, cute, cute. Tall, tall, tall. Need I say more? Go for him, girl!"

Fern sagged in relief. Amanda didn't know. Nothing had slipped out, words or magic, thank the Golden—oops! Fern picked up her text, shoved it into her pack, slammed the door, spun her lock and swung her long hair out of the way to shoulder the pack.

"Ha! I knew it. You're blushing." Amanda—whose creamy cheeks never reddened—grinned and punched Fern's now tingle-free arm. "Tell him quick, 'cause he's only here for the school year, and senior year is gonna fly for us."

Fern leaned against her locker, not meeting Amanda's grin and *not* fanning her neck. Her olive skin would hide the worst of it. She'd shared a lot with Amanda over the years. But not that after seventeen years of living like a human she now had magic. Or that she used a portal to visit her gran on a hidden island thousands of miles away in the Irish Sea. Or that she was now in charge of Gran's magical Meadows habitat. But Beri was a harder secret to keep.

One she didn't want to keep.

Smiling, she turned her head, knowing Amanda was watching. "I might talk to him."

The short brunette squealed. "Yes! Then when you go to Scotland to visit him, *I'll* visit you and find my own hunky Scot. But no redheads for me. We'll make mine tall, *dark* and handsome."

"Ireland," Fern said as she scanned the throng of students jostling their way toward freedom.

"What?"

Oh, she'd said that out loud without thinking. "He lives in Ireland now."

"So you have talked to him," Amanda said as she hopped in place. "See him?"

She had little hope of spotting anyone before Fern did. Being six feet tall helped in some situations.

Amanda tugged her arm. "Talk to him before you get on the

bus. You've got five minutes alone. Then during the ride up the canyon, you can fall into him on the curves, maybe even grip his hand and keep holding it."

Fern snorted. "Yeah, right." But the fact was, she *was* waiting for Beri. They usually touched base in the corridor after school, just to make sure Beri had everything clear or that nothing *unusual* had happened that they needed to call Mom about.

"What's the matter with getting cuddly with him?" Amanda asked. "I know you've never had a boyfriend, but you get used to that warm, fuzzy feel fast."

Ha! Fern could tell her plenty about warm *magic*. Not. "I'll think about it. My mom, you know." She rolled her eyes for effect.

"There he is," Amanda hissed, stopping short of pointing at the broad-shouldered, green-eyed, freckled redhead who towered above the other students. "I mean, look at him. Perfect for you. Tall."

"Hey, Mand? Could you give me some space with this? Like you say, it's my first shot at liking a guy who's…" *Perfect.* She couldn't blurt that. Not yet. "Tall."

Amanda sobered. "Maybe your only chance to date a guy you can look up to," she said in complete seriousness. "Glad to see you've pulled your nose out of the flowers and are going to do *something* about your social life. Call me later, okay?"

"I will."

Amanda dissolved into the crowd as Beri plowed through it, catching her eye and tilting his head in the opposite direction of the buses. Then he headed that way, with a glance back and an insistent frown.

What was going on? She shoved off her locker, elbowing her own broad-shouldered body between packs as she rounded corners a couple of yards behind him. At a back exit crowded with jocks, Beri held the door open for her.

He smiled, and she melted. Warm. Fuzzy. Everything

Amanda had said. But she didn't put out her hand, and neither did he as they headed toward the playing fields. They couldn't risk touching until absolutely no one would see.

"What's up?" she asked.

"Merlin called. One of the rips is expanding. I must get back as soon as possible to lend my mag—aid," he said firmly.

Crap. He'd caught himself, but Dad's "call" had thrown Beri off. Merlin—her newly found dad, *not* the Arthurian wizard—had raised Beri after his parents died, and so they "called" each other using magical thought-speaking that came naturally for anyone who had grown up in a wizard family. But not her.

"During class? That must have been fun," she muttered.

Beri blew out a breath. "Had me looking around to check if he'd come into the room. The lass behind me thought I was making eyes at her, so then I had to deal with both conversations at the same time. I'm still nae sure what I said to her."

Great. Fern would give Dad the bell schedule and instructions to call only during class changes. And she'd accelerate their plans to let people know she and Beri were together. The idea to wait until she had more control of her magic had gotten old fast. "He should have had Mom text me," she said. "What's happened with your gap year, the *rumspringa* break?"

Beri shrugged one shoulder. "The agreement was it'd start once the worst rip was repaired—this one. Or as of my birthday."

August thirty-first. In a couple of weeks, Beri would turn eighteen, and the crazy demands would stop. He could just be a student, and they'd have more time together.

"Merlin wants you to attend as well, for your training. They will pick us up along Boulder Creek, that path through the woods we discussed."

Fern groaned. Yeah, they'd discussed it, but never picked an exact place. That's where students sneaked off to smoke. "It would've been safer to meet right next to the building."

With their long-legged strides, they were on the path in minutes. Her parents weren't there. Avoiding the lingering cigarette odor, they walked to the street, turned around and walked back. The smokers and students walking home had cleared out, and Beri lightly touched her elbow.

It wasn't a random bump and when he looked questioningly at her, she nodded. He slid his hand down and laced his fingers with hers.

It felt so right that she sighed. Then she immediately looked around. Still no sign of her parents. Beri pulled her off the path —okaaay, they prooobably had a few minutes—and around a tree trunk. They bumped together, and she wanted to put her arms around him, but the tingling had started, and it was all she could do to hold her magic in its storage core. Still, Beri bent his head to hers, so Fern began closing her eyes—and caught a movement behind him. As she swung to look, her chin smashed into Beri's ear.

"Youch," he snapped.

And she spat, "Mom!" because it was Mom coming around the tree, wearing her ragged work jeans, her brown hair braided and falling past her hips. Her petite mother might be only five feet tall, but she certainly hadn't been on the path seconds ago. "Uh, hi," Fern stammered.

In answer, Mom tilted her head and narrowed a disapproving look at their clasped hands.

"What—crap." Something green trickled over her finger. It could be candy, gum, anything—but it wasn't. Fern balled her hand, sucking in her magic. It withdrew into her cores, and the tingling stopped, just as her dad poked his head around the tree, too.

"Brilliant," he said cheerily. "No one about. Let's go." He gestured them closer with a short, reddish-brown glass rod fastened on a leather loop that he wore around his neck. The peregrinator for magical travel could pass for a new-age pendant. If Mom ever let him go into Boulder, he'd blend right in—long black hair and beard, leather trousers and a homespun shirt, the collar cream against olive skin a little darker than Fern's.

"Dad could have warned you they were here," she muttered to Beri and pulled him with her, not letting go of his hand despite Mom's frown. No point now.

Dad put his hand on her shoulder so both she and Beri connected to his magic, and Mom clasped his arm. The glass peregrinator in Dad's hand glowed. Magic flushed from it into a globe around them, and the pereport started. Leaves and branches, then buildings, buses and cars whirled outside their protective barrier—they could see out as Dad directed the teleport, but no one could see them.

As they lifted above the Flatirons of Boulder, Fern closed her eyes to block the blur of mountains and canyons—the ups and downs of Colorado's Front Range were way too high for her stomach. In a minute, the scent of pine replaced the city, and a soft branch brushed her cheek. She opened her eyes in a grove of ponderosa pines that hid them from the neighbors' prying eyes.

Giving a huff, Mom hurried off, along a zigzag of lichen-covered granite. The path led from the trees at the back of their property to the modern log cabin she and her mom had lived in since Fern was three years old.

"What?" Fern asked as they descended the slope. "She can't be that mad I had one little slip. Is it because she caught Beri and me together? Or because of having to pick us up by…" *Magic?* They didn't say certain words outside the closed doors of their cabin. "She knew you might need to someday."

"'Twas the parade of elders coming through her house," Dad said. "Looking for Beri."

"Through the…" *Portal?* No way. The magical passageway

that only Fern had been able to operate for the past year was now reconfigured to open with a spark of magic when Beri came over from his home on the Isle of Giuthas for school. Dad had set that up for just them…or so she'd thought. *It must work with any spark of magic.*

Beri grimaced, but Merlin raised a hand. "Not your fault. Problems along that rip escalated today. Once they started, the council discovered its breach is tied to the Pines. They need you to…help because of your work with those trees."

While Beri and Merlin discussed that *help*, Fern rushed ahead and caught up with her mom past their cabin.

"Sorry about the elders breaking your rules."

Mom didn't stop walking. "Merlin will handle it. You say naught, just do what your father suggests for tonight. Otherwise, keep your magic contained." She glanced at Fern's hand. "I shall put on a quash when you return."

A quash was the equivalent of a magical grounding. Fern bent to her mother's ear. "It was one spark," she hissed. "It would have been nothing if you hadn't snuck up on us. You can't quash me, not if I'm going to the conference in Bonterra tomorrow."

"We shall discuss it when you return Sunday," Mom replied. "I need to get back to work."

Fern stopped, while Mom crossed the wooden footbridge over the creek that split their property. She disappeared into the garage art studio on the other side, where she was flameworking glass for a large order. Fern knew not to push it, and now she had a reprieve to come up with another excuse.

"Fern!" Dad called from the cabin's door.

Together, they entered the portal—a doughnut-shaped opening of spinning magic—and emerged in Gran's bathroom on the isle. Dad didn't loiter in the empty cottage, but picked up a lantern and headed outside. The moment he left, Fern threw her arms around Beri's neck. He encircled her waist, and for a precious thirty seconds, they hugged with a full flush of magic.

"Give it your best," he whispered in her ear. They pulled back the magic, easier once they had mixed it for a moment, and followed Dad. Exchanging energy with Beri was the one thing her magic did well, without any effort.

Night had already fallen. Beri unfurled his wings and lifted off, disappearing into the dark.

"'Twill be good for you to lend your magic to the repair efforts." Dad pointed to the ground. "Reconnect your magic to your habitat and fill your cores to take as much energy as you can."

Fern shoved her fingers into a flower bed beside the cottage and pulled her Meadows' energy into her magical channels.

Dad paced as he waited. "I should warn you, people may be testy tonight. Many have complained that your return to your studies has slowed the flow of your habitat's energy to the common pool we use for hiding the isle. I've assured them your commitment remains strong, but it doesn't help that Beri spends half his hours abroad before he's officially on his break."

Beri chose that. I'm only responsible for my parts of this. Still, that hurt. The isle was seven hours ahead of Colorado, which meant after getting home on the bus, she either had to do her Meadows work in the dark, or not at all. Lately, it'd been not at all. Channels full, she straightened. "Would it help if I pulled some every day and…whatever, bottled it to pass along?"

Dad shook his head, but with a smile. "Maintaining your production requires an actual interaction with the habitat. Plant your seeds, harvest something, work with wildlife—" He snapped his fingers. "The beehives!" His excitement flickered rust-brown magic around the glass peregrinator in his other hand. "Before you leave in the morning, we can check the hives for mites. With tens of thousands of bees in each hive, a magical touch will connect to millions—"

"Dad?" She hated to bring this up, but opening beehives still made her nervous, despite how reassuring Dad tried to be about the protection of the bee suits. "You don't want me magically touching bees. I haven't exactly proven myself with anything besides plants."

He stroked his beard. "Anything will do. You could light the smoker and fan the smoke while I remove the frames—"

"I had hoped to seed eight new wildflower patches before fall. Don't we have a rip repair to get to?" She clasped his arm.

With a grunt of exasperation, Dad flushed the glass rod with his magic, and Fern closed her eyes for the pereport. "Still, the bee chores need doing," he resumed, and she knew they'd arrived. "It's getting late in the season, and they are a Meadows responsibility. We can't put these things off because of your school hours."

Fern said a noncommittal, "Huh," and looked around—as much as she could. The dark silhouettes of trees surrounded them, so they were in the Forest habitat. Dad handed her the glowing lantern and guided her to a spot between two trunks. Bending, he lifted his hand between them as if raising a shade, because handling magic was like that for him. It'd have taken her much longer to find this broken boundary, let alone get inside.

This was nice, arriving with her dad. In the two weeks since they'd met, he'd taught her a magic lesson every day. She hadn't gotten much better at working her magic on things besides plants, but she'd finally started to know the father who'd missed her as much as she'd missed him.

Dad stepped through the opening in the barrier, then gripped her elbow to help her follow him inside. "Mind your step."

The ground on this side trembled, and a hundred feet off, a golden patch of light shone like a forest fire. As they pushed through the underbrush toward the light, its color shifted to orange, then blue. Shadowed figures moved, backlit like the tree trunks. A *pop* sounded. The people froze in place. Strands of color spun upward like the ribbons the dance squad waved at the football games, but these kept going up and up, escaping among the branches.

Those ribbons were pure magic. Lots of magic.

Magic needed to hide the island.

3

A FRAGILE HOLD ON POWER

As Fern and her dad hiked closer, the glow over the forest floor winked out. Higher, the floating energy ribbons lit the dark like multicolored Christmas lights.

"Catch them," a man shouted. Feather-winged figures launched into the air.

The wizards chasing the magic strands were the enclave's teens. Fern recognized only a few by name, including her twin brother. Raven darted to collect the brown ribbons, his ponytail of black hair streaming wildly. Others chased gold, yellow and various blue ribbons, likely their habitat's magic. That left the red and the green magic to flutter higher, until at last, Raven and a guy with tousled hair who'd been gracefully gathering pinkish-orange strands went after them. Many fizzled and disappeared before they could catch them, the magic lost to the ether.

Where was Beri? He should have been after the green magic.

Or she should have been. *Why can't I do this yet?*

Fern sighed. Having magic, but no wings, was a huge disappointment after discovering she was descended from these people called the Windborne. Her mom might have raised Fern as human after Mom had run away, but wings would prove that Fern's magic was as good as any other Windborne's.

Even if I had wings, I'd be afraid of falling from the sky and probably kill myself trying to fly.

In the clearing below the fliers, shadow figures lined both sides of a stream, standing amid knee-high clouds of yellow magic. Fern identified the particular energy before spotting her adept friend, Willow, a blond witch who was also seventeen. She paced back and forth along the near streambank, sweeping her hands over the ground and pushing her magic at the water. On the opposite bank, Willow's father was doing the same, their magic seemingly pressing inward while other wizards held their hands downward. They made it look easy, but the amount of Forest magic they controlled surpassed any other color visible here.

Willow's mother wasn't here. Shouldn't the witch in charge of the Forest be present for the repair on her land?

"Time," called Sir Humus, the head of the island's wizard council. The flying wizards dove to the ground, gusts rising from their huge wings. When the last was down, he shouted, "Clear."

Hands lifted, and a rumble shook the ground. Then the stream split open. Light burst skyward, water crashed over the banks and tree roots snaked in ever-branching tangles.

Fern stumbled back, clutching at Dad. This was *the rip* they hoped to fix? This crevasse?

The wizards surged forward, magic streaming from their hands. The Forest wizards threw walls of yellow magic to block the waves, while others thrust various blue magics to the water. In the chaos, emerald-green energy lassoed the out-of-control roots—Beri's energy.

Fern blinked in surprise. She'd known he was a talented apprentice, passing all his trials, but he was working with the adults? Pride swelled for him, tangled with a bit of guilt. She shouldn't have grumbled that he was needed tonight.

Beri corralled the rampant roots alongside the elder in charge of the Pines, Lady Pina. The tall, thin woman, who'd seemed robust a few weeks ago when Fern first met her, looked frazzled tonight. Her lined face was pinched, her knobby fingers curled and trembling as her orange magic released. Her thin streams of pale light pushed the roots underground again.

The wizards calmed the water to more like a stream, and Fern could tell the rip was actually along one side of it. The water tumbled down *and up* a series of rocky drops that didn't match up with the heaved ground on the broken side. An ice-blue mist rose off the water, different colors of magic knotted within it.

"Those are the tangles we're sorting," Dad said.

Fern nodded. Yeah, the island's shortage of magic let its magical shield slip. Sliding magic pulled magic from other spots and then snarled and wore through into rips.

"Before the Forest and Streams wizards can seal the rip in their boundary back together, they must release everything that's not magic from those two habitats. But the Pines magic—the roots—has so much power, they can only counter it with more Pines energy. Lady Pina doesn't have enough available, which is why they requested Beri's magic. Yet it doesn't appear the Pines magic is breaking up."

That's right, she hadn't seen the Pines' blue-green ribbons among the others the teens caught. Beri and Lady Pina merely held the roots underground. The next step seemed to be starting.

The Forests had edged the streambanks in yellow clouds again, confining the blue mist to the streambed. The Streams wizards rolled their hands, making their mist rise, fluffing and loosening the knots of magic to individual ribbons. The graceful boy who'd gathered the pink strands crouched with a woman on one bank and washed waves of pinkish magic through the mist.

The colorful ribbons flushed onto the banks like high-tide debris.

Dad pulled her forward, into the yellow mist. "Here's where you can help. This close, you should be able to call the Meadows magic with yours." He flung out a hand, fingers spread. Ribbons of the same reddish brown as his magic leaped to him.

Fern pointed her fingers toward a green ribbon rising with the yellow mist. *Come.* It veered to her, not fast, but she caught it…just as the yellow magic thinned and disappeared. The ribbons fell, and their muddle billowed into a blinding flash of white fog. It sizzled over Fern's bare arms, stinging.

She swatted the magic, her yelps drowned among others and the cries of several people shouting, "Willow? Willow, where are you?"

She'd been right here—

Fern heard someone retching nearby. Holding the lantern high, she batted away the fog and spied Willow leaning against a tree.

Uh oh. "Dad? It's Willow." Without waiting for an answer, Fern tripped through the undergrowth. Before she reached her, Willow put up her hand.

"Come no closer. My little brother came down with this stomach bug last night and Mam today."

Willow's father flew past Fern, landed and put his arm around his daughter. He smiled weakly at Fern before looking past her. "Merlin, please pass on my apologies, but that's all the Forests can do tonight. I've got to see my lass home and hope the rest haven't fallen ill."

Fern gave Willow a sympathetic wave before they turned away, and Fern caught her dad's arm. "Who can step in to take their places?"

"None can." He grimaced. "Since Forest habitat covers seventy percent of the isle, 'tis our largest energy pool. Their magic is also directly connected to this rip. Perhaps the evening's work has removed enough magic that the rip can be held with Streams magic for a…" He trailed off as Lady Roda approached, looking furious.

Lady Roda, the Wizard of Wildlife, *always* was furious, in Fern's brief experience. Maybe pulling her hair into a tight bun gave her a headache. Anyway, Fern had already decided to make herself scarce when Dad patted her back and said, "Go on."

He intercepted Lady Roda. Sir Humus joined them. Without the Forests, the rip was a torrent of wild colors, so Fern hung out between it and the argument her dad was now in, propping herself against a broad oak and hoping not to be noticed.

Well, darn. Tomorrow she'd been going to the forestry conference with Willow, her mother, Raven and Lady Pina. Would they even be able to go? Her help with the rip wouldn't be a lot, but Lady Pina surely couldn't leave. Maybe Raven could still get away. She'd have to talk to them…

Raven had gone up to their dad, and he was holding his stomach.

Uh, trip canceled. She wasn't that surprised, since Raven and Willow were prebonded and never seemed to be without each other. Sir Humus and Lady Roda backed away, then returned to the stream. The wizards began shouting directions about spells Fern didn't understand.

Fern crossed her arms. She'd been looking forward to going to this magical conference and seeing a Windborne city, but there would be other trips. She watched Beri, still at Lady Pina's side, his magic weaving a barrier with the rest of the elders, mainly in the Pines energy. Beri had never planned to go since plants weren't his thing—animals were—and he needed to study for tests in both algebra and American history, subjects he knew nothing about. Now he'd be here, she supposed. She could help, too, and help him study, along with studying for her own exams.

A number of the wizards had completed their parts and were leaving. Raven had spotted Fern and was coming over. The pair who had washed away the mist with their pink magic had looked in Fern's direction several times, and now she recognized the woman. Lady Sedge of the Estuary had talked to Dad before she and Beri had prebonded. It'd been awkward. She'd tried to arrange an introduction to her son Oyster, but the guy had never turned up. So that was him? He was scowling until he noticed her watching, then he sobered up his expression behind round wire-rimmed glasses. Despite his earlier flying, his linen shirt was tucked neatly into dark trousers, topped by a vest. The only thing not in place were the unruly curls touching his stand-up collar.

He said something to his mother, then stalked off. With a last glance toward Fern, Lady Sedge turned away, wings erupting from the back of her short jacket. She delicately held the folds of her full skirt as she flew away.

Raven arrived and leaned against the trunk of a tree yards from her.

"Sick, huh?" she asked, but he waved dismissively, then turned and vomited.

Fern stepped back. She didn't really want to get too close if he was that ill, but felt like she should do something. "What can I—"

He swiped the back of his hand across his mouth. "Nothing," he panted. "Dad's gonna take me home, too." Breathing still ragged, he slumped to the ground against the tree, sitting with his head tipped back and eyes closed.

Separate from her, Fern hoped.

Beri walked up, glanced at Raven and shook his head. "I helped this lad with some deer the other day, though not as close as Willow helps him, thank the Orb." Beri nudged Raven's knee with his foot.

"Worth it," Raven muttered.

"Mistress Fern?"

She started and swung around. Lady Pina had come up behind them, quieter than a crackle of leaves. Her boots and the hem of her dress were caked with mud, and her face was ringed with a frizz of hair escaping from her single braid.

The elderly caretaker of the Scots pine groves gave her a faint smile. "I shall see you bright and early tomorrow, I trust, if you have not been exposed to this illness as well?"

"Oh, no, ma'am. I mean, I haven't seen the others for days. But can you go, with the rip and all?"

She looked back over her shoulder, and Fern followed her gaze. The air above the rip now glowed in the blue-green magic of the Pines. "I daresay I have done what I can. With the Pines pulled into this boundary, we used my reserves to suspend the rip. Even Mimosa didn't express optimism this could be repaired quickly, and she is the youngest of the habitat managers, save you. While we give Mimosa a few days for her and her family to recover from this illness, I can also honor my commitment to the Arboriculture Committee and introduce you at your first magical conference."

The trip was still on. Fern squared her shoulders She was going with Lady Pina, and that'd be cool. "I look forward to attending with you."

"I shall meet you at Lark's, then. Eight o'clock sharp."

Ohmigod, that would be one a.m. Mountain Time in Colorado. Fern opened her mouth, then closed it again. She couldn't complain, but how the heck was she supposed to get any sleep when she wasn't a bit tired and it'd still be light at home?

A smile twitched at the corners of Beri's mouth, and she wanted to poke him. Well, she deserved it after teasing him for falling asleep at weird times—like *any* time he sat for more than five minutes.

"Tha' is a mite earlier than Fern is used to, ma'am," he said. "You may have to send Lark to fetch her."

Lady Pina rubbed her forehead. "I gave the time second thoughts myself, but apparently, my talk has been scheduled first, so there is no getting around it. Your contribution of putting our photographs on that tiny machine will help liven things up for the morning."

Fern smiled. Creating a PowerPoint and backing it up to a flash drive equaled magic to the isle's wizards.

"I must admit," Lady Pina continued, "energy work outside my own habitat has become harder than in my youth. The magic is no longer free-flowing enough."

"Are you sure that wasn't just the *view* of youth, Pina dear?" Dad asked as he came to stand with them. "I recall being rather enthusiastic about attacking magical issues when I was the age of these three. Now"—he shrugged—"I send Raven. If you'd take on an apprentice—"

"Yes, yes, I know." Lady Pina's lips tightened into a thin line. "In good time I shall find the proper wizard. I shall see you in the morning, Mistress Fern." She turned and walked back to the stream.

"Bye," she said, but no one else did. "Did I miss something there?"

Dad looked at Beri, who still had his hands in his pockets and wasn't meeting Dad's gaze. The familiarity of their positions made the pieces pop into place—the same mood came over Mom and her when Mom was counseling her. Unease prickled over Fern. She stepped closer to Beri, making him look at her.

"You passed your trial last month—in a grove of ancient pines. *You* were supposed to be her apprentice. Instead, you and I prebonded, bringing your magic to the Meadows."

"Nay, it was not settled that I would take an apprenticeship with her."

"She hoped you would."

"Aye."

Merlin put a hand on Beri's shoulder. "Pina appreciates your help all the same."

That made Fern feel even worse.

4

MORE THAN ONE COULD HOPE FOR

Bonterra City

Any time Cor smiled, the conference people gave him a funny look. Aunt Syl always said his smiles came off as forced, and his sister teased that if he wasn't smiling, he looked annoyed or bored. Unless people were talking about trees, Cor *was* annoyed or bored. He couldn't smile on demand. After the seventh wizard frowned, he settled for a nod and holding an open hand toward the auditorium doorway. "Keynote speech? Starting in ten minutes."

They'd flooded in, eager to hear some witch talking about lichens in their Scots pines. Big deal. The estate pines were covered in them. The second talk by Sherwood Forest's Windborne expert in English oaks was the one he was keen on. Those oaks were at the top of his list to work with.

During a lull, he drifted a few feet to the registration table run by a number of academy students, volunteer gofers like himself. Even after their orientation breakfast, he still felt uncomfortable. The forestry and natural resources students all seemed to know each other and, except for one bloke he hadn't seen again, were all white or Asian. And mostly witches.

"Anyone covering Sir Garrick's talk?" he asked.

"Me," said a witch with short curly hair whose name tag read *Penelope, Forest Management Candidate*. Each volunteer had one.

His *had* read *Cor, Gruen Institute for Magical Arboriculture*. He'd conveniently "lost" that one and instead had handwritten just his name on paper he'd magicked to mimic a tag. It looked decent stuck on the lapel of the green estate blazer that he had to wear for formal events, along with black slacks and shiny shoes that made him feel like a dork. He'd worn the whole getup today.

"Would you be willing to trade?" he asked her.

Her face lit up. "If you take my field trip from one to three so I can attend the grafting workshop at two."

He had the two o'clock slot free for lunch, so it was only a matter of her taking his one o'clock. "Which?"

"City highlights including the Gruen Estate."

A snicker escaped him.

She smiled sheepishly, her pink cheeks dimpling. "Yeah, I signed up late. It's the dregs."

Even more so for him. Perhaps the other person assigned to Garrick's talk would have a more interesting trade. A group was approaching the lecture hall doors. "Let me think about it," he told her and darted to his post.

A few minutes later, the witch willing to trade joined him. "Would you like to get lunch later?" she asked.

How, when neither of them was free until four—oh. Was she trying to make a *personal* connection? He hadn't been paying enough attention. "Rather late for lunch, four, don't you think?"

She grinned. "Tea, then. I know a lovely place around the corner. Potter's? If you're from out of town, you need to check it out."

He cocked his head. "This isn't a bribe to get me to trade?"

She waved her hands. "Hey, no. You asked me, remember? I just thought maybe we could talk, tree research and stuff, you know?"

Pine pitch, as his dad would say. Flattering that an academy student was hitting on him—and one older than he. But he didn't look his age, sixteenth year, and he wasn't keen on girls. Moving places often with his family, he'd been able to dodge overtures at more than friendship. This witch was the most outspoken who'd ever approached him.

He ushered in another lecture attendee and side-glanced to her again. He did need a trade in order to attend the oak session. And it had been years since he'd been to Potter's. Their scones were good. "I, uh, could…"

"Brilliant."

What was her name again? He looked at her name tag. *Penelope* pointed to the front doors to indicate where to meet later and returned to her table. An older wizard in a neat suit approached, looking uncertain.

The man was also black, and empathy welled up in Cor. It might be that the wizard was merely lost, but whenever Cor found himself in a place with few or no other black folks, an edge of worry nagged at him. He'd seen fewer than a dozen black wizard attendees the entire morning, and the same number of folks of mixed heritage among the three-hundred-some attendees.

"Keynote speech," he said to the short man with copper-brown skin who'd tied one long dreadlock around the rest to hold them back. "Starting in eight minutes."

The wizard gave a nod. "Yes, yes. Excited to hear Lady Pina's talk. How about you? Will they let the student volunteers listen in?"

"Yes, sir, Mr.—" He glanced at the name tag…well, well. "Sir Garrick. I'm looking forward to your talk as well. Securing the

Sherwood enclave amid the humans' popular Sherwood Forest must be a tricky bit of magic with your old oaks."

Sir Garrick laughed. "Nice of you to say so. I've had the benefit of working with other folks passing along that magical history. Love to get more young wizards on board if you've an inclination—"

"I do, sir." Blast, he'd cut the man off.

Sir Garrick produced a business card. "Contact me."

Cor smiled, a real one this time. "Thanks." This invitation hadn't violated his parents' rules against using their family name for personal gain. So far today, he'd remained anonymous; he'd recognized a few attendees from his parents' work, but none noticed him without them.

A line began to form at the door, and Sir Garrick tilted his head. "My cue to find a seat. Lady Pina of the Pines isn't one for using pretty photos, but don't miss her talk."

"I won't, sir." Definitely not, so he could keep up a conversation with Sir Garrick later. Cor gestured folks along, giving his now-routine nod instead of speaking. Sir Garrick had an internship waiting for him, he could feel it, another black man looking out for him. As Dr. Linford began his welcome speech, several latecomers rushed up, and Cor had to hold open the door that he'd been told to close.

Lady Pina had begun speaking when he finally slipped inside behind the last person. "The Isle of Giuthas, Gaelic for Isle of the Pines, is located twenty-seven kilometers from the Scottish mainland," she said.

Blessed Orb, now this witch's popularity made sense. Giuthas was famous for its forest habitats. Cor had seen that information on the foundation's listings when he'd done his research. Plus, he always noted mentions of Scots pine trees, because his dad and his siblings were named for them. He'd not bothered to research the isle's forests further for an internship, because the island was totally locked down by the residents. No Windborne were allowed to casually travel there.

The lights dimmed, and the first image popped up. Sir Garrick had been wrong about this witch and photos, if this shot of the mountainous island was a sample. Cor edged along the dark aisle, looking for an empty seat.

"Windborne have had the isle secured since 1672. At only forty-one thousand hectares, its energy supports a small population. Management is traditional, and the original plant species thrive in all habitats, which of course the Scots pines are of particular note. The groves have endured since before the ice age swept most of the United Kingdom..."

At the back of the room, Cor propped himself against the wall and looked toward the screen again. Pines, but... He blinked. Their proportions in the photos looked all off. Was he seeing things?

She clicked to a new image.

I'm not. These weren't Scots pines like he'd ever seen, on the estate or elsewhere.

These were monster trees.

The next image flicked onto the screen, a Windborne in flight next to what looked like a tree growing—

"A single ancient tree typically hosts eight to fifteen additional trees in its branches, bringing the biomass and its living energy to a level comparable to one of Bonterra's energy-harvesting plots."

Bloody freakin' insane. The kilowatts of magic from that tree— tree system?—equaled an acre of land? How many of these giants were on this island?

After a few more images and she switched to close-ups of plants and animals living in the boughs, then to the main topic, the lichens. And not like the kinds that grew in the Gruen trees, if size and frilly edges meant anything—some looked as large as platters. It was hard to tell considering these tree *branches* were the size of an entire tree on the estate.

Cor's head spun. This put him out of his tree, as Dad would say, and into another of his crazy urges. He had to see these trees—no… *I have to work with them.*

What was that witch's name? When the lights came up, Cor memorized the old lady—long, evergreen dress, skin the salmon-white of birch bark, hair braided into a rippling, gray ironwood branch. Right-o, between that and her breathless talking, he'd recognize her again.

"…so please extend your thanks to Fern for setting me up with this push-button display of our groves."

That sounded like the end. As Dr. Linford thanked her, Cor had wits enough to race down and get the doors and nod as folks left. He checked the schedule placard for her name—Lady Pina of the Pines—and put himself on the inside of the auditorium to see where she went. Nowhere yet, since a crowd had converged on her, including students.

Cor frowned. They better not be asking for internships, too.

Someone poked him in the arm. "Hi."

It was another student, one studying owls, whom he'd met this morning. *Li, Ornithology Candidate,* her name tag reminded him.

"I'm your replacement. Do you have a minute to tell me more about the nesting at the estate?"

"Uh, maybe later? I need to catch Lady Pina."

"Good talk, huh? What was her…"

"Thanks for coming early." Cor headed down the aisle.

Most people had left. Another student still hung out off to the side, while a youngish wizard in a baggy tweed jacket repeatedly pushed up his glasses as he listened to the old lady's answer. Definitely a scholarly type, not a hands-on worker like Cor. He'd be more suited to a remote island.

As Cor walked up, so did Dr. Linford. Cor fell in behind the waiting student, a tall witch about his age with long, walnut-black hair and dressed sensibly in trousers. She had a printed name tag, but he couldn't make out what it read.

Another witch trotted down the aisle, a paper fluttering from her polished fingertips. She passed him as if he didn't exist and rapped the first girl on the arm. "Hey. You made it."

They proceeded to talk in low voices about the conference. Cor stared, trying not to glare, but glaring anyway. They must have seen him. Was she cutting the queue? In her fancy blazer and pink skirt, she must think she deserved extra privileges. "Excuse me," he finally said.

Pink Skirt turned to look at him. "Do I know you?" she asked with a glance to his not-printed name tag, so he looked at hers: *Duffy, Biology Candidate.* "Haven't seen you in the botany department."

"No," he said. "I'm waiting to speak with her." He nodded toward Lady Pina.

She wrinkled her nose in a dismissive way. "Chill your heels. I'm only here to meet up with them later, not get in your way to schmooze."

Did *them* refer to this girl and another one, or this girl and Lady Pina? Would it help him in any way if these witches knew the lady?

Before he could concoct a nicer way to ask, Pink Skirt—with her overdone clothes, styled hair, white skin and cocky attitude —turned her back to him and handed the other girl a map. "This is the route for the field trip. At stop seven, check out my energy-harvest plot for the city. If anything has gone to seed, help yourself. All native species."

The plots—that's why she looked familiar. "Watering," Cor said without thinking.

Pivoting, she snapped her fingers. "That's it. You're the gardener's assistant."

"Actually, I was just helping out that day. I work for the Gruen Estate, and we've got the hydrant keys, too."

"Well, thanks. You saved my grade. Between midterms and summer registration, I couldn't haul enough water by bucket for the seedlings, native or not."

Her gratitude was sincere enough that his opinion of her shifted. "Had a lull in the rain that week," he said, but she'd returned to pointing at her map.

The other girl, however, gestured him ahead of her.

"Don't you want to get your question in?" he asked her.

"Oh, no. Please go ahead." Her name tag read *Fern, Heir to the Witch of the Meadows, the Isle of Giuthas.*

Giuthas, the island where the pines were. What the heck did the rest mean? Didn't matter, he'd take the bump in line.

"...we take a measurement," Lady Pina was saying, "but we haven't had one fall in decades, and we certainly don't risk introducing disease by taking a core sample of a healthy tree just to figure out an *age*. It's rather a human thing to determine the value of a tree by age. I prefer to think of them in terms of connections. Connections to the macroorganisms they host, down to the micro. All contribute to their energy production, which is the main concern of Windborne when it comes to a tree of any age. You cannot discount the value of each tree to our livelihood."

Brilliant. This lady had her priorities so straight. He had to talk to—

"I'm afraid we must set up for the next speaker," Dr. Linford interrupted Lady Pina. "Could you continue this enlightening conversation in the corridor?" He flashed a smile and tilted his head to Cor. "Cor can show you out."

"Yes," he said a little too enthusiastically and swung into his usher wave.

Lady Pina followed his direction, but the wizard in the baggy tweed jacket, pushing up his glasses, kept pace with her. "I'm quite keen on seeing these unique specimens for myself."

"I'm sure it'd be of value to your research," Lady Pina said. "Send me your questions, and I'll try to answer."

The man bobbed his head. "Thank you. Thank you very much for your consideration."

They'd reached the door, and the bloke walked off, apparently not realizing she hadn't actually said he could come *see* the trees. *That gives me the chance to get that invite.*

"Lady Pina? I'm Cor." He stuck out his hand. "Impressive species you're managing over on Giuthas. It must be a delicate balance to support the big trees and yet still harvest the energy for the island's shielding."

She placed her delicate hand in his and shook firmly. "Thank you, young man. I do my best. I hope you're enjoying your time at academy?"

Shoot, should he say he wasn't a student there…or just move on? "It's a grand place."

"What are you studying?" She began walking down the corridor, but this was an invitation to talk, even though the tall witch was still waiting. She followed a step behind them.

"I have a, um, project researching the difference in species capacity to hold magic. The most promising is a study group of rowans I've saturated. They'll hold my spells, including a self-energizing protective barrier I developed. The trees have maintained it for a month now against anything I throw at it. Insects, sticks, dogs that want to use the trunk as a fire hydrant, a kid I paid to try to climb it. I'd like to test a lightning strike, but I can't in the city."

"You've sealed off the tree?" she asked, like she'd heard wrong.

"No, no, not sealed it against wildlife. Just harm. Creatures that would naturally use the tree can breach the barrier. Fourteen species, so far, including fungus and lichens. I am continuing my observations."

She paused and lifted a brow. "Oh? Who is your mentor?"

If he said Master Harold, the truth of this *project* would come out. "I-I'm looking for one. Would you consider taking me on for an internship?"

She shook her head and resumed walking.

Damn, wrong answer. Now he had to give her something closer to the truth. "I've been on the conservatory staff at the Gruen Estate for a few months. If you'd like a reference, Master Harold can vouch for my diligence in my tasks." That was the truth at least. "I have branched out"—he cringed at the terrible pun, his usual exchange with Master Harold—"into applying the experiment to a number of exotic species..." He pulled out his mobile, yanked out the earbuds and scrolled to an image of several little trees in a line, each a different color. He held it out to show her.

Lady Pina looked at it with raised eyebrows, then back to him, her lips pursed. "I cannot take apprentices. Come along, Fern," she said to the tall girl.

Cor stopped. He knew when he'd been dismissed. As they walked off, the girl turned back, her lips twisted in what he thought might be an apologetic smile.

Okay, the tall girl—*Fern*, he had to remember this one—and Pink Skirt definitely knew Lady Pina. But how could that help him get work with her Scots pines?

The map. The field trip—Fern was going to be on it. *Bloody blast it—*

Cor spun around and rushed back down the corridor. Where was that flirty witch who'd wanted to trade?

5

THE BONTERRA TOUR

Fern hurried after Lady Pina, who had promised to introduce her to the manager of a wet meadow on the mainland. But that wasn't as important as leaving that guy hanging. Cor had hidden it well, but she'd seen the excitement in his honey-brown eyes, then the flash of disappointment. Trees were important to him, the same way wildflowers were to her. Like her, he wanted this.

"Ma'am?" Fern matched Lady Pina's pace. "His project sounded amazing. Is that kind of magic for tree protection usual?"

"Been experimented with, so not unusual. It's in the spell work that the truth would come out if it actually could be self-energizing. That's what would save a wizard effort, to set it up and leave, doing a monitoring every week or month or couple of months. That would be a gem."

"Then why didn't you get his number?"

"A number?"

Oh yeah, this elderly—and simplistic-living—wizard didn't do phones. "Find a way to contact him, or at least set up a time to meet him later this weekend. Lunch or something?"

Lady Pina shrugged. "My hands are tied."

"No," Fern said boldly. "You found a way to help me when you liked my project."

Lady Pina shook her head again. "You had Lark looking after you, training you. You were on the isle…any number of beneficial reasons."

"He seemed very hyped, er, *interested* in trees. I bet he'd work hard, and you said yourself the work has become harder for you. I'm sure it's been difficult with Beri on the Meadows now."

Lady Pina didn't answer.

The corridor had mostly emptied. Fern swallowed. This wasn't something she'd bluntly asked someone before, but Lady Pina wasn't a person who was afraid to speak her mind. *I hope she doesn't mind if I do, too.* If Cor was as hard a worker as he was enthusiastic, then he could replace Beri, which would make Fern feel a whole lot better about stealing him from the Pines. Fern grasped Lady Pina's arm so she had to stop, very aware of how her olive fingers appeared brown against Lady Pina's pale skin. "Is this because he's black?" she asked quietly. She'd been subjected to discrimination herself in the past.

Lady Pina's eyes widened. In the look of confusion on her face, Fern could tell it wasn't.

"Are you accusing me of prejudice? Because I have the same Mediterranean bloodlines in my ancestors as you do. They just aren't reflected in my looks."

Like they hadn't in Raven, even though he and Fern were twins. Plus, honestly, Fern's skin had enough "whiteness" that she'd been largely shielded from racism.

"No, it is not because he's black," Lady Pina confirmed. "I'm not saying that to hush you. It's because of where he's from, what he's used to. He works with city trees, and they are controlled by a council with a goal of farming their energy. It's entirely different than our wild, natural setting where our folks rely on each manager. I simply don't want to waste my time on a city youth. You saw him, dressed with spit and polish, with fancy picture devices and those listening things for his ears. He said fourteen species use his test tree? They should number fifty or more, even in this setting. A wizard like that has more on his mind than caring for trees and their inhabitants."

"He's no more dressed up than Duffy is, and it's probably what they told him to wear to be a volunteer here. I know events like this are picky. Plus, Duffy has come from the mainland and Bonterra Academy—right here in the same city."

Lady Pina frowned and pulled her arm away. "He doesn't know our ways." She stalked into the next room without checking if Fern followed.

Well...shoot. Gran wouldn't have noticed what Cor looked like if he'd talked that way about birds. Fern didn't know Lady Pina well, but her list of lame excuses left Fern with an annoying sense that something more was keeping her from considering Cor.

That afternoon, when she and Lady Pina arrived at the bus for the Bonterra tour, Cor was there. He was handing out maps alongside the guide, an older wizard, who greeted everyone. Lady Pina peeled off to speak with several others who turned out to be friends from other enclaves. After introducing Fern, she forgot about her while they talked about wizards they all knew. Lady Pina wasn't going on this particular tour to see the city. Lady Mimosa had suggested the trip because it was Fern's first time in a wizard city, and she was attending to keep her company. Supposedly.

So Fern hung at the edge of the group of adults. She could board the bus...or just go talk to Cor. What had happened with Lady Pina wasn't her fault, and yet she felt bad about it. Worse, every time she looked his way, and he was staring—not at her, but at Lady Pina.

By the time she'd decided to just say hi and ask about his project, Lady Pina motioned to her to join the queue to get on the bus. At the head of the line, another man had stopped to ask Cor a question about going somewhere in Bonterra. Fern got on the bus. What could she say to him anyway? She wasn't the one making apprenticeship decisions... For the Pines. She *could* make them for her habitat. Hmm, she'd have to think about that one. If only Gran were here to advise her.

"Take a seat, any seat! We're right on time," said their guide, Mr. Acer—Acer, the genus for maple. Easy to remember for a scholarly man sporting thick blond hair. Though they didn't have the species growing in Colorado, last week Willow's youngest brother, Maple Sugar, had proudly shown her his namesake, the field maple. She'd exclaimed over a leaf already yellow for fall.

"Our first stop is minutes away, so don't get too comfortable," said Mr. Acer, a man clearly into his tour-leader role. "We're headed for the historic city center and Bonterra's prized Everlasting Oak, the first sessile oak planted in the settlement 'round the turn of the century in seventeen hundred. At a girth of 19.2 feet, the Gruen Estate records put our oak at the largest in the United Kingdom, but of course we can't claim that record."

This produced a chuckle from the crowd.

"I'm sure many of you are familiar with the tale of the Everlasting Oak, but allow me to repeat it for the visitors to our great city. In the seventeenth century, the Windborne were fairly complacent in making extensive flights across country, especially the young wizards. Clarence the Courageous, along with his best friend, Drennen the Determined, became quite proficient at navigating air currents to conserve their stamina and proposed to a group of like-minded wizards to explore this area north of Yorkshire. As will happen, an argument erupted, and the two went their separate ways. During this split, Clarence found this valley and soon afterwards met a local witch with whom he wished to spend the rest of his life. Love prompted him to show off this glorious dale and declare his love at the top of a hillock of polished bedrock—which today we know was left by the glaciers that scraped this land, but that's another story.

"Marion agreed to bond. Yet, before they could complete what at that time was an unencumbered ceremony, the two encountered Drennen, grievously injured and seeking help for a third friend who had been captured. Clarence forgave his friend and acknowledged that if the comrades hadn't separated, they would not have been easy prey. He healed Drennen and roused a search party. They succeeded in freeing their friend and several other young and inexperienced witches and wizards who had been captured with the intent of enslavement.

"The perpetrators, who had come from across the waters, were magically banished, but the area needed a stronghold, especially if Clarence was to protect the family he and Marion hoped to raise. An idea hatched within him. He gathered the people of these separate enclaves on the hilltop where he had first proposed a life together to Marion. As part of their bonding ceremony, the couple planted an acorn before all assembled. They invited, 'Remain, plant your roots as we plant ours and keep good company forever among friends, so peace and harmony may protect us and ours on this good earth.' Thus, the Everlasting Oak was sprouted and Bonterra established."

A witch behind Fern sniffled. "I've heard that tale since I was a wee girlie, and it never fails to choke me up."

"My ma tells it different," said a warlock nearby, and an argument erupted.

Fern rolled her head against the window and stared at the stone houses passing by. She did not need a rundown on every Windborne's version of this old story. When the bus stopped a minute later, she was the first out of her seat and down the aisle.

Looking out the door, she stumbled on the steps. She hadn't been on the "tree" side of the bus when they drove up, so had had no warning. The park was as Mr. Acer described—a rocky hill topped by a spreading oak—but she hadn't expected the sheer size of such a tree. The limbs alone were the diameter of the trunks of the Ponderosa pines back home. The trunk could house a one-room apartment as easily as the Scots pine on the Isle of Giuthas did. That the mound was surrounded by shops in old, stone row houses was sad, but at least the natural ground around the tree extended twice as far as the limb spread. It didn't even look stomped to death, though there wasn't a fence.

"Excuse me?" someone huffed. "Others would like to exit the bus as well."

"Sorry." Fern swiveled to apologize and came nose to nose with Cor. He was inches shorter than she was, but his indignant attitude made up for it. She needed out of here, fast. Three strides got her away from the bus, but she didn't stop. Ahead, worn stone steps led in a spiral up the mound on which the oak grew. She took them to the top, where a stone walk circled the outer limbs.

Mr. Acer hurried the others along behind her. Fern moved around to the far side. She couldn't remember what type of oak Mr. Acer had said this was, but she could take a leaf back to ask Mimosa. Several feet away, a nice mahogany-colored one was caught in a clump of the tall grass that carpeted the ground. She stepped toward it—

Smack! Fern slammed into a solid surface, bounced off it and stumbled across the stone path. Beyond, the hillside fell away, and she threw out her hands to catch herself—

Magic buzzed over her, jerking her to a stop. In midair.

She sucked in a breath and squinted against the blinding, pulsing light of the five or more energies suspending her. Everyone began talking at once. Several wizards ducked close and asked what had happened.

"Ohmigod," she mumbled. *Why me?*

"Here!" An arm shoved through the magic, sending sparks flying. The wizard grasped her hand in a strong grip and pulled her up and back onto the stone walkway. "Reel it in, everybody," he muttered.

The various magics snapped back to their owners. It was as if the sky had suddenly gotten cloudy. Fern blinked to adjust her eyesight and found herself once again facing Cor.

"Being the oldest in the city, the tree is protected," he said. "Magically protected. From your accent, I gather you're not from around here." His tone was deadpan. No hint of sympathy, but neither was there ridicule. Curiosity traced his face.

"Uh, no. Colorado."

Then Lady Pina jostled Cor aside. "Mistress Fern, you could have been severely injured and are most certainly lucky that so many saw you fall and took immediate precautions, but are you all right?"

Fern drew a breath, then inserted, "Yes, I'm fine. Thank you, everyone, for your help." She made sure her look around included Cor, but added, "Thank you," to him alone.

Lady Pina's cronies clucked like mother hens around her, then, thankfully, Mr. Acer resumed his lecture. But Fern couldn't focus. She'd made a fool of herself with a klutzy accident. Just what she needed, to be the center of attention when she knew so little about forestry or magic. At least it had been a physical accident. No one knew she was bad at magic.

The next stop was at an older home to view an imported monkey tree. After, a small park with a native wet woodland along a stream. Next, a stand of native birch trees, then another specimen tree on an estate. Mr. Acer was an interesting lecturer, combining the different tree facts with how they came to be planted or saved. He also kept things moving, shuffling people aboard the bus for questions during the drives along the route that had been planned to the minute.

After the first two stops, Lady Pina re-immersed herself in talking with her friends and forgot about keeping an eye on Fern. Several people then asked about her enclave in Colorado and how she'd come to be in the UK. Working with her grandmother, instead of her mother, to restore the Meadows would raise too many questions, and she couldn't go into the whole thing about not growing up there. Mom had warned her not to discuss her life or magic with outsiders. Windborne didn't allow nonmagical children in their enclaves past the age of three.

This was when she really needed Willow or Raven to run defense for her. What Lady Pina should have been doing if she hadn't been absorbed with her friends. Instead, Fern stared out the window. She spotted the student gardens that Duffy had described. It would've been interesting to sit next to Cor and learn more about them and his gardening work, but he always got on the bus last and sat wherever there was an empty seat, which hadn't been next to her yet.

Many interesting plants besides trees grew at the stops—wildflowers and grasses—possibly some that might do well in the Meadows. Unfortunately, most were done flowering, so she had to hazard guesses about their plant families. Lagging at the back of the group, she surreptitiously collected seeds and recorded leaf details in her notebook so she could look up the plants later. For sure Duffy would know the plants on her plot, and at last they came to it.

Everyone piled out of the bus again, and Mr. Acer led them across the street to the garden.

"In an effort to improve energy production on every square foot of Bonterra land, the city council removed the more ornamental plantings. They drafted the academy botany students to propose higher-boosting energy plans for their landscape beds. The best were developed with brilliant success!" Their blond guide beamed enthusiastically and continued on about species used for the harvest projects—stuff Duffy had already told her.

Fern stepped away, peering at the wildflowers and shrubs filling each of the raised planting beds with trees in the center. Tucked into an odd-shaped corner between businesses and an apartment building, the park didn't get much traffic this time of day. In fact, the only people along the street were an older woman with her shopping and several teenagers propped against a lamp post. Maybe dog-walkers visited after work—if Windborne kept dogs?

"Spend a minute admiring the garden," Mr. Acer said. "Then, I've brought binoculars along for views of the river's floodplain, including the copper beeches that grow on the hillsides. The bridge provides a good overlook when we've no time for a hike down."

As most of the group left, Fern opened her backpack and retrieved her seed-collection envelopes. Sprays of little white flowers dotted a bed on the far side, away from prying eyes. An aster. It took a minute to find a dry seed head. She snapped off that one, filled a few more envelopes with other seeds, then spotted the milkweed. Yes! She didn't know what kind, but it wasn't the species they had in the Meadows. She found one closed pod, but the rest had burst open already, so Fern pulled tufts of the silky, white fluff that still had the seeds attached from the thorns of berry canes—which she'd never appreciated before this.

Finally, she had enough to plant in one of their quarter-acre plots. Wouldn't Gran be surprised? Fern closed the envelope, put it in her pack and swung it onto her shoulders again. Surely they'd be leaving soon, so she'd better head to the bus. Sounds of a far-off car engine and a couple of guys calling to each other filtered to her through the raised beds. Only then did she notice it was oddly quiet in the little park.

Fern's stomach turned with a bad feeling. When she emerged onto the street, her fear came true—the bus had left.

Left her *alone*. In a strange city. A wizard city. She looked up and down the street…just in case. Missing the bus to gather seeds wasn't going to go down well with Lady Pina. Did her phone have service here? She dug it out of her pack. Yeah, three bars. If she called home, what could Mom do? It'd be better to call the conference hotel, but she didn't know the number, or how to look it up. Not to mention, this was embarrassing to admit she was left behind. Maybe she could find a way to the Gruen Estate, the last place they were going to today.

Okay, she'd walk to a gas station and ask—duh! Fern mentally whacked herself. The staple of every modern city didn't exist here—Dad had said the few cars and public transportation here were all electric. But she didn't see any bus stops.

The adjacent business was vacant. The next was another apartment building. Should she go farther looking for help or stay put? Fern wiped her sweaty hands down her slacks. None of her usual solutions would work here, so she had to hope Lady Pina would miss her and figure out where she'd been last.

She returned to the garden and, with a sigh, pushed aside the asters spilling over the sides of the nearest planting bed to sit on the wall. Nestling among wildflowers offered a little familiar comfort.

If only Beri were here.

Two guys from the lamp post started strolling her way. Like typical human teens, they wore T-shirts, slouch jeans and sneakers. An unzipped black hoodie topped the black guy's clothes, and the white guy had on a leather vest. Fern kept her gaze focused on where the street disappeared into the distance, like she was waiting for someone. Still, from the corner of her eye, she assessed them. Local kids would know where to turn for help. But revealing she was alone *and* lost made her nervous. She'd have to go with her gut, maybe open a conversation with…clothes?

The guys stopped several yards away, not quite looking at her. She didn't quite look at them either, just enough to tell the names on their shirts weren't familiar. Bands? A type of wizard emo movement? Even a lame comment would work to lead to asking if there was a bus back to the city's downtown.

She stood up, ready to do it. But as she did, the guy in the vest glanced at her, then back down the street, and lifted his chin. The others peeled off the lamp post and ambled forward, a boy and a girl.

What was going on? Fern snapped off a browning aster stalk to make it look like she wasn't paying attention to them, but then the vest guy pivoted and closed the space to her.

"Whatcha doin' on our streets, witch?" he asked, his voice loaded with gleeful challenge.

Crap.

6

TRUSTING THE RIGHT PEOPLE

Fern's gut churned way past warning to flashing red alert. *Nope, not asking for directions, not admitting I was left behind, not to these guys.* She shifted her body into her wrestling stance, feet spread, arms loose. When she did this—usually—most people found it hard to approach her, a broadly built six-foot-tall girl.

The guy stopped, far enough back that he didn't have to tilt his head to meet her gaze. Much.

She stared down, not breaking her competition stare when the hoodie guy backed him. He didn't look as tough. His lips twitched, tellingly. He didn't want to be here, or at least facing her.

Good.

The first guy didn't twitch. He smoothed back his slicked hair, looking like Danny from *Grease*. His eyes were eagerly alight.

Bad.

Both were short. Both were skinny. She hated admitting she was large, but she probably had thirty pounds on them, definitely eight inches in height and muscles built from the heavy labor of gardening. And her wrestling team training… Oh.

None of this meant squat in the Windborne world. Magic topped muscle every time, a lesson Raven had impressed on her *after* he hadn't fried her when they'd fought. Double crap. Although she might not be able to do complicated spells, at least she had enough power to burn someone. She opened a core.

Green energy jerked loose and raced to her fingers. She clenched them in time to stop from sparking. *Calm. Calm. I've gotta be…* She centered herself by running the aster stalk between her fingers. The surge slowed to an even flow that partially filled her channels.

She opened her other cores, too. It didn't hurt that the flush of magic always made her feel powerful…and somewhat light-headed. Dad hadn't warned her about this sensation, but once Willow's complaint about her brother Ches' magic going to his head had led to Willow cautioning, "More magic in your head, means less in your fingers to work with." So she knew to move the energy down to her torso.

The other two teens were almost to them. He was white and blond, nearly Fern's height. The girl was short, maybe Latina. Neither looked like they were in shape.

Just keep walking. Fern's fingers grew numb where they gripped the aster stem… *Just keep walking.*

They didn't. The stem broke in her hand, and with a start, she saw its worn brown had turned a fresh green.

With that break in her stare, the leader asked, "Witch? You hear me?"

Her arm was tingling. She was totally going to blow the *No Use of Magic Against Others* rule in Bonterra. Then Mom would quash her for sure. "I hear you."

"Brilliant. You here alone?"

"Waiting for someone."

"No good for you to be alone here. Right, Cara?"

The brunette in a skirt and leggings murmured agreement, but the blond guy snorted.

"So here's the thing, witch. I'm Marty and this is my area and my tribe and there's only two ways we let anyone else be here. You pay or you join."

She'd left her purse back in Colorado and had only a few bucks on her. If she went back to saying nothing, could she stall and hope the bus returned for her?

"You want to come with us?" Marty asked. An edge of taunting pleasure filled his voice.

Leaving was not an option. She could prevent them from dragging her out of here, if she had something to grab on to. She could even lock herself to it with her magic, couldn't she? What to use? She casually looked around. No poles. Crap. What kind of a street was this? No light poles, no electrical poles, no signposts, nothing but...trees. Okay. Plants, very useful Natural poles.

"So, you plus us equals no alone. Get it, little lost witch?"

Marty was past letting her stall. Abruptly, Fern leaned forward, raised her shoulders and stuck out her elbows, a wrestling trick to make herself look as big as possible. "I get it."

Each of them took a step back. As they did, Fern bounced backward and stepped up onto the raised bed with her long legs. Crushing asters—*sorry, Duffy*—she shoved her way toward the tree, but the next plants didn't give, and her slacks caught—damn. Berry bushes.

"Hey, you're goin' the wrong way." Marty laughed—and he'd lost his tough-guy accent.

Thorns jabbed her thighs. She lifted her leg and tried stepping over the berry canes. Then on them. There were too many. The tree was...just...out...of...reach...

Close rustling meant they'd also climbed the bed.

She twisted to push through, thorns dragging painfully across her thighs. "Youch!"

Laughter erupted. "Told you, you're better off with us." Marty and the hoodie guy were only feet away. "Just come along." He waggled a finger at her.

Blood beaded across the back of her hand, the stinging mixed with tingling, and her hand turned green. Fern clutched it to her chest, hiding the evidence that she was losing it big-time. Leaning forward, she got one hand to the tree trunk, but crossed canes and thorns anchored her in place. She pinched the one digging into her leg between her finger and thumb and lifted—

The cane flushed bright green. The color moved rapidly over the stem, out the smaller branches and into the leaves. New shoots sprang from every tip, and the stalk grew heavy in her hand. Fern dropped it, but already it reached to her chin. "Ohmigod!"

"Well, I never been called a god before, but I kinda like —spells!"

"Would you look at this? Nice, witch." The hoodie guy picked a berry and popped it into his mouth.

"Slick, you git. This is not the time to feed your fool face."

No, but it was time for her to make more of these überberry bushes. Fern poked the cane in front of her—*grow*—then pivoted and tapped another.

"Hey now." Arms high, his leather vest protecting him, Marty inched closer. "Come on, Slick, Bret, help me." He reached through a gap and snagged her backpack.

Frantic, Fern pointed. Green sparks erupted from her fingers.

Marty blocked them with a red-orange shield, same as she'd seen Raven do. "So that's how you wanna be?" He sneered. "Right-o."

"No, I, uh—" Fern cringed just as he raised his hand. Ducking a flash, she stumbled into the thorns. His bolt of magic sailed over her. "Help!" she shouted. "Help!"

"Ain't nobody to hear, greenie," Slick gloated. He'd edged closer while she wasn't looking, joined by the other boy.

Three of them against her. Maybe she couldn't work a blast, but the plants were responding—if her magic held out.

"You git! Grab her foot and get her out of there."

Scrambling, Fern pulled her legs in tight. She flushed green magic. *Grow!* The plants it touched grew like Jack's beanstalk. She swept her hands in a circle and did it again and again. *Grow! Grow!* A green wall surged higher around her, thick and leafy, with tightly crossed branches and three-inch-thick stems. The ground rippled under her rear—the roots were swarming like moles.

"It works," she breathed.

"Marty? Slick?" said the girl. "You're rippin' your clothes trying to get to her."

"Who knows what kind of mess is in there, spiders and such, ye ken?" the other boy added. "A lotta trouble there."

Marty laughed wickedly. "No trouble," he said. "Least not the kind a little magic on magic can't fix." A red glow sprang up on the other side of her plant wall. Leaves curled, burst into flame and dropped. The stalks caught fire and burned in orange crisscrossing lines that sizzled closer.

Fern threw up her hands and shot back magic. The wall of plants flared green. Slick stumbled back, beating at his hoodie front and turning it blue. The red faded and disappeared.

Yes! But the canes between them were now black.

Branches snapped to her left. She shuffled away just as the fire flared again. Fern blocked it with her magic, dousing the red flames, but they'd gotten closer and hotter this time. Moisture slicked her face, and her nice blouse stuck to her back.

"Marty, let's go," Slick whined. "That witch isn't worth it."

"I agree," said a deep voice. "This witch isn't worth your trouble."

Cor? Fern stood and peered over the blackened brambles.

Yes, Cor was striding across the street in his dress clothes, his earbud wires snaking toward his ears. Their gazes met, and he rolled his eyes. Great, he hadn't come back out of the goodness of his heart. But he *was* here…and defending her?

Slick paused on the wall. Clearly, he'd been leaving, but was now looking back hesitantly. Marty popped up in front of her, sneering again.

Fern flinched, then immediately straightened and narrowed her gaze at him. She raised her hands.

Cor said, "Particularly not this witch."

What did that mean? She'd been ready to trust Cor, but should she?

"Cara?" Marty said. "Tell him to get lost."

She'd lose her edge of looking tough, but Fern opened her mouth to beg him not to. One look froze her tongue.

Cor was smiling at Cara, and it wasn't a nice smile.

7

A PROMISE

Cor's cheek muscles were aching, but the smile that Aunt Syl hated was working on Cara. He'd never gotten into a fight with her, but he didn't want to find out what she could do. The wide-eyed witch backed up enough to give him room to pass, bumping into Bret, who dropped a few blackberries. Where had he gotten those this time of year?

Cor kept walking. Not his first choice to put his back to them, but he did. Up in the bed, Marty was eyeing the tall witch with her glowing, green hands, a ball of red energy forming behind his back and out of her sight.

They better not catch that birch tree on fire.

"Do it, Cara," Marty said.

"Tell him yourself," Cara yelled from farther away than she'd been.

Cor didn't turn, but Marty did. Slick appeared from the far side of the black mess that had been the energy plantings, saw Cor and stopped. His lips were stained purple, and he cupped a mound of berries against his hoodie.

Marty lifted his chin at Slick. "Take care of him."

"No way, man, I had enough the other night."

"I don't care. I want her, so get your ass in gear." Marty turned his back on Cor.

By the look on Slick's face, things were going down the loo for him. He made a wide circle to avoid Cor, jumped off the wall and trotted away.

Well, well. It'd been worth his time to stand up to Marty, aside from collecting the beechnuts. Cor mounted the wall. The tall girl was smart enough not to look at him, and he moved silently up behind Marty. "Sorry? What did you say?"

Marty spun, throwing out a close blast, but Cor was ready, blocking it with a gold shield and striking at Marty's legs as the shield rose.

The girl shrieked and ducked. Bloody good thing, because Marty fell into the wall of plants and Cor dove after him, taking a fist to his jaw and a kick as they tumbled to the charred ground, but finally getting a good hit back with a stunning blast. Marty lay there. Cor grabbed his foot and dragged him off the bed. Marty crumpled to the sidewalk. Cor pulled him up and retrieved his magic at the same time.

Marty slowly shook his head.

Cor didn't wait for him to be able to think. He poked a glowing finger to Marty's belly. "You've scared a visitor and made a bloody mess of someone's project. I'm reporting it unless you walk with your hands in the air straight down Wolman Street. Don't stop until you enter your building."

Eyes barely focusing, Marty raised his hands, and Cor shoved him in the right direction. Marty stumbled off. Thank the Orb, the street was deserted, though a few curtains were moving at windows on the upper floors. They had to get going before security came, 'cause for sure it was. At least he looked enough like Slick that people might think that bloke had been fighting Marty.

A mobile rang...in the middle of the messed-up berry

bushes. The tall girl answered with a muffled cry. They didn't have time for calls. He leaped back onto the wall and headed toward her incoherent muttering. Something green was beneath the charred tangle. He didn't remember her wearing a green coat, but it had to be her. Using a burst of golden energy, he shoved the debris aside—

"How the hell did you do that?"

"Who's there?" called her voice from inside a hickory nut. He'd swear it was real, except it was the size of an armchair.

"Cor van—*Cor*," he said. "We need to leave." It was one thing to spell trees or fling magical light shows at midnight, but an outright magical fight in daytime violated city policy.

"Okay," she said, then quieter, "I'm gonna be okay, Beri. Someone from the conference is here to get me. I'll call you tonight. Thanks." Louder again, she said, "You might want to stand back. I—just in case."

He took a step back. "Right, then, let's be going."

The nut shimmered, then dissolved, leaving the tall girl sitting there, her knees pulled up to her chin, mobile in one hand, fingers poked into a transparent shell that disappeared, too. She looked at her hand, closed the last of the magic into it and whispered, "Wow," like she'd never seen something like that before.

He raised a brow at her. "Hickory nut?"

She stood up, pushing aside the last of the tattered vegetation, some of it smoldering. The plants bent at the merest touch. It was as if... No, they couldn't be. She lifted her foot, and the plants parted like the Red Sea. Yes, they were deferring to her.

She slid the mobile into her pocket and gripped her backpack straps. "I, uh, collected them last weekend. First thing I could think of that had a protective coating. So I wouldn't get hurt in your magical fight." She gestured to him. "Are you okay, Cor?"

Her hand was shaking. Not as calm as she wanted him to

think she was. Neither had he fared as well as in his last encounter with Marty. His trousers were ripped, and his blazer had burn marks over it—so much for his docent getup. He swept a hand over himself and magicked into clean clothes, black jeans, T-shirt and his leather jacket. *Spells*, not the jacket. He changed it for his older green blazer.

"Yes, thanks"—he looked at her name tag—"Fern. You missed the bus."

She looked around. "Where did those—"

"Gone." He didn't want to talk about the fight. Maybe it'd go away. "Did you plan to continue on the field trip?"

"I—yeah. Thanks for coming back. The fight, too. I really appreciate you getting rid of those guys."

The wail of a siren sounded in the distance.

He stared up at the birch. He could hide there, but could she? Likely not. But with those long legs, she ought to be able to keep up with him.

"Let's go, unless you'd rather do some explaining." He waved at the disaster of a garden bed.

She groaned. "Sorry to be so much trouble." She bent and put her fingers into the ground. New blackberry canes sprouted from the ashes, flushing out leaves in a bright spring green. In a matter of minutes, the burnt remains were hidden from view. She shooed him off the wall, followed herself and perked up the crushed flowers the same way. Straightening, she rubbed her hands together. "There. Now Duffy won't be totally pissed at me."

"This way." He started a fast walk up the street, looking back again over his shoulder. The damaged garden bed looked no different than the others now. "If you have that much power, why didn't you just stop them yourself?"

"Look, this sounds like a wild tale, but I'm a beginner at magic. I only found out I'm Windborne two months ago."

He snorted, but the siren drowned it. She kept pace, and they reached the only car parked on the street, a green Smart car. He rounded the driver's side and yanked the handle.

It didn't budge.

"What the—" He patted his pocket. The key wasn't there. Had he dropped it?

"Did you lose the key in the fight?" she asked.

"We'll have to go back," he said impatiently. "Or on." The siren wailed again, closer this time. He turned—

She grabbed his arm. "You changed clothes. Is it in those pockets?"

"Curses." He magicked the pile of clothes into his arms. The door lock clicked with the key in range. Driving was new this summer, so keeping track of the automatic key was, too.

He flung open the door and threw the clothes in the back. "Get in," he called while hitting the unlock button. The car started at the touch of another button.

She folded her long legs into the cramped foot space and said, "Seat belts," as he started to pull from the curb.

He groaned, but put his on to stop the beeping and accelerated slowly—no need to draw attention, or get a speeding ticket. Bonterra had strict rules for the few electric cars allowed—and luckily the estate had managed to acquire one. Borrowing it to find this visiting girl had been quickly approved.

"Really, though, thanks," she said. "If those guys had figured out I have little control over my magic, I'd have been trapped. I owe you. Big-time."

He glanced at her—clearly using another of his threatening looks, because the girl who towered over him by a half foot leaned away.

"A favor," she clarified. "If I could…repay you for your ruined clothes? Trade plants? Grow some nursery stock for you?"

He found her name tag again. *Fern, Heir to the Witch of the*

Meadows, the Isle of Giuthas. If she lived there and had a title—whatever that meant—how could he use this favor to get in with Lady Pina?

"Replace your earbuds?"

Cor touched his ears—huh, they were gone. His mobile? He put out his hand and retrieved it from his damaged blazer and another set of earbuds from his dresser top at home. He dropped them into the console. "It's fine, thanks. The clothes are…" He shrugged. "Those are things. I'm far more interested in…"

She looked at him warily.

He made a turn before answering. "How exactly did you arrange to work for Lady Pina?"

"I don't work for her." She blew out a breath. "I manage the Meadows, but all the habitats are so closely connected on the isle that they wanted me to understand more about the Forest."

"Does anyone work for her?"

"Lady Pina? No, not regularly."

"That's the favor I ask of you in return." He paused longer than he needed to at an intersection. "I want to work for Lady Pina in the ancient pine groves."

"I can't give you that. It's not my habitat."

"You are a habitat manager on the Isle of Giuthas, correct? Witch of the Meadows?"

"Heir to the Witch." She tapped her name tag. "Doesn't mean I…I'd have to check around before I made any decisions for the island."

"But you know the people who do?"

She shifted in her seat. "Of course I know them—"

"That's more than I do. You can convince them to let me work in the Scots pines. Lady Pina needs to train someone to take over for her. Let's be frank, she doesn't have long to get her act together. You'll be doing this crowd a real favor by getting things all set for the day she dies."

"That's rude," she snapped.

"Maybe, but you can't say it's not true. You all are going to be up a tree, literally, when she dies, and no one knows the ways of her habitat." He knew that from an emergency the foundation had been called in on.

"That's not true. There are people—wizards—on the isle who know what she does."

Cor smiled, then stopped, because it was *that* smile again. He remembered a few things about the island from this morning. "Not nearly enough of them. Population for the Isle of Giuthas has been dropping the last forty years. A rare habitat like the Scots pine wildwoods that have survived for centuries under Windborne care does not deserve to be compromised because of some antiquated idea that only a family member is suited to manage it."

She didn't say anything the rest of the way to the estate. He drove up to the gate, waving to Barnaby, and parked the car in its slot behind the gatehouse. They got out, then he had to duck back in to collect his mobile. When he came around to face her, Fern stood with her arms crossed, tall and frowning. He wasn't about to let this favor go.

"Look, let's cut to the chase here. I'm knowledgeable about Forest species and habitats. I'm magically skilled, with a strong ability for trees. And I'm interested in this ancient grove."

She nodded like she agreed. "So you want me to arrange an apprenticeship for you in Lady Pina's Pines habitat."

"That's the idea. Do you promise to help me?" He extended his hand.

She met his handshake. "Yes, I will."

The magic to set the pledge raced down his arm and through his fingers to hers. She blinked at the green and honey energy surrounding their clasped hands.

"Oops," she said. "Sorry. I must not have put my magic

away." She withdrew her hand. "I'll try, but I can't promise they'll agree."

What did she mean, she'd *try*? She'd proposed the favor and *pledged* to arrange it. Unless... Cor cocked his head to peer at her. "You weren't kidding about being new to magic, were you?"

8

SOME THINGS LEFT UNEXPLAINED

"If I could control my magic, I'd clean my clothes, too," Fern snapped. All that showed Cor had been in a fight was a dark mark on his cheek. "I don't make *that* many mistakes, and I'd appreciate it if you kept it quiet." She jerked her head toward the guard peering curiously around the gatehouse.

"You might be surprised," Cor muttered. "I, uh, will have to hold you to that pledge. Can't undo it. But right now we best find Lady Pina and let her know you're all right. She was rather in a dither when I offered to fetch you. Come on."

Something about the way he said the pledge bit was fishy, but Fern kept quiet. He'd rescued her from a sticky situation, which seemed to be how she met wizards. It was more important to find Lady Pina. She trailed him around to the front of the gatehouse.

A guard in a pressed green uniform accepted the car key, and a second held open a massive wrought-iron gate. Above, scrolled lettering read "The Gruen Estate." High stone walls extended down the street in both directions from the gate's tall stone pillars, and trees blocked any view. It looked like they took security seriously, but Cor walked through confidently. She followed, and they strode up a cobble drive covered by arching rowan trees. Toward the end, the view opened to a towering stone…

"It's a castle," she said stupidly.

"It's an estate house with towers," he said in his deadpan way. "No moat."

"But it has crenellations around the top."

"At the time it was built, defending yourself with arrows was a daily thing."

"What about magic?"

"The arrows were spell-cast to explode."

Oh.

"The grounds are better."

She tore her gaze from the castle. Trees didn't only line the drive, they filled the grounds. Visitors walked the stone pathways winding among hollies with lower limbs sweeping the ground, peeling-bark birches, broad evergreens and stands of deciduous trees. Most were underplanted with flowering shrubs, ferns and other natural-looking vegetation, so many shades and shapes that Fern didn't know the names of.

"I guess I missed Mr. Acer's description of this."

Cor waved. "The arboretum dates back to 1738, the year the main house was completed and the conservatory and greenhouses started. Clarence didn't wait to plant the grounds—eight-point-two hectares of them, if you want that detail. He'd collected various species on his travels across the British Isles and the continent—Sherwood Forest, Taiga Forest, the Black Forest, all the famous forests. Many were grafts that he rooted himself. It took him decades of trial and error to get the sun and shade conditions correct to imitate their natural conditions so the long-term care would be easier. He raised and lowered the perimeter wall three times, finally leaving a mix of heights."

She laughed. "Really?"

"Really. It *piqued* the neighbors, according to his diaries, but after fifty years, the trees had matured and overgrown it to the point that no one could tell anymore. It'll be faster if we fly up the drive." Dark brown wings were unfurling at his back.

This time, she looked away. "I'm good with walking."

"You honestly are a beginner at magic?"

"Yeah." Could he please just drop it?

Ten minutes later, they mounted the front steps. Cor asked another green-uniformed guard where the tour was, then rushed her through a broad hallway past room after room of heavy oak furniture, landscape paintings and Tiffany lamps.

"Wow," she exclaimed. "Is the upstairs as fancy?"

"Mostly foundation offices." He pressed a panel beneath a grand staircase and led the way spiraling down a musty stone stairwell, lighting his fingertips against the dark.

"This better not be a dungeon you're trapping me in," she whispered.

"Heh," he snorted. "And foil your promise to get me to Lady Pina's forest? No way. It's called the catacombs, which just sounds better than wine cellar, another of Clarence's hobbies."

His accent was British, but he sounded more like a Boulder High student than Beri did. "Where are you from?"

"Bonterra, but my family traveled a lot when I was little, so my accent got diluted."

"More like your slang vocabulary expanded. Did they—"

"*Shh*," he said suddenly. "Voices echo down here. I think I hear them."

She didn't hear anything. His golden glow trailed past a lot of closed wooden doors, and a minute later, the cobwebby hallway turned a corner. The room it opened into was clean, well-lit and lined with wine bottle racks. People were filing out the far side, ushered by Mr. Acer.

"Where have you been?" he exclaimed. "Lady Pina is upstairs making calls."

"Ohmigod, not my mother," Fern muttered. "I need to stop her."

"Just lost her way," Cor said, "She's fine…" He stepped toward the crowded doorway, then pivoted back the direction they'd just come. "I'll stop her." He dashed back into the dark hallway, his glow bobbing.

"Come along." Mr. Acer clasped her arm. "I'll keep an eye on you this time."

She'd have preferred to go with Cor.

The group gathered in an upper corridor where a female tour guide waited at a heavy metal door. "The armory holds the collection of van Gruen family weapons: swords, daggers, dueling pistols, rapiers. Only three people can enter at a time. Please circle from the right wall to the left, so one my may enter as another leaves." She pushed open the door and gestured to those at the head of the line to begin.

Fern waited at the back with Mr. Acer and looked around for Cor. He had to have found Lady Pina by now.

"Labels will indicate the type of weapon," the guide continued, "the owner and the name they gave the weapon, if any. Of special note is the collection centered on the back wall, placed by Clarence himself so no others would grab them by mistake during a siege. This section includes his favorite weapons collected during his travels with his sons and, of course, his famous broadsword, Leafbringer. Forged with joint spelling by Clarence himself, the dwarf Windborne foresters of the Black Forest, and the Wizard Zora of Sherwood Forest, Leafbringer contains a magic said to work for the forester's blood descendants alone."

She nodded at this before continuing, "The blade will slice oak as if passing through butter. A touch of the blade will seal living wood cells against disease, insect and fungal infection. It is the blade Clarence used to take his cuttings and grafts and the tool he used to wedge open the soil to plant them. Every tree on the estate is said to have been planted as a centimeters' thick cutting, which as you can see worked like magic."

A rumble of laughter rose from the crowd, nearly masking approaching footsteps. Cor accompanied Lady Pina—who of course didn't look happy.

Fern stepped away from the group. "Thanks, Cor. I'm sorry I missed the bus, ma'am. Did you call my mom?"

Lady Pina lifted her hands. "What could Heather have done about it from Colorado? No, I had Bonterra's wizard security on the line as they searched the vicinity of where I last saw you."

The sirens they'd heard? Fern met Cor's gaze. "Sorry," she said again. "I went to look at an academy project garden that Duffy planted and lost track of time."

"Or the bus?" Lady Pina hugged Fern around the shoulders, her frown dissolving. "I understand about your keen interest in plants, dear, but do try to be more careful. You don't"—her gaze cut to Cor—"*know your way around.*"

No point in keeping it quiet. "Ma'am, he knows how pitiful my ability *to find my way is.* I owe Cor a huge favor for getting me back. If you could help out with that, he'd like to study our pines..."

Lady Pina had already begun shaking her head as she stepped toward the line to see the armory.

Fern grasped her arm. "But he *really* rescued me," she whispered. "A couple of wizard guys had me cornered."

Lady Pina stared past Fern toward Cor, still managing to look down her nose. "This is the truth? You didn't orchestrate some—"

"How would I have done that?" Cor spat, and immediately a look of horror flooded his face.

Fern cringed. That wasn't the way to talk to an elder, and he knew it.

"I-I was working," he said, trying to recover. "For the conference."

"He had no way of knowing *when* I would wander off. Give him a break." Fern crossed her arms. She shouldn't say it, but… "You're being unreasonably stubborn about blocking outsiders from a resource everyone admires."

"The very reason it's still a resource," Lady Pina huffed and bestowed another frown on them. "I suppose we can make an exception for a visit. This young man's project did outline a deep interest in trees."

"Very deep." Cor nodded. "Like, my life."

By now, Fern could tell he meant this, but Lady Pina smiled a rather patronizing smile, her gaze pausing on his shiny boots and the phone stuffed into his blazer's breast pocket.

"Considering you live in the largest wizard city in the United Kingdom, I doubt it. Leave instructions with Fern on how to contact you, and I will make the arrangements for a visit." She gave a final nod and joined the armory line.

Fern tilted her head that they should follow, and he fell into step with her. "You nearly blew that one," she muttered under her breath.

"Thanks for the save."

He truly did want this, and she had to admire his persistence. Still, he wasn't telling her everything, and he'd have to if he wanted more of her help. "The elders running Giuthas are strict, but it's worth your time navigating their rules to see the isle."

"I'll be careful. Appreciate you holding up your end of the pledge to get me this first step."

She side-eyed him. Heck, he was dreaming if he still thought he could pull off getting an apprenticeship. But that wasn't up to her. She pulled out her phone. "Give me your e-mail."

He glanced at Lady Pina's back and shook his head. "Tomorrow, when she isn't around. I'll find you in the afternoon." He gestured her ahead of him into the armory. "As a fellow plant enthusiast, you need to admire Leafbringer, Clarence's pride and joy." He pointed to the back wall.

Amid other shiny swords, the lit one in the center had a short blade made of brown steel engraved with a bough of leaves, each one a different species. The darker hilt was set with square-cut emeralds winking between bronze crossed feathers and the twigs of the bail.

It was a beautiful thing, certainly created by a plant lover.

"Did he really heal trees with it?"

Cor grinned, the first sincere happiness she'd seen in him. "So they say."

Cor accompanied the tour back to the conference, when all he wanted to do was race to Aunt Syl's cottage and pack for the trip. He checked the bus for trash and forgotten items, then did the same in the lecture halls with the rest of the volunteers. At last, they gathered for the coordinator to review schedule changes. He waited at the edge of the group, surreptitiously checking his mobile.

Finally, the warlock said, "Good day, folks," and Cor bolted for the door.

Someone caught his arm. "Hey, Cor?"

Bloody hell, it was the witch from this morning, the one who'd traded duties with him—Penelope.

She was removing her name tag. "Did you forget we were getting tea?"

"Right, I did," he admitted while walking out the door with her. Potter's was on the way to the estate. How could he make his lapse in memory not seem so bad? He didn't want to hurt her feelings. "I have to pack," he said while trying to think of some reasonable excuse that wouldn't involve arranging another get-together.

"You're leaving?"

Right, that would do. "Yes, I unexpectedly had something come up today. Sorry, but I don't know when I'll be returning."

She looked so disappointed, and he was hungry…

"See here, I can take a half hour before heading home."

She talked. He listened. And exactly thirty minutes later, scones devoured and tea cooled, he said, "I've got to go."

"Want to get together again next week?" she asked.

Tell her. "Don't know if I'll be back…" He stood up, suddenly too warm. So did she, and he tried desperately to form the words. "I…" *Don't want to see you again if you want to prebond.* "I'm not"—*into witches*—"I'm sixteenth year."

"Oh," she said, frowning. "I'm, uh, eighteenth. When's your birthday?"

They were out the door. He stuffed his hands into his pockets and looked down the street. *Just tell her.* "I…can't," he said and walked off.

Great Orb, what was wrong with him? He knew people who had no problem saying they were gay. His parents and sister knew and didn't care. Aunt Syl was gay, too, and the rest of the estate staff accepted it. Many probably assumed he was, wearing earrings and all. Why couldn't he just say it when he needed to?

Because of the two times he had, a witch had burst into tears the first time, and the other, the guy had punched him and told all the other kids. It'd been a miserable summer in that enclave.

Cor dropped his blazer on a greenhouse table and finished potting up the eight juniper root stock that Harold hadn't finished. Putting his hands in the soil, handling the fresh little trees…that always calmed him. He watered all twelve and found the right places for them. The edge of his failure was starting to peel off, so he watered, yanking the hose around the conservatory to douse all his personal plants.

"A bit wet for a bristlecone, don't you think?" said Master Harold from behind him.

"I got a spot," he blurted. "Or a chance to try for one. I'll need to leave tomorrow."

Master Harold took the hose from him with a grin. "Saw you'd planted up the bonsai. They've all sprouted new needles. Didn't leave Leafbringer in some corner the rest of us won't find for a week?"

They had? He glanced at his hands. Orb take it, his energy was charged. "No. Didn't use it."

Harold had switched off the water and dropped the hose. Cor bent to retrieve it, but the older man clasped his elbow. "Tomorrow, you say? Did Syl agree?"

Cor groaned. "Help me talk to her? Please?"

They climbed to the third floor, his guts twisting, and stood in the doorway of Aunt Syl's office. When his father's younger sister—thirty-three, single and an economics major—looked up from her computer, they lowered into the sterile chairs before her crowded desk.

"I have an invitation from Lady Pina on the Isle of Guthas to visit her ancient Scots pine grove," he said.

Aunt Syl's fine black brows rose above the frames of her purple glasses, but Harold softly said, "Make it happen, Syl," and she got on the telephone.

He had to talk to his parents, Harold talked to them, they talked to someone else, or maybe several someone elses. Cor sank lower in the chair, waiting. He'd sneak out if he had to. His parents called back, but spoke only to Syl, who nodded repeatedly while glancing at Harold, who was snoring quietly now that he'd done his part. Finally, Aunt Syl stood and stretched and removed the band holding her waist-length dreadlocks. They fell around her shoulders, the usual signal that she was ready to go home. The phone rang again, and she handed it to Cor.

"You may go," his father said. "We trust you to know if the situation is safe, and from every account we've heard, this is a stable population in an enclave difficult to gain access to. Congratulations on your invitation."

His dad wouldn't be saying that if he knew the real circumstances. But no one had asked. He was going before that old lady had a chance to change her mind.

"Tell your sister where you'll be and report in every two days," Dad was saying and added cautions about working within other wizards' enclaves, policies Cor had known for years.

"Thank you," he breathed and hung up. "I have to call Hazel and tell her I won't be here."

Aunt Syl's head swung around. "How long will you be gone?"

"Don't know."

Her jaw tightened. "I'm scheduled to speak at a meeting in Belgium two weeks from now. I expected you to be here when Hazel comes home that weekend."

His older sister was attending sessions at a program for magical art in another enclave that ended every three weeks and sent the students home for the break. Hazel was a decent artist, and this program seemed to be working out with her anxiety. When she returned to the estate, she needed a family member on hand in case she hit a crisis—he and Aunt Syl had shared the responsibility this summer. Two weeks. That seemed like forever from now, and if he had to be honest, by then Lady Pina would have decided she didn't want him there. "I'll be here for Hazel, don't worry."

"Come along and call her from the house," Aunt Syl said. "While I get dinner on."

She'd not only heated the leftovers, but had eaten and washed up by the time Cor finished listening to Hazel and assuring her he would not forget.

After all that sitting, he visited Toots and flew with her beneath the invisible dome of the magical shielding that hid Bonterra from humans. With the early hour he had to report to the conference the next morning, Cor had to get everything ready tonight. Instead of returning to his aunt's cottage, he went to another building that served as his family's storage unit. Walking between the shelves, he pulled down a larger day pack and took it to his clothing trunk.

What do I need to stay someplace where I have no idea where I'm staying?

9

CREATING A SHORTCUT

Fern skipped the evening social and did her homework. When she fell into bed, bizarre dreams interrupted her sleep. She was flying over rolling green countryside that looked nothing like Colorado or the Isle of Giuthas because of the farms, stone walls and hedges. She dropped into patches of forest that she seemed to know and visited with the people there like they were old friends. But when the dream suggested that she was going to stay overnight in the woods—like, camp—Fern woke herself up. Uh-uh. That wasn't happening. This outdoor girl went only so far when communing with nature.

The Sunday sessions—including a tour of the botanical gardens—went by without any hitches. Fern made sure of that by sticking close to Lady Pina. She seemed to have forgiven Fern and didn't say anything about missing the bus or Cor coming to the isle. Oddly, neither did Cor. She saw him several times, and they said hello, but he was always busy, and he still hadn't given her his e-mail address.

After the last session, she searched the volunteer area on the main floor, but no one knew where he was, so she went up to grab her stuff and met Lady Pina in the lobby to check out. Fern asked if Cor had contacted her.

"I have nae spoken with the young man."

"Then how will he get a message to us about the visit?"

"They are just…sent."

"I don't even know where he lives."

Lady Pina shrugged and greeted another of her friends. Cor had said he'd get in touch with her, so she shouldn't worry, but Fern went to the conference information table and left her e-mail for him.

While she was gone, Lady Pina had gotten drawn into conversation with more people. Again. Fern smiled politely. "Meet you out front?" Lady Pina nodded, and Fern escaped through the front doors to an entrance courtyard.

Leaning against the wall in the sun, stood Cor. A black pack, a little larger than her school pack, sat at his feet with a longboard propped beside it. Looked like he was heading home as well.

"Hi," she said. "I looked for you earlier. I need your e-mail or something so I can let you know about the visit to the isle."

Cor squinted at her. "Why? I'm going with you." At that, he slid his pack straps onto his shoulders and picked up the longboard.

"You can't. She didn't arrange anything yet."

"Why not?"

"Too busy visiting here. You better not push your luck."

Cor rolled his eyes and made an annoyed sucking sound. "I have no luck with her. She won't give me the time of day."

As if to demonstrate, Lady Pina exited the hotel, strode up to them, nodded at Cor, but spoke to Fern alone. "People are gathering for a last tea, and I wish to attend if you don't mind if we delay our return?"

Crap, she didn't want to sit through another one of these meals where no one would talk to her. Fern pulled out her fail-safe response, one every high school student kept handy. "I have a test tomorrow."

Lady Pina looked confused.

"At my school, uh, human academy? I have an exam, a, uh, judging of my skills—" That was it! "They are checking if I have the proficiency to continue my studying there."

"Ah, so this is an important event in the day of a human?"

"Yeah, my mom would be really upset if I don't do well. But I hate to ruin your tea plans. Can I go back by myself?"

Lady Pina appeared to consider this for a moment before extending both hands and swirling up a ball of her orange magic in each. Seeing it this time, Fern realized it was the exact color of the Scots pine tree bark. In one, the orange sticklike glass on the leather lace appeared, the peregrinator they'd used to travel to Bonterra. In the other lay a glass pinecone on a silver chain.

Fern started. Mom made the delicate brown glass ornaments every summer to sell at winter holiday art shows. This had to be a piece of her mother's flamework. But how did Lady Pina come to have it?

Before she could ask, Lady Pina touched the two pieces of glass together. A flash of orange hopped from the stick to the pinecone. "This glass will hold the isle's entrance magic for my use for a short time." Lady Pina looped the chain with the pinecone over her head and handed Fern the stick-shaped peregrinator. "Use this peregrinator to return to Hillux, but leave it on Lark's kitchen counter so I can retrieve it after I have confirmed the location of the café."

It was easy enough for her to leave it in Gran's cottage. Yet Fern hesitated. The warmth of the glass was fading in her hand.

"You remember where the pereport station is and my instructions to you earlier?" Lady Pina asked.

Yeah, mainly because Mom, Dad and Gran had gone over peregrinator use multiple times upon learning she'd be making this trip. "It's in the next block down." She pointed in the correct direction. "Just, I feel bad you'll have to come to the isle to get it."

"Worry not, the cafés under discussion are next to the station, each preferred by my various friends for different reasons, and I welcome the opportunity to avoid the end of the discussion." Lady Pina smiled. "Now you run home to study for your judgment while I move my friends out the door and ascertain we will be having tea and not dinner in Bonterra." She pivoted on her heel and walked back inside.

"Thank you!" Fern looped the leather lace around her neck, just as she'd always worn the glass teardrop she used for travel from Colorado to the Isle of Giuthas. She turned to go and ran smack into Cor, her chest slamming his nose. Face warming, she jolted back and mumbled, "Sorry."

He looked dazed and was now staring at her chest. *Argh, boys!* Fern sidestepped him, her face now burning up. She just better go. "See you," she said and walked past him.

"Wait!" He caught up and walked beside her, up the tree-lined avenue.

Side-glances she sneaked over the rest of the block confirmed Cor wasn't taking his eyes off her. *This is ridiculous!* Fern stopped before crossing the street. "Cut it out."

His gaze jerked up. "Huh?"

"You're staring. Rudely. And following me."

His face shifted to the stony look she'd come to know over the weekend. "She *gave* you a peregrinator for the isle."

Oh, that was the reason for his stare. Right. He'd had all weekend to stare at her and hadn't. She closed her hand over the glass. "I do have to get home to study."

He opened his mouth, closed it and smiled. "Brilliant, let's go." He crossed the street.

What choice did she have but to follow? It was the only route to the station where all pereporting was done.

Still, she slowed. Should she just take him? She had enough

to do with school and chores, and this would save her the hassle of e-mails and arranging how to get him to the isle. That somehow was tricky with the enclave's shielding. Gran had an extra room, or maybe Beri would help with a place to stay for this guy—which would probably be only overnight. Gran would know the best way to approach Lady Pina, so when Cor went to the grove for a visit—which she *had* agreed to—he could persuade Lady Pina to give him a trial. That would fulfill Fern's favor to arrange everything.

By the time they reached the station, she'd convinced herself this was the right thing to do. Cor might look like a Goth, but he wasn't too sullen and had done nothing to dissuade her. Before Fern knew it, they had approached the counter, been issued a stall and were walking through its door.

It worried her a little that she was moving forward on this without asking, but Cor looked confident as he held out his forearm. Perfectly ready for the trip...except for the longboard tucked under his other arm.

Unable to keep from smiling, she waved to it. "There aren't any streets on the isle. Nothing is paved."

"Oh." Frowning, he gripped it in both hands. The board lit with honey-colored sparkles and disappeared. He looked lost for a moment, then his poised expression returned as he held up his arm again.

This guy didn't quite have it as together as he wanted her to believe. But it was simplest to lay one hand on his bare wrist, take the peregrinator in the other and say, "To the Isle of Giuthas."

Of course, she visualized the front porch of Hillux as the orange light swirled off Lady Pina's peregrinator and expanded into a portal. Cor stepped forward to go through, but it was wrong. She pulled him back. This wasn't Gran's cottage. It wasn't even the Meadows. The image of a windswept rocky area with short bushes looked familiar, though. Crap, Mount Lookout. They'd hiked on the Giuthas mountaintop before school started.

"Not there. Hillux!" She held tightly to Cor as the image blurred with a green haze. *Hillux, Hillux!* She thought of the smell of the wildflowers, the tangy breeze, the constant chirp and buzz of the birds and insects. The view cleared, its scene shifting... Fern held her breath until—there!—the grassy dome of Hillux appeared, the stone steps leading off the earthworks that surrounded Gran's cottage. It wasn't exactly on the porch as she'd wanted, but that was okay. Anyplace in the Meadows was better than hiking down the mountain, through the woods and across the ridges.

Her fingers tightened on Cor's arm. "This is it. Come on." They stepped through the circle of light and into the tall grass. Everything was just as she'd left it yesterday morning—the smell, the sounds, the feel.

Cor turned to take in the Meadows, the two forested mountains between which their valley lay and the Irish Sea on the far horizon before facing her again, frowning. "You're holding out on me."

"What?"

"The magic you just worked—you're better at it than you're letting on if you can control a peregrinator."

"I didn't want to end up over there." She pointed to the highest of the mountains. "Landing on the top of Mount Lookout would have been a lot of trouble."

"Ach, not nearly as much trouble as you're in now," resounded a fast-speaking, high-pitched voice as ropes of multi-colored magic appeared above their heads and whipped into a magical cage around them.

10

RED TAPE

The Isle of Giuthas

Fern whirled. The cage surrounded them—no escaping it physically. But did they even want to? Outside it, a weird, blinding light—magic?—zipped over the hilltop, preventing her from identifying who had trapped them.

Cor pressed into her side. "What have you done?" he growled.

A sinking feeling grew in her stomach. Her parents had told her to be careful in Bonterra, but this was her home enclave. "I don't know. It's never happened to me before."

"Mistress Fern?" The mysterious voice snapped out her name from the right. No one was there.

"Y-yes?" Why did she have to sound so scared?

Above them, the voice said, "I'm surprised." Then, from their left, he said, "I was assured you would be no trouble."

The wizard was moving, but Fern couldn't get a good look at him because the light was always in her eyes—oh, duh. The person *was* the light...at least right now. Wizards could do that?

Cor was frowning, so she didn't want to ask him. "Wh-who are you?"

"Why did you alter your passage?" the wizard-light asked from near their ankles.

Fern looked down. "I-I—"

"It's against the rules—"

She and Cor twisted to look behind them, tripping into each other.

"—if you are bringing a stranger to the isle."

Cor grabbed her arm. "Hey, are you trying to get me banned? I don't appreciate being treated this—"

"I'm in trouble, too, *if you didn't notice.*" Frowning, Fern shook him off. He reminded her more of Raven each moment they spent together.

Like Raven, Cor didn't back down under her glare. He jerked his head, flipping his curls to the side, his honey eyes glinting. His look said, *Well, fix it, then.*

So, drawing a breath, she called into the space overtop of Hillux, "Show yourself! It's too hard to talk like this."

"A moment."

A sound like the wind blowing through power lines surrounded them. But Giuthas had no power lines. Seconds later, a small figure shimmered into view.

"This is the closest I can come to meeting your request, Mistress Fern. During my watch, I must stay alert," said the man.

He had light brown skin and looked like an elf, though she doubted he was. His ears weren't pointed, just large and sticking out. Or maybe his face was narrow, hard to tell because of his flailing auburn-red ringlets. Worse, he sparkled—which color, or colors, weren't clear—and bounced from foot to foot, even in midair. The guy was a jittery mass of movement, and it didn't help that the glowing cage ropes stood between them.

Cor elbowed her. "Get on with it. I don't like being a sitting duck."

"You are nae sitting. Nor are you a duck. Both can be arranged, if you prefer." The man raised a hand.

Fern darted her hands to block him—stupid, really, because she hadn't tried magicking a shield—but she flushed magic like she had with the protective hickory nut. Or tried to. Nothing came out. Just as well, because the man was smirking. "We, uh, this must be a misunderstanding. This is my grandmother's house, the Meadows, where I…" Hold it, *she* was in charge of the Meadows. Why was she stammering around when she belonged here? "I was just coming home, to *my* habitat." Cor elbowed her again. "And bringing a friend with me."

"Aye, that I did nae miss, and therein lies the problem, Mistress Fern," he sneered. "Your friend here is nae approved to visit the Isle of Giuthas."

"How do I get him approved?"

"You speak to the council. They approve the visitor. They submit the person's details to the Watchers."

This sounded like a lot of red tape, which—her heart sank— was probably what everyone meant when they said the isle was secure. She must not have triggered this guy's radar when she first accidently came through the portal because of her blood relationship to Gran. "The Watchers?"

"The Watchers are the wizards charged with keeping the isle secure," said Raven.

Fern spun around, her despair lifting, though he was frowning. "Thank goodness, you're here. Tell him who I am."

"Fee knows who you are."

"And?"

"Fee doesn't know who"—Raven jerked his chin at Cor —"that wizard is. You broke a rule."

Cor grunted, and she elbowed him this time. "Can you get someone to fix this?"

"Suppose I have to if I am to have my promised lesson." With a shake of his head, Raven rose into the air and glided down the side of Hillux.

Oh yeah, she'd promised Raven a computer lesson this afternoon. He must have been waiting—and oh no!—he was going home, to *her* home, which meant…

"Dad," she shouted. "Get Merlin." But he continued toward Gran's front door, darn her pigheaded brother. Classic Raven. He lived to create conflict.

Mom stormed up Hillux's steps a minute later, her long hair pulled into a thick ponytail with the curly strands twisting into knots like Fern's stomach. She skidded to a stop outside the cage as Raven ran up behind her, still trying to explain. She raised her hands—

The little Watcher squealed and winked out. Fern couldn't blame him.

—only to shove something at Raven. He caught it. *A cookie.* Fern could smell it from here. One of Dad's huge oatmeal spice cookies.

"Who is that?" Cor whispered.

Mom flipped up her palms and flashed sage-green energy—

Cor yanked Fern down. "What the hell is she doing?"

Freakin' bloody nutcase. Hands gold and darting, Cor flushed a barrier around them. Solid. Safe.

"Fee," shouted the nutty witch. "Show yourself!"

"My mom," Fern muttered. "Get off of me, so I can—what is this?" Seated, she pushed at the barrier he'd spelled for himself and then for trees, imprinting the golden film with a green handprint.

"*That* is your mum?" Of all the answers he'd expected, that wasn't one of them. Parents didn't behave this way. Fern was just as bad, thrashing at his magic and stretching it. He grabbed her arm. "Cut it out. It's a protection. I'm not letting your dodgy island wizards put me out."

"This is thin. How can it—"

A *crack*, like thunder, sounded. The cage shook and flickered, but his barrier merely rippled like a leaf had landed on a pond.

Fern's eyes widened, and he couldn't help smirking. "It only looks thin. It absorbs energy blasts—*like the one that just hit us*."

Her mum and the security wizard were yelling back and forth, all of it along the lines of "How dare you attack my daughter?" and "I did nae attack her."

Despite that, Fern scrambled to her knees and pushed toward the cage ropes, stretching the barrier farther. Outside, the Watcher flashed back and forth, and the nutty witch blasted after him.

Curiosity won out. "Of all the—here. Just keep down." He pressed his palms to his magic, reforming and shifting it. Together, they crawled over to the ropes. "Please don't stretch it again."

"Thanks," she murmured. She watched the witch pace like it was a demonstration she had to duplicate. Her sage energy streaked to wherever the Watcher paused.

"I've never seen my mom throwing magic around."

"Seriously?"

"Honest. Told you I only learned I have magic a month ago. Mom kept hers hidden from me while we lived in the human world. I don't think Raven has seen this either." She pointed.

The black-haired warlock was ducking the blasts, wincing when the witch hit the cage, but looking as curious as Fern.

Her mum still hadn't hit the Watcher, and that was making her angrier. At least, Cor figured it had by the way her hair was alight. His sister's did that when she got mad.

"Does she have to make up for it now?" he asked sarcastically.

"It's kind of funny, in a scary way," Fern whispered, "considering she's wearing clothes I've seen her in for years. That's what she wears for flameworking glass. She must have been working and came in to get a snack."

Indeed, the ripped jeans and faded sweatshirt were a typical human outfit—but not the scorched canvas apron. The witch stopped suddenly, drew in her magic, crossed her arms and tapped her foot.

"Oh crap, this is bad. The last time I saw Mom do that was when I was twelve and pushed a discussion about meeting my dad too far."

"I am losin' my patience, Fee," her mum said in such a low voice that Cor had to strain to hear the words. "Ye canna avoid me, so 'tis better to appear and let us have this out."

Fern's lips parted in awe, and so had the bloke's with the hair like hers.

"That's some tough witch," Cor muttered. "That your brother?"

Fern side-glanced at him. "Yeah. Twin brother."

"Nice he's stuck around to support you."

Fern rolled her eyes.

Nothing happened for the space of several heartbeats, then the whine of a massive power collecting sounded and Fee winked into sight. Brilliantly quick, the witch darted and landed a finger on him. One finger, on his shoulder. The jittery man shuddered to a stop.

He was as small as Master Harold was large. This Watcher wasn't that old, though certainly his parents' age.

"Ach, Heather!" he howled. "I canna stand it when you do that."

"Well, we have something in common, then, because I do nae like what ye have done to my daughter. My heir is nae to be treated such."

"Your heir has breached security."

"Surely you know it was a mistake."

"Have you gotten a good look at the wizard with her? There is a distinct possibility the lass has been coerced."

"I resent that," Cor snapped, the words out of his mouth before he thought about how his tone might sound to white folks. He cringed. *Bloody stupid to spout off to elders I don't know.* He had to fix it. "She acted of her own free will and could have left Bonterra without me."

Fern snorted, and they turned.

Cor sucked his teeth. "You want out of here or not?" he said under his breath. "You need to agree with me."

"Yes," she said quickly. "I brought him here as a favor to see the Pines. Lady Pina agreed to a visit."

Then, for all her craziness, Fern's mum rolled her eyes at Fern and turned back to the odd little man. "From what I see, the boy looks like any teen attending Fern's high school—er, lower academy. What do you say to giving these kids a chance to explain themselves before jumping to conclusions and"—she waved at the cage—"locking them up?"

Brilliant. With that, he ought to start looking *normal.* Cor flicked the barrier. It broke apart and, with a sweep of his arm, blew off. He stood and helped Fern up.

Slowly, and clearly reluctantly, Fee nodded.

"Excellent." Again, her mum gestured to their cage.

"Watch yourself." Cor pulled Fern with him into the center of their enclosure. The multicolored ropes sizzled and snapped out with a loud *pop!*

"Humph," Fern snorted. "Dad preaches preserving energy to me, so why didn't either of you suck those creations back to save your magic?"

"He was showing off to your mum," Cor said.

"And you?"

Cor crossed his arms, then uncrossed them as he recalled Harold's advice.

"Can't do it, huh?"

He couldn't, but he wasn't admitting it.

"So, ah, Heather?" Fee looked very pointedly at his shoulder, where the witch's finger still pressed into him.

He couldn't step back from her?

Her mouth quirked up on one side, and she lifted her finger. Purposefully, as if it weighed several pounds.

"Coooool," Cor murmured. "I wish I had that going for me."

Fee was flickering at twice the rate of before, like he was under a strobe light. He spun around Fern and Cor like Toots figuring out how to bite into a rabbit kill. Then he stuttered to a halt again in front of the witch. In a stage whisper that carried, Fee said, "I still say there is a distinct need for caution with this foreign lad."

Cor's shoulders tightened, but Fern's mum smiled at the small wizard. "When is your next break? Perhaps you should get off the isle for a look around the rest of the world. It'd give you a better perspective on today's youth."

"Bah!" Fee spun into a sparking tizzy again. "The rest of the world amounts to naught when it comes to protecting our precious isle. Tha' includes the portal to the human world that you so carelessly keep."

They had a portal like that here?

Fee stopped before Fern's mum. "Perhaps *I* should show *you* exactly where your portal defenses canna stand against the invasion of those from the human world who seek to harm you and the heir who means so much to the honorable Lady Lark."

Maybe Fern's mum wasn't such a nutter after all—she was both open-minded and able to manage the Watcher. Cor peered at Fern. "You? He's talking about you, the heir witch?"

Fern ignored him, while her mum continued to smile. "Certainly, Fee. When would you like to visit?"

"Tomorrow at noon?"

She nodded. "I shall come to fetch you. Now"—she glanced

toward Fern and Cor—"I shall leave you to inquire of my daughter and her guest their intentions." She took the cookie from Fern's brother and turned toward the steps down the hillside.

Fern darted over and intercepted her. "Uh, Mom? What am I supposed—"

"I'm sure you can handle this."

"Mom?" echoed her brother. "Shouldn't you stay and hurry Fee along?"

She looked him in the eye. "No. You best leave as well. This is Fern's business." After a last glance at Cor, she left.

Fern and her brother looked at each other. "I don't mind if you stay," she told him.

"As much as I'd like to, I can't cross her." With a glance to Cor that was creepily like the witch's, he followed her down the hillside.

Cor walked over to Fern, and the Watcher…sort of did. He bounced in and out of sight, alternately peering at them and leafing through papers on a clipboard. At last he stopped in the middle, rolled back the top papers and, with a flourish, produced a pen. "Guest's full name?"

"Corylus van—Avellana," answered Cor.

"Ah-ah! The resident wizard must provide your information!" Fee glared at them.

"Corylus Avellana," Fern said.

"Enclave of domicile?"

Bonterra? she mouthed to Cor, and he nodded. "Bonterra."

"Age?"

Sixteenth, Cor mouthed and she repeated it.

"Wizard responsible for guest?"

"Um, me." Then, under Fee's stare, she said, "Fern Fields."

Fee stopped shimmering long enough to blow a long, exaggerated sigh, punctuated by his eyes lifted skyward. "Mistress

Fern, heir to the Witch of the Meadows," he droned as he wrote. "Location where the guest will reside during the visit?"

She bit her lip. "You know the Scots pine grove just a quarter mile northeast of—"

"Nay!" Fee spat. "The guest remains in the habitat of the sponsoring wizard. Location where the guest will reside during the visit?"

"At Hillux," Fern answered, her eyes wide.

Fee wrote it down. "Reason for visit?"

"He wants to have an apprenticeship on the isle."

Fee's flickering escalated, and they both took a step back.

"Pardon me?" He advanced on Fern, and Cor flushed magic to his fingertips.

The Watcher looked pointedly at his hands.

Cor withdrew his magic to his cores and crossed his arms, tucking his hands beneath his backpack straps. "Sorry."

"He, uh, Cor wants to pursue apprenticing on the Isle of Giuthas with one of the habitat wizards."

Flipping the clipboard, Fee slapped the papers together. "Such a thing is unheard of. Visitation denied."

"Hey!" Cor said. "That's not fair. You haven't even given me half a chance."

Fee started tsking, and Fern laid a hand on Cor's arm. "My mistake. Cor will be helping me with projects in the Meadows."

"Projects? What kind of—hold on a second." Fee disappeared.

"I don't want to work with grass—"

"*Shh!* He might come right back!" They both glanced around, and Fern leaned down to whisper, "Or even still be here. Now who had better agree with who? You *want* to work in the Meadows if that's the only way he'll let you stay."

Fee returned as a glow at the top of the steps, and seconds later Lady Pina marched up behind him.

"Mistress Fern, Fee tells me you still have my peregrinator and are still in need of it."

"Indeed, she is," Fee said from beside them. "She will be returning this lad to—" He flipped through his pages. "To Bonterra."

"No," Fern said. "He can't leave, because he helped me. Remember, Lady Pina? I promised him a visit."

"Nay." Fee slapped his pages closed and tucked the clipboard under his arm. "She did nae request a *visit*. She is seeking work for the lad upon the isle."

Lady Pina's lips thinned as she pressed them together, a look of distaste forming. "Windborne youth in Bonterra sought to force Mistress Fern to do something she did not wish to, and she could not refuse because she does not yet have adequate skills with magic to protect herself." She tilted her head toward Fern.

"Sort of, well…" Fern mumbled, turning red. "Yeah. I mean, yes."

Lady Pina faced off with Fee, though not as aggressively as Fern's mum had. "This is my fault for not having watched my charge as carefully as the circumstances warranted. Lady Heather had warned me, I knew her limitations and yet it never occurred to me the city could be such a dangerous place for a young witch not versed in the ways of the Windborne."

"Well, it wasn't that—ow!"

Cor elbowed Fern in the ribs. "Not now!" he hissed.

"Fee," Lady Pina continued without noticing, "approve this wizard, uh…"

"Corylus Avellana," he said quickly.

Her brows lifted, and she eyed him. "Approve…*Corylus Avellana's*…"

She had to recognize the tree species—common hazel—he was named for. Cor held his breath. That should give him extra points with the old lady.

"…visitation."

"I canna do that, Lady Pina!" Fee buzzed in agitation, his glow turning red and growing to cover half the hilltop. "Only the council may approve a visitation, outside of an apprenticeship trial."

Lady Pina put her hands on her hips with an exasperated sigh. "'Tis my fault the witch is indebted to this warlock, so I will address the council at the earliest opportunity, and in the meantime Corylus is visiting Mistress Fern, heir to the Witch of the Meadows, with purely social intent." She fixed Fee with a glare.

Pfft. Social intent? So much for being named after a tree. Supposed he should be thankful she wasn't glaring at him.

"Mom was wrong," Fern whispered. "There wasn't any business for me to handle, just keep out of the line of fire."

"Thank them," Cor whispered back, "and let's get out of here."

They walked forward. Fern unlooped the peregrinator from around her neck and handed it to Lady Pina. "Thank you."

The lady grasped Fern's hand and whispered something in her ear.

Nothing good would come from more negotiation. He'd been told he could stay, so Cor kept walking. Down the steps of the hillside that turned out to have a house under it and across the meadow to the closest stand of trees. He'd hide until this blew over.

11

NO HELP WHATSOEVER

Fern saw Cor walk off, but Lady Pina was talking and she couldn't—shouldn't!—interrupt. Then Gran arrived, in pretty much a copy of Mom's entrance, since they looked alike. A dozen songbirds accompanied her. *And* Raven *and* Dad *and* Beri. Raven rolled his eyes as Lady Pina continued to rant about her bringing Cor. Gran tried to interrupt, and so did Dad. With the birds circling and twittering noisily, it was easier to step back with Beri supportively at her side and let them all go at it.

Four more wizards from the council arriving didn't improve things. Sir Humus quieted people—and birds—and they listened as Fern told the story again. By the end, *Gran* was glaring at her.

Fee materialized between Fern and the angry wizards, hovering at her height. "There is the matter of diverting your route."

She'd been grateful for his interruption, but *this* was not helpful. "How come I never saw you before? Or heard of you?"

"You've never been in trouble before. You were born here, and because you had no magic as an infant, we never thought to exclude you when Lady Heather was banned. Then, after you *were* here, Lady Lark put out a pesky command that we stay out of your way until she was sure of you. Answer why you diverted your peregrinator's route."

"I'm not sure what you mean," Fern said. "I came straight to the isle with the peregrinator."

"If I may?" Beri asked. "When one of us returns to the isle, Fee, or one of the other Watchers, recognizes the energy of the wizard. But if it's a wizard they do nae recognize, the person is channeled to their station for processing."

Oh. Her stomach churned in a not-good way. "Is that on the top of Mount Lookout?"

Gran's eyes widened. "Aye. You left there?"

"Ay—uh, yeah. Was that bad, uh, that I left?"

As one, they nodded.

Fern scrunched up her nose. "Sorry."

"Why did you go against the proper procedure?" asked Lady Roda, a council member who was both stern and mousy-looking with her pressed clothes and brown hair in a bun.

That Fern was new to this should have been clear, but of course, Lady Roda had to point out all her faults. The Wizard of Wildlife clearly still resented things Fern had done this summer. "I didn't *intentionally* leave the…processing station, was it?"

"You used your magic, did you not?" Lady Roda persisted. "Or was it the warlock? Did the outsider use his magic?"

"It most certainly was the energy of Mistress Fern." Fee's answer reverberated across the hilltop.

"Yes," snapped Fern. "I used *my* magic to leave Mount Lookout, because I thought I'd messed up the pereport and tried to fix it."

"Then you did *intentionally* leave the processing station." Lady Roda punctuated this with a determined nod.

Since nothing else would please her and let them move on, Fern pressed her lips together and nodded.

Lady Roda started to say more, but Gran put up a hand. The

five birds crowding her shoulders squatted, ready to swarm Lady Roda.

"Ach," Beri whispered in Fern's ear. "I feel the same."

The taller Lady Pina stepped between them. "We are bogged down in unnecessary details," she said. "The lass is young. She is new to our ways. She is inexperienced in the use of magic."

"But powerful," said the invisible Fee. "Some type of control—"

"Which is exactly why"—Lady Pina's voice rose above Fee's—"she was offered the position of heir to the Witch of the Meadows *and* is now acting in that position. Let us move on to the matter at hand. Mistress Fern, acting as one of us…" She paused and looked around.

Fern looked, too. Was anyone willing to go against Lady Pina?

"I, for one," Lady Pina continued, "believe Mistress Fern acted with great graciousness and consideration of her position with the Isle of Giuthas. She is young and may not *yet* understand all of our policies, but given the circumstances of the Bonterra wizard's protective service, she acted within reason and correctness. In short, she is a credit to our enclave."

The elderly Sir Snap of the Ponds cleared his throat. "At least as far as *pursuin'* the possibility. I am nae sure we wish to be openin' our limited resources to every person who seeks to use them."

"'Tis a situation we will continue to regulate with the utmost of care," Gran said.

"Yet we should stand behind the agreement Mistress Fern made," murmured Mr. Grouse. "We wish to keep our alliances with other enclaves on positive terms."

This middle-aged and modern-dressing wizard was an ornithologist who did bird research across all the Windborne enclaves of the British Isles, so of course he didn't want trouble elsewhere.

Fern put up her hand. "Cor knows a lot about trees. During the tour, he answered as many questions as our guide Mr. Acer did. He works at the Gruen Estate, with the trees."

"He is a van Gruen?" Sir Humus asked.

"Corylus Avellana," Lady Pina said as if that answered the question. "Many of the extended family work for the foundation. His work corresponds with his interest in our ancient groves. As this situation came about because of my inattention, I have already agreed to have the boy here for a tour and will do so. We will not insult one of the oldest Windborne families, do not worry."

People murmured agreement, and Fern met Beri's gaze. He gave a nod of encouragement. She was on the cusp of letting out her breath, but Sir Snap stepped forward.

The old wizard's mouth twisted within his long gray beard like he'd bitten a lemon. "We mustn't prejudge the young man for yer mistake, or ye while adjustin' to the enclave," he said to Fern. "Yet I find the way ye have sprung this on us distasteful, lass. Young'uns on the isle are brought up to follow procedure. Varyin' from our protective measures brings risk to the enclave. To accelerate yer education of the isle's security, I suggest ye spend three patrol sessions with Fee. Pina might agree to host a tour for the lad, but ye are the wizard who is ultimately responsible for him."

Ohmigod. She had to be responsible for that Goth boy? Fern's gaze flashed to Gran. The small woman shook her head slightly and touched her finger to her forehead. Just like Mom. And just like Mom, that meant, *We'll talk about it later*.

There was no way around this. "Fine. I agree to these stipulations."

"Tuesday, Friday, Monday," Fee said, his high voice reverberating around them.

Sir Snap looked up and grumbled, "A little less forceful the next time, if ye please?"

What could she do, but agree? "After school lets out," she said. Great, something else to look forward to on Tuesday besides her test.

Heads nodded, and people turned away. Beri slid his hand into hers to squeeze her fingers, his magic flushing to greet hers. Fern released her breath, just as Beri snatched his hand back.

"What in the name of the Blessed Orb have you done with your magic?" he bellowed. "Is that…did that lad—"

Everyone snapped around. Beri held up a blob of energy at the tips of his fingers, her spring-green magic streaked with an amber glow.

"You did," Beri spat, his distaste clear. "You're carrying a pledge to him."

A DONE DEED

Fern stared at Beri. How—and what—had she magically pledged to Cor? It couldn't be as serious as bonding, the Windborne version of marriage. Not after the applications she and Beri had had to fill out for just a *pre*bonding trial.

"No way," she said, wanting it to be true. But there was the proof, her magic threaded with the honey-colored magic she'd seen Cor use.

Crap.

"What does this mean?" She reached for it, only to be pushed aside. Dad pinched the ball of magic from Beri's fingers. He held it up and turned it this way and that, the other wizards gathering around to see. His rusty-brown magic poked in like a needle taking a biopsy to check the golden parts. He lowered it, only to put his hand on her shoulder and run the same inspection through her channels.

"You agreed to this," he said.

Lady Roda laughed, her arms crossed. "You couldn't have provided better proof that Mistress Fern is as naïve about magic as she claims."

"So what—" Fern started, but Gran's birds shot skyward

again, forming a threatening cluster around Lady Roda. She and Gran lifted their hands at the same time, and the birds dispersed.

"Family matter." Gran shooed her hands at Lady Roda and the other wizards. "Leave us."

They did, unfurling their wings and flying off. Gran and Dad gave mysterious side-glances to Beri, who still looked angry. Raven sidled over and took the magic from Dad.

"I don't see an agreement," he said, but Dad prompted him where to look—like this was a magic lesson—and his lips twisted. "Sorry, mate," he said to Beri.

Fern fought the urge to put her brother on the ground. "Sorry for him? What about me? Someone tell me what this means!"

Beri snatched back the magic and returned it to her, and Dad gestured for Beri to answer.

Great, another lesson.

"You have entered an agreement with that lad, a magically binding one," he said through gritted teeth. "I do nae understand how this could have happened at a Windborne conference, but Bonterra is a city, and they all have hidden dangers, human or not. What did he trick you into?"

You're telling me. She pressed her fingers to her temples. What had happened? The bullies, wrapping herself in the hickory shell —which none of them had even noted—Cor fighting, leaving in the car, offering a favor… Oh. Hold on. Their magic had leaked —or had it been a leak? Cor had said something odd after they'd shaken hands, about *trying*. The words came floating back:

"So you want me to arrange an apprenticeship for you in Lady Pina's Pines habitat."

"That's the idea. Do you promise to help me?"

"Yes, I will."

"Crap," she muttered. "And I gloated to the scammer that I didn't make many magical mistakes anymore."

She told Gran, Dad, Beri and Raven about her promise to arrange an apprenticeship and Cor trying to clarify that she had agreed to do more than *try*. They had her repeat the wording several times, Gran shaking her head and Beri turning so red his freckles popped.

She put out her hands helplessly. "I didn't understand what it meant to promise—"

"Pledge," Beri ground out.

"*Pledge* something to another wizard." Surely Beri had to understand this.

He shifted back. "How much does the lad want this apprenticeship?"

Cor certainly hadn't hesitated to travel to a place he'd never seen, even knowing how much Lady Pina was against it. Though, since he'd tried to bring his longboard, he hadn't understood exactly how remote or rural it was.

Fern rubbed her aching head, knowing she was in for it before she answered. "Badly."

"Then you are stuck carrying his magical reminder of this pledge until you fulfill it to his satisfaction," Beri confirmed. "Until you do, your magic will nae work without him."

***

The next morning, dew droplets gathered on Cor's cheek and rolled, chilling his neck. He squirmed, seeking another angle to protect his face. But his sleeping bag wouldn't move, caught somewhere between him and the lines he'd linked to his harness to make sure he didn't fall out of his bivy sack overnight. The rush of the wind through the needles and the twitters of the birds were a glorious replacement for the rumbling tour buses and calls of the estate staff that had filled his mornings this summer.

He yawned, stretching a hand to wipe away the wet and

settled back in to sleep. The birds had quieted, so he ought to be able…

The birds had quieted. His eyes flashed open, and magic flooded to his hands.

No one was in sight, just the boughs of the Scots pine he'd strung his bivy sack in last night after finally finding one of the groves. But the woods were too quiet.

"Dammit," he hissed.

"Aye, my feeling exactly," said a deep voice with a Scottish accent.

13

ONLY WHAT WAS PLEDGED

"Orb take it." Heart racing, Cor shoved magic out into a shield—

Snap!

His magic shattered, another energy taking its place, and Cor stared up at a bubble as yellow as a ginkgo's autumn leaves.

A quiet—and definitely feminine—voice said, "Don't taunt him."

He craned to search…

A blond witch stood on a branch above his head, upside down from his angle, her loose hair fluttering in the breeze. He crooked around to see her better. Her wings were unmagicked—she wasn't bothered by being two hundred feet in the air.

She nodded to him. "Sorry for the early meeting, but 'tis better for us to approach you before the elders do. We've come to ask that you release Fern from this spell."

His first thought was, *Who is "us"?* It was simpler to answer, "Can't. Not when she *agreed* to help me. That's how a binding pledge works."

A head popped up beside his. A redheaded bloke pressed his

freckled nose right up to the yellow shield, and Cor leaned as far back as his bivy sack let him, magic racing his channels.

"We may live in the countryside, but we are nae stupid about magic," the bloke snarled. "You can undo it if you choose—"

"Beri." Another wizard dropped from above on arched wings. "Give him a chance to answer." It was the bloke who had fetched Fern's mum. Right, her brother, same walnut-black hair.

"He did answer! That was a nay." But the redhead retreated after Fern's brother prodded him.

Walnut Hair had helped when that security wizard caged them, and now he acted a damned sight more reasonable than this ballistic redhead. But would Fern's brother continue to be an ally when Cor refused again? They had him outnumbered. And trapped. He glared, knowing it was a dodgy move. "Tell the witch to remove her ward if you want to continue this conversation."

"There is nae much I tell her to do. That is, if I want her to stay prebonded to me." Walnut Hair grinned in an odd way that didn't match his helpful appearance. "And I do."

"And 'tis the magic of *my* prebond you have tied up in this ridiculous pledge." The redhead pointed a glowing finger. "You might give a word of thanks to Willow for casting that ward, as it works both ways."

The blonde gestured with open hands. "In these proceedings, I offer you the protection of my mother, the Witch of the Forest."

What the hell was she saying? "I heard Lady Pina has no kids."

"Cut the bilge he canna ken," said a new bloke, and this time Cor wasn't the only one twisting around to search the treetops.

"It means no one can blast you one," added a different girl.

He glanced at Blond Witch, an unexpected ally, but…the *four* others were her friends, not his. With the new arrivals' distraction, Cor tested his fingers against the shield. No shock, and it gave a little. He flared a fingertip spark and pressed again. The witch's magic flared back. He looked up and met her gaze. She shrugged.

He was decent at spell casting, but never had strong energy. Pisser in these situations. He couldn't curse at her for being a bloody peacemaker.

The hidden warlock who'd spoken glided into sight. He wore knee boots and a dagger at his hip, and grinned like this was a stage performance he'd dropped in on. "I told her not to follow me over, but my sister isn't much on listening."

"And miss a fight? Nay."

Overhead, clumps of needles shifted, and a head ducked between them, a cascade of brown braids falling to surround dusty-tan cheeks. Her coloring, blue eyes and cocky grin matched her brother's. "Ahoy," she said. "I'm Coral."

"Cor," he said automatically, while shoving up into a sitting position and trying not to rock the hammock too wildly. "Corylus."

She whooped and fluttered to the side of his bivy. "Corylus and Coral! Now if that doesn't have a nice ring, I don't know what does."

He frowned. Coral was close enough that he could correct her—*Corylus and some other* warlock, *if you don't mind*—but he didn't. Then two *more* wizards flying up distracted everyone again.

Blast, seven wizards—*white* wizards—surrounded him. This was worse than the time his family had been the only black folks in an entire enclave. His parents' advice scrolled through his mind: *Stay calm. Mind your words. Identify potential allies. Don't argue with elders. Walk away.*

Ha. Dad would never have given him permission to come here if he'd imagined this happening. Nor would Cor be allowed here again if he told him. Gaze darting and assessing the seven teens, he recognized one of the newcomers. Today, she wore khaki work clothes. "You were at the conference," he said to her. "Pink skirt."

"Yeah, good to see you again, too, green blazer. Fern told me what you did for her." She flipped her polished nails around at the others, pointing accusingly. "Did any of you bother to get the entire story? Because I'd run into those chaps myself and had to get security to patrol when I was going to be working alone in that section of town."

Blond Witch began explaining to Pink Skirt how upset they all were, and between the two standing up for him, Cor felt slightly less uneasy. The last wizard fluttered closer. Sandy-brown hair falling in loose curls and tawny skin the color of Toots' facial feathers—that could either be a healthy tan or his natural tone. Behind round glasses, his eyes…were they pinkish? Freakin' flights, what color was his magic?

Did it matter? Curly Hair was part of their group, and they'd designated Cor *persona non grata.*

"You," Cor interrupted Blond Witch. "What's your name again?"

"Willow, heir to the Witch of the Forest. Perhaps we should introduce everyone."

He put up a hand. "No point. I can't remember names. I get that you're all concerned. Like she said, I did a favor for Fern, so I need a favor back."

"Need?" asked Redhead…Fern's prebond?

"I *want* a favor, okay? I couldn't get on this island without it. Willow"—*Orb, help me remember her name at least*—"I accept your offer of protection from Fern's fan club. Get on with what you want to say and leave."

She frowned and waved a dismissive hand toward Coral. "We are nae going to *fight.*"

"But it looks that way to a city boy who blasts street rats in Bonterra," said Pink Skirt. "Let him up." She turned to him. "I'm Duffy, and I totally empathize with you being a new person here. I've visited my uncle for years on Giuthas and am still only tolerated by those who were born here."

Blond Witch—Willow—crossed her arms. "That's not true. We've included you since your trial approval—"

"That's the point. Only since I was approved was I asked to do stuff like help search for him with the rest of you."

"And we have found him. This was supposed to be a conversation between Beri and Cor, you understand?"

Pink Skirt put up a finger. "Seriously, you all are having Beri confront him instead of Fern?" She shook her head. "Fern isn't going to like that."

"Not confront, just talk."

A throat cleared. "To do that, the rest of us need to clear off," said Curly Hair. His brown wings carried him gracefully backward, and it took seconds for Cor to realize half the others were flying away as well. Tossing him a smile, Curly Hair spun to follow.

Suddenly, being trapped in his sleeping bag was downright embarrassing. Cor pressed the heel of his hand to his forehead. What had they said, the ward was protective? Then all he had to do was sit tight until these three gave up.

"What is it you wish to achieve with this favor?" asked Red—prebond bloke—*Beri*.

Cor uncovered his face. The three hovered a respectable distance off his camping spot. "Why should I tell you my reasons?"

The bloke fisted his hands, the green of his magic showing between his fingers. Walnut Hair pulled him back. "Because if you do nae, I'll see to it you're kicked out, binding pledge with Fern or no. Raven promises to help." He tilted his head toward Fern's brother. "Willow is here because her mother is curious if this expertise in arboriculture you claim to have is actually something that might be of use to us."

He acted like he had some pull here. *Raven*, Cor repeated. "I want to work with these trees. When will Lady Pina be able to show me around?"

"Believe it or not, the head of a habitat has work to do after being gone for three days. Apprentices"—he gestured to the three of them—"take over the routine chores. Like tours for folks who push their way in."

Cor tugged at his earlobe where his earring should have been. Made sense. Lady Pina hadn't wanted this, so he was gonna have to say something brilliant for Willow to pass on to get anyone's attention. All right, that set his goal for the day. "Appreciate you doing it and interrupting your work and all."

Willow smiled kindly. "Would you like a few minutes alone before we begin?" She pulled off the magic with a touch of her finger. "We'll be at the base of this tree—"

"The top," Beri said. "'Twill give him a better overview of the isle." He flapped his wings and rose out of sight.

"The top, then." Willow unfurled her wings and followed. With a curt nod, so did Raven.

At first, Cor just listened to Willow's unhurried commentary. He stuck close to her as they flew him over the Isle of Giuthas, pointing out the coves formed by the two mountains' ridges. These protected spaces had preserved the Scots pines during the ice age that swiped the giants from Scotland, Ireland and northern Britain. Some held only a dozen trees. The one he'd bivouacked in had thirty. The largest was twelve hectares on the southern side of the taller Mount Lookout.

"Lady Pina lives in this main grove," Willow said. "We shall visit it last. We thought you might like seeing some of the research first."

No, but visiting multiple groves was on his list. He nodded.

They landed in a midsize grove, and Raven added details to Willow's descriptions of the habitat's soils, needle litter, moisture and understory plants. Beri leaned against a trunk with his arms crossed, silently glaring across the hummocky forest floor, as he'd done throughout the tour.

They flew up to the first branches, fifty feet up. The lighting was incredible. Cor hovered among the trunks to figure out why. The spacing between trees varied, like in other forests, and the boughs in the canopy still spread to touching. Maybe it was because billions more needles broke up the sunlight? The light filtering through them had *so* far to go to reach the ground that it made him think of the European cathedrals he'd visited with his parents. Distance seemed surreal here, the feeling mystical. If only he could have been alone for this flight.

He glanced up. The three stood on a branch, talking, not paying attention to him. Cor flew horizontally instead of upward, slowly flapping between the massive trunks, fitting his hand in the deep orange bark furrows, spiraling out until he reached the oak-covered slopes, then returning to pinewoods. A red kite lazily glided past, silencing the songbirds. In a few minutes, they resumed their calls. With a sigh, Cor put some effort into his strokes and rose to the lower branches, found the one with the others and alighted.

"For someone who wants a tour," Beri snapped, "you could keep up."

"Beri!" Willow glared at him. "People appreciate wild lands in different ways. He clearly thinks it's nice enough to spend time looking."

Not nice. *Glorious.* But he just nodded.

Beri side-glanced at him. "One of my study areas for the last six years."

"Six?" Cor choked out.

Willow elbowed Beri, and photographs appeared in his hand. "Salamanders and lichen." He grumpily offered them to Cor.

He flipped through the images of salamanders, but he couldn't get his mind off photos he'd shown someone else—*tried* to show. "But..." How could he say this? "You take photographs? Lady Pina sniffed when I showed her my project images." He pulled his mobile from his pocket and waved it.

"She won't be impressed by something on *electronics*," Raven said, "but that doesn't mean the rest of us don't use them."

"We have a research facility with a library," Willow added. "We document our species and their changes in population, range, health. Different folks study what we believe is affecting our energy, from the base of the habitat up."

"The lichen?" Cor asked.

Beri nodded. "It's a very productive species in an ancient tree, catching airborne nutrients and eventually building the soils that allow other plants to seed and grow."

"You do that, plant seeds in lichen?"

"Often, they are there before we can get around to doing it," Beri said. "The birds defecate them all over the branches."

"Including the smaller pine trees I saw growing among the ancient trees?"

"Nay, those just fall. But the blaeberry bushes all come from birds."

His freakin' ignorance was showing. Of course bird poop ended up here. His owls didn't eat berries or seeds, so he hadn't thought of that. "Right-o, can I see?"

They showed him more lichen than he'd ever wanted to see, berry bushes, orchids, grasses and wildflower clumps dangling hundreds of feet in the air, a colony of bees that likely never visited the ground wildflowers, trees on tree branches, salamanders hanging out in little damp crevices, snakes in dry ones, mice, red squirrels and a sleeping pine marten.

"A tawny owl pair nests on the estate in Bonterra," he couldn't resist telling them.

"Do you band the nestlings?" Raven asked, which launched a demand that he contact their visiting ornithologist.

"The estate has an arboriculture focus. It's not like they're against bird research, but likely don't want to take the time…"

They were looking between themselves again.

He threw up his hands. "What? I'll ask them to now that you pointed it out." But he felt as though he'd somehow failed some test, and the urge to prove himself rose. "Say, can we have a look at this tree's energy?"

Beri waved to a normal-sized Scots pine growing on one of the branches below them. "Go ahead."

Cor dropped to its base, an easiness coming into his body. He didn't visit a tree without inspecting it to some level. Usually by brushing the leaves or needles, testing the strength of limbs, or checking its bark, but sometimes clasping cones and picking out seeds to examine, even rolling the underlying soil between his fingertips. Often, his inspection was an energy check. Now, he let this pine register in his senses. Magic flowed to his fingertip, and he touched a spark to the cambium.

It circled the tree. Lines of light traveled up and down the tree's fluid system, reaching the branch tips and spreading through the needles to set them aglow. At his feet, the magic flowed into the tangle of roots embedded in the branch of the main tree. They ran past Willow, but didn't quite make it to the main trunk.

A grin crept over his face at the soft blue-green glow that matched the pine's needle color. "Quite healthy," he said. "No dead limbs. Appears to be an insect infestation along the outer branches, midway up."

"What?" Beri leaped off the branch and flew upward. He returned a minute later. "Pine spittle bugs. Not bad for a tree this size." He rubbed a hand over the back of his neck. "Been a little busy the last month. Must have missed it."

Cor covered his smile by tugging at his earlobe and letting the tree energy fade.

Beri nodded. "Fair. Considering you have been here less than a day."

"Fair? I'd like to see you do better."

With a shrug of one shoulder, Beri flicked a hand in the direction of the main tree, and the entire thing—two hundred and fifty feet of it—lit ablaze like he'd thrown a switch.

Cor stumbled off the branch and had to catch himself by the wing.

The tree magic snapped out. Raven leaned against the trunk, laughing.

Cor clenched his hand to stop from punching the bloke. "Suppose you can do that, too?"

Raven reached out, but as he streamed a line of magic, Willow batted the space between them, sending brown and yellow sparks flying.

"On your own," she chastised.

He crossed his arms and scowled at her a moment before pursing his lips and whistling an ascending note. A rushing sound rose after it, like the breeze picking up.

Cor braced for another light display, not the falling darkness.

Birds. Hundreds of birds descended on them. He threw up an arm as the flock dove, but none attacked. They landed in the surrounding branches, several on Raven.

"I can light them up, too, if you like?"

"S'all right," Cor said, trying not to sound breathless. "I believe you."

"Scottish crossbills. They eat mainly pine nuts." Raven lifted his hand. The birds rose with deafening *cheeping* calls...and white falling from—

Crap. Literally. Cor waved up a protective shield as quick as the others. Raven chuckled as whitewash rained down on the magic crowning their heads in honey, yellow, green and orange brown.

Beri cursed. "Some warning would be nice."

Cor turned to Willow. "What can you do?"

"Naught so inane as that show-off."

"She can light the entire forest," Raven said.

"Not this one, the oak-birch forest my mother manages, but that's not entirely my magic."

Beri and Raven snorted in unison, and Willow silenced them with a frown.

"We best go," she said. "My mother and Lady Pina wish to meet Cor for a luncheon at her grove."

Willow launched herself into the air. After a startled second, Cor flapped hard to catch up. "Why didn't you say so before?"

"The invitation just came."

"Because?"

"Because I told Mam that your interest in trees is sincere and you weren't kidding about being able to detect tree energy."

The lunch was a simple salad of greens, vegetables and pine nuts. But the food didn't matter much compared to Lady Pina's house. Carved from a fallen pine, the rooms lined up one after another, with round portholes of old limbs forming deep-set windows. Berry bushes grew from a carpet of moss over the "roof," so Cor expected damp and moldy walls behind the round door cut from a cross section of another tree. However, the interior wood was smooth and polished, not at all musty. In the living area, they sat at a simple wooden table before a stone fireplace. To one side, he glimpsed the kitchen. The door leading the other direction was closed.

"How many rooms total?" he asked.

"Eight," she answered. "Hollowed by my great-grandfather using only an ax and hand tools…" Other descendants had made improvements over the years, added a bathroom, solar and so forth.

This is brilliant. Though he itched to take photos, he kept his mobile in his pocket and minded his manners.

When Lady Pina began to eat at last, Willow's mother asked about his work in the conservatory and his family.

Blast, he had to avoid that discussion. "My dad preaches the policy that if we have to rely on family to get something, then we haven't actually earned it. So, if you don't mind, I'd prefer to answer questions only about myself."

Lady Mimosa set aside her fork. "Very well. Why do you want this position?"

I love trees didn't seem to be a good enough answer, so he said some nonsense about the biggest trees in the world, and if these were here and the redwoods were on the other side of the world, he had more of a chance working with these than those.

"Yet you are here for a visit only." Lady Pina stood up. "Time to see our largest grove."

Outside, she unfurled her wings and rose to fly with slow, steady wing beats. Lady Mimosa gestured for him to fly ahead, so he did, and Lady Pina introduced him to the trees in her grove—there was no other way to phrase it. She gave the age, size, biomass, health concerns, and energy production of each. She never stopped, and at the end of an hour's tour, he was exhausted. They had circled back around to her home. "Do you have any questions, young man?"

"During your talk at the conference, you said the Scots pines provide over half of the energy for the isle. What happens if one falls?"

Her eyes narrowed. "We spend considerable energy ensuring that none do," she snapped, clearly affronted.

He raised his hands. "I don't mean to be rude, but is that possible?"

Lady Mimosa put a hand on Lady Pina's arm. "It has prevented a number from toppling. To answer your question, if one falls, its energy will be redirected into others."

Lady Pina sniffed. "None have fallen since I was a child. When a clearing like that forms, we move others to fill the gap as soon as possible, protecting against red deer browsing on the young trees. That seventy-year-old gap is practically unnoticeable."

"Are you raising new trees to replace the ones that will eventually—" At the lady's rising brows, he quickly amended, "Are you raising new trees anywhere?"

She waved him to follow, and they flew to an edge of the grove he hadn't yet seen. Ten rows of pines in clay pots stairstepped back, from the youngest sprouts at the outer edge to eight-foot saplings nearest the grove.

"Nice," he said. "Looks like some of these are ready to be planted. Have you tried to expand any of the groves?"

"There is no room for expansion without affecting other habitats." She gave him a thin smile. "Every available slot for a tree is filled."

Just like every available apprenticeship slot, apparently. He nodded. "Thank you for showing me around."

"Now that you have had your visit, you may release Fern from the pledge, and I can return you to Bonterra."

"I'll talk to Fern tonight," he said and left it at that.

14

THERE IS NO TRY...

No note from Beri was waiting for Fern when she returned from school alone. Mom knew only that Beri had pulled one of his ten allowed *it's urgent* cards with her to skip today.

"The second week of school?" Fern wailed before slamming the studio door and stomping across the bridge to their cabin. At this rate, he'd get kicked out before Christmas, despite indulgent breaks for exchange students.

He hadn't left a note in Gran's cottage either. Gran's guinea pig, Hilda, circled Fern's feet and begged, her long gray and white fur whipping around. Fern picked up the little animal, got a piece of lettuce from the refrigerator and fed Hilda while she checked the counters again. Even if Beri did have a phone, she had no way to reach him on Giuthas without magic. Her magic was still inside her—yesterday, she'd tested that a gazillion times. It was just useless. The pledge to Cor just meant she couldn't do any spells on her own—not that she'd learned that many yet—and worse, she couldn't connect to the Meadows.

Gran, Dad and all the elders had realized that before she had. Gran would be able to use the magic that their habitat now contained, but without Fern—the heir—no new energy could be generated. Fern wouldn't be of any help in repairing this rip, unless Cor accompanied her so her magic worked. She'd suggest that, even though she hated the idea of looking even lamer than she already was. They shot down the idea. No one wanted an outsider witnessing Giuthas' problems.

Mom, as the Witch of the Meadows, *could* bail her out. But two weeks ago, when Fern had taken this position and established her magical connection to the Meadows, Mom had made it clear she wasn't returning. So for right now, Fern didn't ask. Neither would she confront Cor. *I agreed to this. I'm going to work with him and get him an apprenticeship.*

As soon as possible. Before the elders decided to replace her.

Maybe there was a bright side. Maybe since the pledge limited her, she'd be able to *see* Beri in her magic like he kept describing she should. Leaving Hilda inside, she went into the field out front, put her fingers into the soil, closed her eyes and thought of Beri, and his magic.

Nope. She tried to push magic out anyway. *Beri? Can you hear me?*

That didn't work either. Crap. She had an hour before she needed to start homework, so she might as well do the bee feeding Dad wanted. Taking a jug of sugar water, she went to the bee shed and dressed in a bee suit. Sweating already, she approached the first hive, and then stopped to recheck her zippers and pants legs tucked into her boots. Dad had said she didn't need to smoke the bees to calm them when filling the jars, but she was ready to run if any started to fly at her.

She lifted the first hive's lid. A few bees were walking around the feeder base, but none paid attention, so she lifted the feeder, moved away a few paces and refilled the jar. She put the feeder back in place and returned the lid. Okay, that wasn't so bad. After the second, she had a system and her mind went to other problems, like how she was going to get Cor back to Bonterra if she didn't have her magic, couldn't find him and he didn't want to go.

She had one more feeder to fill when Beri walked up and nonchalantly asked, "What did I miss today?"

Clenching her jaw, she gave him a rundown, finishing with, "What did I miss here that was so urgent?" As if that wasn't more important!

"I wanted to keep an eye on this chap." He shrugged. "Mimosa wrangled a meeting with Lady Pina. She gave him a tour and told him that he could release you and go home."

"Then where is he?"

Beri looked into the distance—thought-speaking. "Willow says he flew around different groves this afternoon. Touching the trees. He's very focused on trees."

"That's a bad thing?" she asked, then realized, "Oh. It is if you're dealing with a habitat as a whole."

"Lady Mimosa said in that way he wouldn't make a good apprentice for Lady Pina because he'd be exactly like her. Trees above all, the rest of the plants and critters ignored."

"Huh." Fern tipped the last feeder into place, picked up the jug and left the bee yard.

Beri took the jug and put the cap on while she removed her gloves. "Let me." He gestured to her neck and unzipped her veil, setting the netting and pith helmet back off her head. Blessedly cool air washed over her clammy skin, and Beri leaned in and kissed her.

When they parted, she was breathless and even warmer. "Thought I was all nasty with his binding?"

"Just your magic. I missed seeing you today."

She laced her fingers with his. "I wish I could have gone on the Pines tour with you."

"You'll be able to eventually, if not by flying, then by peregrinator."

Not him, too? "You don't sound so sure I'll fly."

"Ah, was it a lack of flying that kept you from joining the bloody mob surrounding me this morning?" The question came from above, in Cor's British accent.

"People surrounded you?" She spun toward Beri. "Did you guys—you didn't!" *OMG, I can't believe…* Her magic surged, and she balled her fists…before realizing no sparks would fly.

"Ganged up on me." Cor landed. "Tried to strong-arm me into leaving."

Beri's hand flew up. "We did nae touch you." At Fern's glare, he added, "Physically or with magic. We talked."

Cor crossed his arms, looking smug. "That required *seven* of you?"

"Seven," Fern repeated. "What would Mom say—"

"Don't you dare tell her," Beri warned. "Mimosa knew Willow was checking on him."

Darn, she couldn't. "He. Is. My. Problem," she huffed. Mom had made that clear. "I will work out his departure."

"I'm not leaving." Cor pounded a fist. "This is the most amazing forest I've been to. You promised you'd get me an intern—*apprenticeship* here." He stepped closer, trying despite his shorter height to glare down at her. "Have you tried? You weren't even here today."

Beri came close behind her shoulder. "Don't push it, mate."

"I have school," she said through clenched teeth. "And unlike some people, I have to pass. On top of studying, I have chores." She gestured to her bee suit.

Cor didn't back off with the two of them looming over him. "I'll do chores for you while you butter up the old lady.'"

Beri huffed, and Fern reached back and grasped his arm. "First off," she said to Cor, "you don't refer to her as 'the old lady.'"

"She is Lady Pina, the Witch of the Pines," Beri said gruffly.

Cor's hands flew up. "Right. I'll try to call her Lady Pina."

"Try? Like you're asking Fern to try?"

Cor stuck out his chin.

Beri crossed his arms. "I ken you have an issue showing respect, after the way you tricked Fern. Yet I'd think Lady Pina's position as an elder in this enclave and the head of the habitat you wish to work for should garner her *something*."

Cor shoved his fingers into his hair and stretched several coils. "Bloody—fine, I get it. She's important. Lady Pina. Got it. Chores. I got that, too. What do you need done? Feed the bees?" He reached for the jug.

Fern let him take it. "You know what to do?"

"Yeah. We—they keep bees at the estate."

"I'm done for today, but…"

"What? I'll do it."

Cor sounded exasperated. He also sounded sincere. If he helped plant—and held her arm like he had during the pereport —she could use her magic for her fall seed planting. Fern nodded. "More sugar water needs to be made and the feeders filled again tomorrow. I have seed heads to collect from various parts of the meadow and others to put down. I'd have to show you the map and locations, but everything is labeled already. You know how to plant wildflowers from pots?"

"Never done flowers, but it can't be too different than trees, right? Dig a hole twice the size, break up any root-bound areas, back fill to keep the root ball at the surrounding soil level, plant and water."

Exactly what she'd been about to show him. The tightness in her shoulders eased, and she rolled them back. If he did her chores, she'd have the time to pursue his apprenticeship. "I add compost to give them an extra boost. Can you also see to the watering for the next week?"

Cor grinned. "As long as you make sure I'm around."

Pfft. "I'll talk to Lady Pina right after I show you the pond planting."

Beri cleared his throat. "Start with Mimosa. She met Cor

today and…" He crossed his arms again, fingers trailing a spark of green. "I must love you, Fern, because I canna believe I'm helping this scammer, as you called him. Mimosa and Lady Pina are friends. She'll listen to her suggestions."

An hour later, Fern had met with Lady Mimosa—who'd told her Lady Pina valued action, but was slow to accept anything new—and had had supper with her dad. Well, she hadn't meant to go to his house to eat, but he'd started making her sandwiches while they talked—mainly about how she was going to have to be patient with Beri.

"Beri? What does he have to do with it?"

"Your magic is tied up in this pledge when he's just getting to know you—'tis nae something a wizard wants to see happen to someone he loves and then not be able to do anything about it."

Fern balled her fists under the table. No, Beri couldn't, and he'd made it clear that he was mad at Cor. The sooner he admitted this was her problem to deal with, the better. "Dad? Beri and everyone else can't continue to bail me out magically. Let's talk about what *I* can do. Would meeting with Sir Humus help?"

"Perhaps after you complete your sessions with Fee."

Ugh. It was like having court-ordered community service.

"No one approves of the methods Cor used to gain entrance, but they've stopped blaming either of you for the misunderstanding. You couldn't learn years of Windborne norms in two weeks."

Fern laid her head on the table. "Even I can see I had a bull's-eye painted on my forehead in Bonterra. Sucker."

Dad patted her on the shoulder and set up a meeting for her with Sir Humus. When Dad returned her to Hillux so she could go home, Cor was sweeping the kitchen, Hilda chasing his heels and wheeking. He was ignoring the begging guinea pig—but then, he had his earbuds in. He lifted his chin when he saw her, then magicked the dustpan to his hand and collected the pile of dirt and hair.

Nice. This would help Gran, but she pointed to her own ear to get him to remove his earbuds. He did, pipes blaring a lively tune before he turned the music off.

"What was that?"

"Celtic folk tunes?"

That wasn't what she'd expected his music to be. "Did you feed her?"

Hilda stepped on his now-still foot. "A little," he admitted. "Carrots."

"How many?"

"Um, four. But we shared the first."

Fern picked up the guinea pig. "You've had today's ration and tomorrow's." She tapped Hilda's pink nose. "It's hay for you for the rest of the day." She put her in her basket under the counter. Probably he was checking out the fridge when Hilda started begging. "Have you eaten since yesterday?"

"Other than Lady Pina's lunch today, I brought protein bars. That gets old quick."

She took a cloth-wrapped sandwich from her bag. "Here. Leftovers from what my dad made for dinner."

He peeked at the sandwich. "Sprouts, tomato and cheese?"

"Yeah, I'm vegetarian. Are you?"

"No." He took a bite and chewed with an appreciative nod. "But I could be. Would that help convince Lady Pina?"

Fern rolled her eyes. "No, you can't lie."

He shrugged. "Wouldn't be a lie. Just an eating preference while I'm on an island where it's a thing."

"It's not a thing with everyone, but I'm glad you're using her name." She told him what Lady Mimosa had said about Lady Pina valuing people who acted on their plans.

Cor brightened. "I got your pond plants planted, and more bee syrup is cooling in the fridge. Also, it's time to put the mouse guards on the hives, so I found them in the bee shed and did that."

He had moved fast. She opened the drawer where she and Gran kept their Meadows gardening plans and pulled a map from the fall planting file. "Can I show you the planting for tomorrow? Or at least some of it. I have homework, so I can't walk all over the Meadows."

"What that bloke said is true, then. You can't fly?"

Fern pushed through the door. "Nope."

"Why not?" He jogged to keep up as she strode northward into Upper Meadows.

"Don't know. My magic is new."

"Strong, though, from that thicket you grew."

"Plant magic."

"Grounded magic. You nervous about flying? Sailing through the air with nothing holding you up but your own will?"

She side-glanced to him, trying not to reveal how his description knotted her stomach. "Thanks. I might be now."

"It's all right," he said quietly.

They crossed several hills without talking. He didn't start going on about how great flying was, or what she was missing, or push to ask what she'd tried so far. He didn't know about the practice exercises Dad had given her to do, or Mom's resigned advice to not push it, or Beri pressing his palms to her shoulder blades and urging her to move magic to them. He'd seen her major fail with hiding from Bonterra's bullies, and by tomorrow he'd find out she was also afraid of the bees. What did it matter? It might just be nice to have someone to talk to who didn't care if she wasn't a magical prodigy.

"I am afraid of heights," Fern told him.

"Rock-climbing."

"Pardon me?"

"You ever been rappelling?"

Just the memories of seeing climbers they'd come across

during hikes to the Flatirons in Boulder made her shiver. "Like off a cliff? No way."

"Like in a rock-climbing center where you'll feel safe about your anxiety with heights. And flying."

She stopped. "How do you know about those?"

He stopped, too. "We have them in Bonterra. There's one where you live?" He gestured back to Hillux.

"Yeah?"

"Let's go sometime. I can coach you through it."

"You rock-climb?"

"Usually, tree-climbing, but yep, my entire life. My parents couldn't keep me out of trees, so they got me lessons and gear so I'd be safe."

"Are you?"

"Certified instructor." He pressed his hand to his heart. "Honestly. That's not an exaggeration." He pulled out his wallet and showed her a card. "I can pass a belay test at any place you've got and then work with you. We'll have you swinging down from the top to give you a sense of what it would feel like to be airborne."

Fern chewed her lip. It was worth a try. Might even be fun. "Okay, Friday I'm free after school." She eyed him. "But the real issue is, can you pass my mom's human-immersion test to go into the human city with me?"

Cor rolled his eyes. "I think I'm good with that."

Fern beckoned him to follow her. "You have met my mom, remember?"

He groaned. "Not that short witch doing the intense muttering?"

"That's the one."

15

WHEN DOING YOUR THING IS THE RIGHT THING

Cor didn't see Fern the next day, Tuesday. Only her scowling prebond...*Beri*. One glance from him when he walked through the hillside house, and Cor decided it was time to water the pond plants. When he returned, Beri was gone, but Fern didn't come. The next morning, her gran—Lady Lark, he reminded himself—gave him a note from her and a marked map and envelopes of wildflower seed. She walked over the Meadows hills with him and showed him how to score the ground with a hard rake and scatter the seed. Fern had also left him a bag of groceries in the refrigerator, making him feel like a lame moocher. He'd pay her back.

He planted the seeds, fed the bees and watered the pond plants, getting caught in a freakin' afternoon rainstorm that popped up from nowhere. That ended the planting for the day. Bored and without his longboard or climbing gear, he swept the house again, feeding and petting the guinea pig. He found himself pulling out his earbuds and talking to her.

Brilliant. He'd never been one to chatter, but when he and his family traveled or were on the estate, there was always someone around to break up the day. Here, his music wasn't even taking up the slack. He'd emptied the dustpan and was standing on the porch watching the rain when a rise in magic sent goose bumps over his skin. He startled back just as someone appeared.

The blond witch from yesterday morning looked just as surprised to see him.

"Hello," she said while putting away her peregrinator. "How has your day been?"

Was this a trick question? "Fine," he said, and when she tilted her head, clearly expecting more, his day of not having another soul to talk to got the better of him. "I've done the planting and bee work Fern gave me, cleaned and organized the bee shed and the garden shed, and now that it's raining, I have nothing left to do but wait and see if Fern arrives to give me more work."

"Oh." She looked thoughtful. "You tend bees? Could you have a look at our hives? My father hasn't had time the last few weeks."

"Is that why you're here? To get Fern to help you?"

"Not exactly." She smiled sweetly. "I came to ask Fern how things are going with you."

Not having anything better to do, he accompanied the witch to see her family's hives. He was too embarrassed to ask her name again, because he should have known it after she'd taken him around the groves two days ago. Oddly, it wasn't raining at her family's farm, a cleverly terraced spot carved into the natural contours of a mountainside. She led the way to a barn. He picked through their equipment and selected what he needed —including their mouse guards—and started to leave.

"Bee suit?" She plucked one off a hook.

"I have a different method."

She gave him a look, but didn't say anything as she magicked one on. They climbed a flight of stone steps into an orchard, where he tried to keep from gaping. The crowns of apple trees spread overhead, their tips just touching as the mature branches reached out in perfect wheels, arrayed down evenly planted rows. Shiny red apples spotted the first row, a darker, duller variety in the next and a sunny yellow in the third. The rows continued at different levels farther back within the valley and up the mountain, different bark, different branching patterns, different leaves.

Bloody brilliant. He didn't care what she thought of his city-bred awe. Cor turned to take it all in. Master Harold would be drooling—and this was just the apples. He couldn't make out the distant species.

Willow had stopped a few paces ahead, waiting with her hands clasped together.

"What..." He cleared his throat. "What varieties do you have?"

"All the usual to provide throughout the year—cherry, apricot, summer sauce apples, plums, pears, peaches, autumn apples, keeping apples. The nut trees are spread up the valley more."

This and nut trees. Cor shook his head. "The hives?"

"Two terraces up. Not quite the middle, but that lets us check on them"—she grimaced—"when my father isn't so busy filling in for Mam, who is dealing with Forest rips. Anyway..." She tilted her head. "I hope they aren't in too awful shape fending for themselves."

Their bee yard was in a clearing between two terrace walls, four hives made up of two hive bodies each and a fifth with three. Additional hive stands stood empty.

"This isn't enough hives for the size of your orchard," he remarked.

"We magic in others during the blooming periods, then move them back afterwards. These are for our honey production." She was messing with the smoker, stuffing the canister with dried leaves from the ground.

"Hold off a minute," he said and flooded his skin with his protective magic.

"That's…interesting," she said curiously.

He held up his arm, the brown of his skin now shimmering with the honey-colored coating of energy. "It's a spell I worked up for tree protection to keep insect pests from the new saplings. Gives them a fighting chance on Bonterra's streets. One day I was too lazy to put on a bee suit and thought, 'Why not?' The bees can't get through, and they seem to be calmer."

"Likely because you're calmer. May I?" She held up a finger and, at his nod, pushed at his barrier. "Cor, this is brilliant. I can only imagine the boost it gives to new trees. Why didn't you show it to Lady Pina?"

He tugged at his earlobe, again missing his earring. "Never had the chance. She's so dead set against having me that I doubt she'd listen." He took the hive tool from the bucket of supplies. "Either stand back or zip your veil. It worked fine with the Meadows' bees, but we should give your workers a few minutes' test to make sure they're good."

He removed the lid of the first hive, pried loose a few frames and lifted one. Full of honey. So were each of the other seven. "I'll check the bottom box, but it's looking like you need to add another body of empty frames. These ladies don't have any room to put their brood for the autumn and winter."

"The bees are carrying on as if you aren't even there," she said. "If you're fine by yourself for a few minutes, I'll collect a box and frames and see if my father has time to talk about your recommendations."

"Make it two more boxes, if you can carry them." He waved her off. The bees hummed pleasantly around his arms, bouncing off his energy, not bothered by it or him. By the time he'd shuffled through the frames of the second box and started on another of the smaller hives, he'd figured out that these must be split hives from this spring.

"Flights," someone said in a whispered squeak. "He *is* doing it without a bee suit."

Cor turned to find three little boys climbing on the stone wall at the edge of the yard.

"Are you supposed to be cursing?" he asked.

The oldest turned red, and the other two began giggling and smacking him.

"No," the blond boy mumbled. "Willow said you'd opened the hives without a bee suit on, and we didn't believe her."

"Aren't you afraid you're gonna be stung?" asked the littlest boy.

"Naw," he said. He pried up a frame. *Willow*. Her name was Willow. Tree name. He should have remembered. Right, her mum was Lady *Mimosa*.

The boys sat on the wall, whispering and watching him go through the hive boxes. He'd finished the last of the smaller hives and had opened the largest when Willow hiked up with a man he assumed was her father. He had blond-brown hair pulled into a short ponytail, a trimmed beard and the same style of pullover shirt and trousers worn by the rest of the fellows on this island, only his were held up by red suspenders.

They set their armloads of boxes and frames on the stone wall beside the boys, and Cor went over to meet the man. Ash— *come on, Cor, they couldn't be making this easier for you with these tree names*—was in full agreement that the hives needed more room. "Common situation with first-year hives. I've just forgotten to attend to them."

"Wouldn't want to lose them," Cor said carefully.

"Not after we had to get replacement hives last year from Merlin. That'd be da—bloody embarrassing to ask again."

The three boys gasped in horror, and Ash pointed at them. "Don't you dare tell your mother."

They began hooting with laughter, and it took Cor a moment to realize the gasps had been in fun at their father's near slip, but the smile on Ash's face and Willow's grin said this was a frequent joke between them.

Cor and Willow, in her bee suit, stapled on the mouse guards and shuffled the boxes to add the empty frames to the middle of each hive. Meanwhile, Ash put the boys to work assembling new frames with wax foundations. When they had enough to fill a last box, Cor added it and put on the hive's lid. They packed up the remaining supplies and equipment, and then everyone wanted to touch his protective barrier.

The middle kid was studying his arm hard, peering this way and that.

"Ever seen anyone with brown skin?" Cor asked him.

"All of the Streams' family, Lady Sedge, Merlin and..." He rattled off a few more. "None of them have lines running through their magic like yours."

This kid was freakin' sharp to see that. "That's part of my spell. It's like the veins in leaves."

The boy scrunched up his face. "If your arms and legs are like the trunk and branches of a tree, wouldn't this be more like the cambium layer?"

"Right-o. I didn't think you'd know about that."

"I like plants," he said, "and I'd sure like to be able to spell like a plant."

Cor squatted down, swiped a swath of magic from his arm and held it out. "Then what tree can we put this on so you can study how it's done?"

"Can it be a hickory? We have one in the yard, and that's what I'm named after. Hickory, but you can call me Kory, same as your name."

Cor laughed. "Well, isn't that something? Except mine comes from *Corylus avellana*. Know what that is?"

Kory looked up at his father.

So did Cor. Something had changed. Ash had been boisterous, but now... *Uh, oh. Should I not have offered his kid my magic?*

"The hazel tree," Ash answered softly as he pressed his knuckles to his mouth, his gaze on his son.

"We have those," Kory said. "But would it still be all right if I use the hickory tree?"

Cor assured him it was, and his father nodded, so Cor tipped the magic into his palms.

The older boys ran ahead, but Kory walked, carefully cupping the magic. When they reached the farmyard, Lady Mimosa was coming down the steps of the house with the other boys, one carrying a canvas bag of apples. Her gaze sought out Cor's with a disturbing intensity before she knelt to listen to Kory excitedly explain the protection spell.

"Mam says we can do it," Kory called, and Cor released his breath.

Heck, he'd never thought of getting permission first—he'd be out of here in a snap if he'd made Lady Pina's friend mad. As it was, this could look like a bribe. Damn.

Cor walked up to her. "Ma'am? I'm not trying to pull anything. He was interested and could see the structure of the spell. I didn't think to ask before offering to give him some." He glanced over his shoulder at Ash. "I-I forgot you're the Witch of the Forest, and I should have gotten your approval. Sorry."

But Lady Mimosa was looking at her partner, her eyes swimming with tears. "Kory says he can see the structure of your plant-related spell," she said softly. "Is it possible you could teach him to copy it?"

"It might take some practice for a kid this young, but seeing the right parts and knowing plant structure helps. He's already got that down, and he says he wants to spell like plants?" Cor looked at her in question.

Kory piped up. "I love plants."

"He does," his parents said in unison.

They were hanging on his answer like it was a big deal. Maybe it was to them? Being Foresters and all, perhaps they wanted all their kids to share their skills. Willow did for sure. Maybe it was just a matter of finding this kid his *thing*, like Cor had trees and his sister had art. "I can help him." Well, for as long as he was here. But they knew that—and it still sounded like a bribe. He tapped Kory on the shoulder and pointed. "Is that your special hickory?"

The kid grinned and led the way. Cor started to follow, but Willow hooked an arm into his and whispered, "Thanks, but my father said to tell you not to expect too much because Kory hasn't—he's only fifth year and not magically inclined."

Oh, that was why… "Got it." Cor knelt beside Kory. "Hold the magic to the tree."

Kory lifted the glowing mass and edged it closer until one side flattened against the bark. Cor cupped his hands around Kory's small white ones. "I'm going to demonstrate, and you do all the things I do. The next time we practice together, you can start to take over. The energy has to sink to the cambium layer and bond to it, but then it has to rise to coat the bark to protect the tree."

"Like cutin, the waxy coating on leaves and fruit?"

"Exactly." Cor eyed Kory. How old was this kid again? "Cutin over every portion of this tree, to each twig tip, each leaf surface, each…you tell me while it's going in so we can cover every part." Cor pushed on the magic with his energy just enough that it sank slowly so the little kid would have time to come up with the whole view of the tree.

Kory's lips formed into an O, and it was a moment before he tore his gaze from his hands to look up into the tree spreading above them. "Twigs, leaves," he repeated. "Down the branches and limbs, the trunk. Over broken stubs, knotholes. The nuts that are forming." He looked pretty pleased for remembering those.

"Keep thinking. There's more," Cor said.

The boy's gaze darted. "Roots! It has to cover everything underground, too, because that's part of the tree."

Cor nudged him, shoulder-to-shoulder. "You got it, little man. Now let's imagine the entire tree and let it spread."

"Will there be enough?" Kory nodded to the remaining glob between his palms.

"Not from what I gave you. We'll put a little more in, and then the tree's energy makes up the rest. It won't be fully formed up for a while." Cor left that vague, so the boy wouldn't feel bad if his first efforts didn't work. Cor pushed a bit more magic, and though the boy scrunched up his face and looked like he was concentrating, Cor couldn't detect any of his magic streaming in. Probably a problem connecting with the tree. Cor pressed his hands to Kory's empty ones for a moment. Then drew back. "I think that's good for a first lesson."

Kory brushed back his bangs and sighed. "Nothing of mine moved in."

The kid was bloody aware. Cor shot him a half-smile and shrug. "You'll have to try again tomorrow."

"But is it really there?"

"Yep." Cor put a finger to the tree. "Just below the bark in the cambium layer, remember?" His finger brought a glow of the mixed magic to the surface.

Kory frowned and copied him. Cor opened his mouth to tell him that this took practice, but a glow surrounded Kory s finger.

The boy shrieked—and so did the rest of his family.

Cor flinched. "Spells," he sputtered. "You people are enthusiastic about trees."

Ash snatched up Kory and swung the boy into the air, then both his parents hugged him, and the others were laughing and hugging him or patting his back, rousingly cheering him on, including another boy—older brother?—who must have returned while they were setting the magic.

"All right, Kory!" The older brother held up a glowing hand, and Kory grasped it in an upward handshake.

"Could you give him a few more lessons?" Ash asked quietly, and Lady Mimosa touched her partner's shoulder, then held out the bag she'd been carrying when she came from the house. "I intended to ask if we could reimburse you for your time with the bees with apples—"

"That'd be great," he said a little too eagerly, his stomach growling audibly.

She tilted her head. "Though you didn't ask for payment, I feel we owe you more. Stay for dinner." She smiled, this time with no question in her eyes.

The next morning, Cor worked alone in the Meadows again, planting seed in yet another field. Lady Lark was off casting spells with her cronies against these rips they kept mentioning. Hours of seeing no one else left him feeling like he hadn't a friend in the world. Would that change if he passed their tests to stay here, like Pink Skirt had? Lady Mimosa had promised to talk to Lady Pina, but could she even get that far? She hadn't offered him an apprenticeship in her Forest, the habitat she controlled. She could, he was coming to understand. So could Fern. But it wouldn't be the same as working with the Pines.

He took a break for lunch, collecting an apple and the cheese Fern had left for him and eating beneath the overhang of the house. There, he was within sight of the porch in case anyone arrived, but not in their way. Today was Thursday, so tomorrow was the climbing day with Fern. At least he could look forward to someone to talk to then. He raised his water bottle to his lips...

Someone was slowly flapping their way up from the south. The person—a man—pivoted his head right and left, looking over the Lower Meadows for something.

Right-o. This chap was looking for him.

Cor pushed to his feet and stepped out from the hobbit house. He didn't have to wave, because the movement caught the wizard's attention. He swooped downward, raising his hand in greeting, his hair bouncing and light glinting off his glasses—

It was Curly Hair.

Brilliant. Just freakin'… Why couldn't he remember people's names, especially this good-looking bloke's?

He arched his wings and fluttered to hover before drifting downward and landing lightly on his feet, just as he'd done on the tree branch. He folded his wings and smoothed his hands down trousers that looked as if they didn't dare get a wrinkle in them.

"Hallo, Cor," he said. "I've been sent to fetch you to meet with Lady Pina."

16

JUMPING HURDLES

F reakin' bloody brilliant. That made this twice as embarrassing. "Can you tell me your name?" Cor asked.

"Oyster of the Estuary." He stepped close and offered his hand.

Cor met his grip. His nails were neat and clean, his palms soft, fingers curling in just an appropriate amount of squeeze, and then he let go. No magic, no threat, but the moment put Cor's head in a muddle, and what came out was an echo of his thoughts the other morning: *nice*.

Too late, Cor became self-conscious that his own hands were rough from digging through the dirt—though he had washed up before lunch. The bloke was saying something.

"Sorry?"

"Most people call me Oy." He smiled, lips stretching over straight, pearly teeth, his wire rims lifting a bit.

Cor had to look away to hold it together. "Oy," he said evenly. "Right," he added while inside a chant ramped up: *Oy. Oyster of the Estuary. Oy. Oy. Oy. Spells, I can't forget!*

"So? Lady Pina?"

"You'll have to lead the way. I haven't got the whole isle's map set in my head."

Oy rolled his eyes. "Likely because she blocked you from her grove."

She did? "Hey. I didn't try to go back or anything. Not after she told me to leave. I have *some* common sense." Thank the Orb, he hadn't—she'd have known.

Oy beckoned and unfolded his wings, ran a few steps and lifted gracefully into the air. Kind of like a ballet dancer, so sure and delicate at the same—Cor shook his head. For freakin' sanity's sake, he had to keep himself together. He hoped Oy was gay, but that wouldn't mean he was available. Or interested. In his experience, light-skinned warlocks didn't find black ones as attractive. At least, not as often as white witches seemed to. And the preppy, soft-handed ones...who knew what they preferred? Likely not a fellow who'd been digging in dirt all day.

Cor sent his excited energy into his shoulders. His wings popped out faster than they should have, and one banged into the porch post. "Damn," he muttered into his shoulder as he pulled it around to his front and checked the feathers. *Brilliant move, man. Just need to bend up a few primaries and ground yourself until you can replace them.*

Oy glided back, making Cor feel like more of an idiot. He took off, flew over the garden compost to toss his apple core and followed. The Meadows valley and several ridges of their tallest mountain had passed beneath them before Cor had figured out how he could ask a question without sounding totally clueless.

"Your Watcher wanted us to land at his mountaintop processing station. These rips Lady Lark is always off repairing, are they hampering his ability to secure the isle?"

Oyster wrinkled his nose. "It's more complicated than that."

"You think I'm not talented enough to understand it," Cor said a little more hotly than he should have.

"I was trying to avoid telling you that I'm not allowed to tell you, mate," Oy said evenly. "Can we drop it?"

That ended the conversation.

They flapped hard to climb the rocky bluff of the mountain. The air cooled and the wind kicked splatters of rain at them. This wasn't the gentle, circuitous route Willow had led them over, so it was either faster or a test to see if he could keep up. Cor was panting by halfway, but determined not to lose pace. By the time they topped the mountain, his vision was spotting at the edges. The updraft caught his wings, and he took the blessed break. His head cleared. The island spread before them, the southern tip of land curved to the horizon, the Irish Sea a cloudy blue on either side. There, protected within a deep cove of mountain ridges, lay the large grove of pines.

Tossing a grin over his shoulder, Oyster flattened his wings, dropped to soar, then tucked his wings and dove. He gained speed.

Cor delayed only a moment, then copied him. The wind rushed in his ears and dragged on his jeans, but the thrill of it raced his heart and energy. Spells, he needed this. The wind was perfect, the slope steep, the spiky tops of the Scots pines the ultimate target. A longing ramped up inside him—

Cor promptly squashed it. He had to maintain detachment. He had no idea what the old—Lady Pina was going to say or do. He couldn't go into this hoping for the world. He'd be crushed like the bug they seemed to believe him to be.

That put a damper on his carefree drop. Shifting from his streamlined posture, he slowed himself incrementally until he was trailing Oy by hundreds of yards. He came upon the Pines—someone else's property—with more caution and deference than he would have if he'd barreled in.

Oy shot over the treetops, slowing naturally and swinging around to wait. When Cor caught up, he pointed to a tree whose top was splintered with an old break.

"Base of that one is where she's working," he called. "I assume you can find your way back to the Meadows after?"

He'd been able to find the valley after other flights. "Yep."

Oy touched two fingertips to his forehead. "Best wishes, then." He turned, flew over the ridge and dropped out of sight.

So...on his own for this. Of course he was. He was the one who wanted an apprenticeship.

Cor made the descent take as long as he possibly could, appreciating the view from the full-on midday sun to patchier light beneath the canopy. He kept expecting to enter the duller needle-filtered light that was typical of the dense groves, but it didn't happen in this one's branches. This tree had the spread of a mature tree, but not the fullness. He spotted a spiraling scar. It'd been struck by lightning in the past. At the last branch of the giant, still a hundred feet above the forest floor, he paused to look at the top of a black cavity that spread in an arch on its way down the trunk.

"I do not have all day to wait for you," called a high-pitched —and very irritated—woman. Below, two figures leaned back to watch him amid the blaeberry shrubs.

Stomach sinking, he glided to land a few feet away. "Sorry, ma'am," he said to Lady Pina and nodded to Lady Mimosa.

She smiled back. "You obviously enjoy being here. We can't find fault in that, can we, Pina?"

Lady Pina harrumphed. She studied him, crossing and uncrossing her arms.

Great Orb, would she just put him out of his misery now?

"I'm told you have skills that *might* benefit us," she finally exploded. "The opinions of others do not sway me, young man. I'm solitary by nature and sure of my energy. I have never needed help from others to maintain my habitat—"

"None of us have," Lady Mimosa said gently, a hand on Lady Pina's arm. "Times have changed as our population grows smaller and the pressures of the human world threaten our resources. We must try new methods, new sources of magic. New apprentices."

Lady Pina harrumphed again, her steely hazel eyes locked on Cor. "I cannot say I like the methods you chose to continue putting yourself in my sights, but it has brought you into favorable circumstances with Mimosa, and I do listen to her. She makes the logical argument that her habitat is brimming with wizards—three fully trained, one on the brink and three more in the wings. Four, if your ability to work with her lad is as promising as she hopes."

He'd thought she was listing Lady Mimosa's staff until the last bit about Kory. This list was her family, and his audience with Lady Pina was a result of his casual gift to a little kid. What were the odds? His mother had always told him and his sister to be kind, but he'd never seen a payoff like this one…*might* be. Giving a slight nod, he kept his gaze on Lady Pina.

"I, on the other hand, am alone in caring for the Pines and, as everyone deigns to point out, stretched thin as I funnel energy to accommodate our shielding needs while also seeing to the issues that time and natural causes bring to our individual trees." She flipped a hand at the gaping cavity in the tree.

"Yet I cannot waste my energy training someone who will take me away from these duties, so I give you one week to meet my requirements. One, I expect hard work. This is not a glamorous position among a unique species that you tout to the Windborne world. It is a job."

That's what I want, a job. His heart began to race with excitement…

"Two, you master the traditional method of energy transfer that my Windborne ancestors have used to harmonize with the vast energy of these living creatures."

She was referring to the trees, right?

"Energy Song."

His stomach dropped, and he asked before thinking, "Sing to the trees?"

"Energy Song," she repeated. "Musical phrases uttered in a recognizable and repeated sequence, synchronized to your energy to integrate with the trees' energy."

Cor pulled out his mobile, opened a note and began typing what she'd said.

"Put that away," she snapped.

"But to remember—"

"I'll teach you. Every morning. You will practice. Every afternoon. My third requirement is that your spiritual presence must be fully invested in this place. Not seeking recognition, other training, the urge to travel or what have you. You cannot be unsettled in any way to work with these vast energy reserves. Organisms of this size will win every time, and their massive energy will remain deep in their cores when it is otherwise needed to circulate and fuel the isle. Now"—she paused and eyed him—"do you wish to attempt to meet my requirements?"

Cor swallowed. "I-I love trees. I would be honored to train and stay."

The way Lady Pina continued staring, he wasn't sure that had been the right response.

Then she grunted. "For someone who displays a protective energy that mimics the vascular tissue of trees, the last requirement shouldn't be too difficult. I'll see you here tomorrow morning."

Tomorrow? Oh blast. He should say yes. He should... "I, uh, can we make it the next day?"

One gray brow lifted.

"I've got five more areas to prep and plant that I've promised to the Meadows." He pulled the map from his pocket, unfolded it and held it out. "Lady Lark is off repairing some rip, and Fern has her human studies. They haven't..." Brilliant, this was becoming a bluster of excuses. He should just shut up and say yes. He frowned at the map, unable to meet her gaze. "I promised to finish."

In the silence that followed, he looked up. Lady Pina was still staring down her nose. Lady Mimosa wore the hint of a smile.

He kept his features frozen. "Afterwards, I can be fully here, as you said." He swallowed.

"This is an excellent example of your dedication," Lady Pina snarled, "if indeed it is. However, if this is some excuse—"

"Orb take it, Pina!" Lady Mimosa exclaimed. "The lad is demonstrating he knows how to work. Even I would be hard-pressed to plant five of Fern and Lark's wildflower patches in a day and a half. Go on, Cor, complete your Meadows work and be here the day after tomorrow."

He went.

Outside the grove, well into the forest covering the ridge top, he stopped and made the notes on his mobile. Three hurdles to pass. Hard work. Energy Songs. Spiritual presence. Or the last was something like that. Probably an out, something no one but she could judge, as an excuse to say no. He blew out a breath. Still, he'd gotten to the next step.

17

ON THE ROCKS

Fern spoke to Beri on the bus for the first time in the two weeks since Beri had enrolled as an exchange student at Boulder High. They'd been too self-conscious about their relationship to do that before.

"We never came to an agreement about when we'd start to appear interested in each other," she said quietly. "Do you want to start?"

Beri rolled his eyes.

She jabbed him with her elbow. "Seriously."

"I am serious. All you have to do is stay in this seat, and you won't need to say a thing to Amanda. She will know."

On the morning rides, Fern had started by sitting with him at their stop farther up the mountain, then moved to an empty row before Amanda's stop to share a seat with her friend as they'd been doing through middle and high school.

"She'll want the scoop later. We have to have the same story."

"We met on the bus. That's the story Lady Heather says to give."

They'd agreed they could avoid questions after Beri was around for a few weeks. "But—"

"Fern? I do nae have the energy to make up anything. Do you?"

No, she didn't. She let her head rest back on the seat and stared at the ceiling. Finally, she turned to him to find him staring at her. She felt her cheeks warm. "It's harder when you're a girl. We talk more about this stuff."

"Just don't."

Darn it all, she didn't want to argue in public. A moment later, his fingers brushed hers, and it was impossible to resist turning her hand over and folding it into his.

"I do want to let people know we are dating, as you call it. I canna say much for fear of making a mistake, you ken? Between these new ways and my duties and that lad's trickery, I have as much to focus on as my en—" He cleared his throat. "As my *efforts* can take."

He'd nearly slipped. Neither of them could afford that.

"If saying little is too hard," Beri continued, "then go sit in another seat. I completely understand."

To do that, she had to take her hand from his. So she stayed in her seat, and when Amanda climbed up the steps, Fern slipped her hand back to holding her pack. She met Amanda's grin with a small smile of her own. After Amanda turned her back and sat down a few rows before them, Beri released his breath.

"Good luck today, then," he said quietly.

Too bad Beri's wish of luck hadn't been a real magical wish—if that was even possible. Fern's day went about as bad as she'd predicted. Amanda had not been easy to distract from the gossip about boyfriend possibilities—and if it hadn't been for the magic issues, Fern would have loved to dish on it. As it was, she took every interrupting ring of a class bell or other classmate's passing as an opportunity to run off or change the subject. By last period, Amanda was on to her, and mad.

Hoping to get to the bus line without seeing her, Fern gathered her notebooks and waded through the crowded hallway.

Amanda appeared at her side. "Gonna sit with him again?" she asked, peering around the hallway.

"I guess. We didn't talk about that."

Amanda nudged her. "Do it. Just assume he expects you to. Then, after a few days—"

"Don't ruin it before I can even get anything started." Fern glared at her.

"Fine," Amanda huffed. "But you're gonna have to tell me this weekend."

"I'm busy," Fern said automatically, and when Amanda's face lit up, she cringed.

She grabbed Fern's shoulder. "You're seeing him, aren't you?"

Fern closed her eyes. No, she wouldn't start lying for this, not when she already had to lie to cover up her other life. "Not sure if we're doing anything—which is why I'm nervous to sit with him," she added through gritted teeth. "I'm taking a rock-climbing lesson this weekend." She didn't need to say who it was with. "Plus, my college essays still aren't done. Come on, I can't miss the bus."

Amanda trotted to keep up. "Okay, then let's get together next week sometime, because for sure you are sitting with him on the bus tonight. Even if I have to kick someone out of the seat next to his."

"Do. Not. Dare." Giving a laugh, Fern swatted her, and when they burst through the doors to the bus lines, there was Beri, tousled red hair visible above everyone else's heads. Their gazes met, he smiled and she melted inside, even with Amanda pinching her arm. Of course she was going to sit next to him. Otherwise, she'd have to talk to Amanda half the way home.

Once the bus dropped them off, Fern sighed. "Amanda wants to come by next week. We'll have to make sure you aren't in the house."

He rolled his eyes. "Because we would be dating if I was at your house."

"If you turned up casually, without being there specifically to see me, it would be odd."

"Just let me know when."

They walked in silence up the gravel mountain road, over their bridge and into the cabin. When the door finally thudded closed, Beri dropped his pack and pulled her into his arms. Letting her own pack slip down and fall, Fern sank against his chest, bent her head to his neck and held on tightly.

"It's just so hard," she whispered. "I feel like a huge liar, even though I'm not lying to anyone."

"Your world is not a place you can truly be yourself," Beri said. "That's why Windborne live like we do."

That made sense, and still everything had changed from her junior year when she'd found out about the isle and secretly traveled there. Nothing magical had come into her life here, and certainly not at school.

"I do nae suppose there is a chance you'd skip this last year of your schooling?" he asked.

She pushed off him. "No!" *No! What the—*

She took a breath, trying her damnedest to calm down. "I mean, what would people think if I *quit*? Pregnant? Cancer? Drug rehab? Died?"

He shrugged. "You have a choice now."

"Really? Because I haven't mastered magic yet. I can't fly. Can't do anything except with plants. I'm like in between, not totally Windborne." She pressed the heels of her hands to her eyes. She needed to keep her options open. "I don't have time for these problems. You were the one who asked for a *rumspringa* to be here."

Beri grunted.

She lowered her hands, knowing full well she was scowling and should shut up. "What?"

"Maybe if you do nae want the problems of dating me, then you do nae want me." Beri spun on his heel and marched to the powder room.

After a moment's hesitation, she stormed after him. "I didn't say that! You don't understand the gossip of high school. You're immune, coming in as an exchange student. Everyone thinks you're cute, that your accent is sweet, that how you don't understand half of our slang is fun." She pushed through the portal on his heels, and they burst out into Hillux's bathroom. 'The girls fawn over you to get you to talk, then try to answer back like they're Scottish." *So* annoying to have to listen to. And say nothing.

Beri turned around, blocking the door.

"But none of them are you," he said, his voice rising. "None of them have *your* sweetness, or care for nature, or are Wind-borne like me. And here, I have to put up with Lady Sedge demanding that Oy test your magic when we all know he's not the least bit interested. And some other lad rescued you in Bonterra when it should have been me there protecting you, but my energy is so in demand on the isle that the elders will nae let me go."

"You should be proud of that," she shouted. "I am!"

"Well, 'tis as much a problem to me as gossip is to you, because 'tis still others talking about me and assigning me a status that I do nae give myself or want." He glared at her. "Do you still think I do nae understand gossip?"

A rapping came at the screened door, and they fell back several steps from each other, Fern warming all over.

Cor opened it, holding up his water bottle. "Just here for water and the next package of seeds. I can't delay." He smiled self-consciously. "I'm starting a week's trial with the Pines, and it's due to you letting me do your chores, then Willow asking if I'd see to their bees. I worked magic with Kory and—"

"Kory worked magic?" they asked in unison.

"With his tree." Cor explained how Kory's part was only a little, but his parents wanted Cor to teach him more. "Lady Mimosa put in a good word for me, and somehow the—*Lady Pina*"—he nodded to Beri—"couldn't deny I might be worth a go."

"A go where?" Beri asked, and Fern had to bite her lip.

Correcting Beri's misunderstanding of the slang would only make them argue more. Guilt poked at her that she was still learning magic and hadn't gotten good enough to help Kory with their shared interest in plant magic. "If you can't get the rest done, I understand."

"I will," Cor said. "I promised. Lady Pina seemed to understand that."

Beri made a sound that wasn't quite a snort.

Fern turned to him. "What do you know that we don't?"

He did his one-shoulder shrug. "If he's keen on being her apprentice, he should put her work first."

Fern put up a finger. "He took on my work first. After she refused him."

"You see it that way. He sees it that way, but Lady Pina sees it her way. Maybe she's not wrong. The Pines are our largest energy producer. We need that energy to repair the rip, especially since…"

The Meadows isn't producing more. He didn't need to say it.

"She is only one person," Beri continued, "especially now that you have my energy with the Meadows."

"Except you're working on the rips, and so is Gran."

Beri ignored her. "It's all in how you view yourself. Why do you think she won't take apprentices? She doesn't think anyone will meet her standards."

Cor frowned. "But you were her apprentice."

Beri snorted and shook his head slightly, like that was a stupid thing to say. And it was. Beri had worked in every habitat on the isle. He'd completed five trials and been given his choice of available habitats to take over when he turned eighteen. But when he'd met her, he'd picked staying with the Meadows. Could he have been Lady Pina's heir? Fern had never asked...

Now was not the time to ask. Not when she could feel his magic rising at her back. Yet his fingers weren't balled when she glanced down. Stiff, but no magic showing. He cleared his throat and lightly said, "Through Lady Mimosa at the start. You do nae have that buffer."

Cor crossed his arms. "You're just trying to make me doubt myself because you're angry that your prebond pledged to help me and you can't do anything about it."

"Do nae kid yourself," Beri said in a low voice. Then he straightened to his full height of six-five.

Crap. Boys posturing. *Magical* boys posturing. This was not good. She'd only seen only one magical fight, and that had been between people who liked each other. Fern threw herself between them.

"You have your trial," Beri said. "Release Fern from the pledge."

Cor glanced at her, then up at him. "She promised to help me arrange an *apprenticeship*."

"This is close enough," Beri ground out.

Cor stepped closer. "Not the same—"

"Don't." Fern gripped Cor's shoulder to hold him back. Sparks fizzled from her fingertips. She snatched back her hand. "Just...don't. Neither of you have time for this. Cor, get your stuff and leave. Beri—" She swung around, but he was already stomping toward the door.

"I have better things to spend my energy on, do nae worry." He let the screen slam behind him.

She glanced at Cor, then followed Beri. Outside, a wall of

waving red-brown wings blocked her from him, and though she called his name, she wasn't fast enough to catch his foot and stop him.

She dropped her arm and watched him fly away.

No, this wasn't good.

Fern didn't see Beri again that night. On the bus the next morning, they each studied for their end-of-week exams. School was not the place to discuss this and neither was the return bus trip. During the walk home, they had begun tentatively talking about school, like adults did about the weather. Then, of all things, Cor was waiting on the bridge between the garage and cabin.

"How did you get here?" she demanded.

"What?" He lifted both hands. "It's an open—"

"Don't say it!"

"By the—ugh." Beri pushed by them, headed inside. "I'm glad he's your problem, not mine."

"Thanks," she snapped at Cor. "Do you realize the trouble you're getting me into?"

He took her arm and tugged her toward the garage. "Right, make me your excuse. Just remember to thank me when my rock-climbing lessons help with your flying, which you will bloody love, seeing as how you're into that bloke. Your mum escorted me over, if that never occurred to you. *She* remembered we were going rock-climbing this afternoon."

Oh, right. Fern rubbed her energy core in her stomach. Mom knew because Fern had asked her to put a quash on her. It seemed reasonable to be prepared in case she got scared while doing this.

At the climbing gym, Fern went to the orientation class she'd signed up for, while Cor showed them his certification card and waited for someone to give him this facility's belay test. Her classmates—mostly parents with kids and a few college students

—were already wearing the rock-climbing shoes, so she hurried to catch up. They learned to put on the harnesses, tie the knots that would rope them in and answer the pattern of calls to use instead of a lot of talk while climbing.

At one point, as they answered their instructor in unison, she looked around for Cor and finally spotted him spidering up a wall, skipping most of the rubberized handholds to reach as far as he could.

Her breath caught. But of course he wouldn't worry. He had his magic, since he'd had to complete as rigorous of a certification in magical control with her mother in order to come into Boulder.

"One more time on these knots, people," their instructor called.

Fern undid hers and looked back at Cor. Fifteen feet up, he straightened his legs in a quick spring against the wall, swung out and glided to the mat. No thud, no buckling at his knees, just the same light landing most Windborne made.

"Off belay," he said and tossed Fern a grin.

He expected her to do that?

"Knots are your security," her instructor repeated. "Have your belayer check your knots until you are super comfortable with your skills."

The class ended, and people split off to climb with the facility staff they were paying to be their belayers, or with friends, like she was doing. Still wearing the harness, she went to the bench behind where Cor now stood with his tester, a middle-aged woman who looked as fit as any of the younger staff, and watched while another staffer was roped into Cor's belay line and climbing.

Fern knew the terminology now, but it didn't make her hands any less sweaty.

"Lowering," called the young man who was climbing.

"Lowering," Cor answered and moved his hands, keeping his

gaze on the climber, answering when he asked for slack. His drop was less dramatic than Cor's had been.

"That's a pass," said his tester. "Hold on a minute, and I'll get your card."

She left, and the staff climber began to untie the knots on his harness. "This your climber?" He nodded to Fern, and at Cor's answer, he said, "Have her rope in and review your calls."

Fern retied her newly learned knots.

Cor checked them over. "Good. What do you say?"

"I'm not ready."

Cor and the staffer laughed. "Whose idea was this?" asked the staffer.

Fern pointed to Cor. "But I agreed I want to try it. It's just…" She looked up at the wall. It might be the shortest beginner wall, but it looked much higher now that she was standing next to it. And she towered above this guy and had a good thirty pounds on Cor.

"I'm heavier than either of you," Fern said. "How can he keep me for falling?"

The staffer tilted his head toward Cor.

He held up the metal thingy attached to his harness. "The way the ropes go through the belay device lets my pull on the bottom rope act as a brake. I never let go. I never stop watching you. What do you say if you slip?"

"Falling."

"And if you feel like there's too much extra rope?"

"Sla—no *take*. Slack is if I need more."

"I'll keep it tight as tight can be, if that'll make you more comfortable. You'll be saying 'slack' with every move."

Fern nodded.

The woman who had tested Cor handed him a red card. "We're hiring. After seeing your test and hearing that, I'd love for you to put in an application. Ask at the desk if you're interested and put a note on it that Libby did your test."

Cor pocketed the card. "Thanks. I'll do that." He turned a grin on Fern.

Oh man, was he serious? Libby left, but the other guy was still there, so she couldn't say anything.

"That's a high compliment from Libby." He nodded to Fern. "Still worried?"

"Uh, no," she muttered. "On belay," she said to Cor.

He chuckled and pulled up the slack in the rope. "On belay."

Fern turned toward the wall. "Climbing."

"Climb on."

Ohmigod, this was really happening.

She climbed. It wasn't so bad. The easy wall of grips everywhere, plus long legs, meant she didn't need to think about where to step. Cor kept the rope taut, just as he'd promised. In fact, it pulled a bit, which urged her onward.

"Might be a good place to try your first rappel," Cor said, breaking into her thoughts.

The rope wasn't pulled tight. She made the mistake of looking down at him—and snapped her head up again, looking straight ahead at the gray wall and red line of rope.

"Fern? Just ease back into a sit, and I'll lower you."

How did I get this high? The rope slacked beside her nose. "Take," she choked out.

It tightened.

"I got you," Cor said. "Sit back and float down."

"Too high," she squeaked.

"Then come down three or four grips, but you'll have to look to place your feet."

If she just sat back into the harness, she wouldn't have to look. Which was the lesser of the evils? Hands sweating, she stared up the wall of colored blobs. Then across at other climbers. The little kids were going at it, the taller college students matching their progress upward. A woman had reached the top, way up, maybe thirty feet to—

"Fern?" Cor said gently. "At least let me know what you're planning to do."

"How high am I?" she asked.

"About fifteen feet. A little over twice your body length."

Pitiful. Okay. She'd forked over babysitting money that she'd rather have spent on new plants. She was here, and with a guy who actually knew what he was doing. "Okay," she said aloud. "I'll rappel."

"Attagirl. When you've got your hands on the rope, give the command 'lowering.' I'll give you enough slack to bend your knees to sit."

With a glance at the rope, she shifted her weight and clenched one hand around the rope. Then the other and quickly said, "Lowering."

"Lowering."

The rope went slack, her knees bent and her stomach dropped with her rear. Then she was sitting, her toes dragging over the grips as she floated down, hands clinging to the rope for dear life. It was slow, so slow that she finally dared a look down again…just as her feet touched the mat.

"Rather straighten your legs and stand?" said Cor from right behind her. "Or do you need a break on the floor?"

She stood. "That wasn't so bad," she whispered.

Cor winked. "You're still on belay."

"Oh. Belay off."

"Belay off," he repeated with a grin and released the ropes. "Way to go." He held up his hand, and she high-fived him.

"Thanks." She couldn't stop grinning. "That wasn't bad at all."

"You're so tall, it wasn't that far," Cor said matter-of-factly. He wasn't laughing at her. "So…" He tilted his head and grinned back. "Belay on?"

She climbed and floated down, climbed and floated down, managing to drop her feet from the wall, then at Cor's instruction, giving a little bounce off it. He dropped her faster. At first, she protested, then on a slower descent, she realized it'd lost the thrill and had to abashedly ask him to speed it up.

While waiting their turn on the other walls, they talked. About the wildflowers he'd planted for her, the caterpillars and butterflies she hoped to attract with the different seeds. How some of the flowers hadn't made it the year before. She bit her lip. "I suppose I should have planted these myself, you know, to give them that special extra boost." She wiggled her fingers.

"Right," he said. "I didn't mess with that. But it's there already, in the soil."

"You can see it?"

"Sure, why not?"

Well, she couldn't if she didn't know the other person well. Gran's and Mom's magic, Beri's and Duffy's since she had worked so much in the Meadows' soils. But not Raven's or her dad's. "I'm not that good yet," she admitted.

"With the help of your plants, you will be," he said. "That's how mine matured. I never have a day go by that I don't touch one of my trees."

"Dad told me I should be interacting every day. I haven't been," she admitted.

He waved his hand in a petting motion. "Only takes a few minutes brushing them, crumbling soil in your bare hands. The places I planted? It'll bring them under your—" He side-glanced at the belayer closest to them. "You know." He lifted his chin. "Ready to get up there again?"

After several hours of climbing, she made her third and last climb to the top of the medium wall and soared down. As soon as he said, "Off belay," Cor smacked her palms. "You rock, Fern!"

She laughed. "Very funny. But yeah, I feel like I do." She put up her hands and high-fived him again. "You do, too. Thanks.

No one else suggested this, and it's been great." She began untying the knots on her harness.

"Think it will help?"

"Well, I'm not scared of dropping while tied in."

He grinned. "Thanks to my promises and good looks."

She rapped his arm. "Thanks to Libby for offering to hire you." He pretended to be outraged. "But seriously, your confidence helped a lot. You're good at this."

"Told you."

"Show-off," she said, but it was to tease, and his grin said he knew it.

He had unhooked from the rope and now stepped out of his harness. "We'll practice up a tree next weekend," he said before carrying his gear to the return desk.

The visual of that... Slowly, she got out of her harness and shoes. A tree. She met Cor at the desk. "Okay, I'm in for next weekend. But it'd be nice to find someone else to...for a..."

He grinned impishly. "You don't trust me?"

Well, that had changed from a week ago. "I do, but...geez. Wouldn't backup be nice? What if a branch breaks?" Beri could catch her...maybe?

Cor eyed her.

Maybe if Willow and Beri were both there. "Okay, that's not likely, but..."

"Stop with the buts. You said you were in." He nudged her toward the door. "I've got the week to help you, and maybe Beri won't be such a bloody ass to me."

18

ENERGY SONGS

Cor arrived early to the Pines and flew below the treetops. The dull light of the cloudy morning didn't reach to the understory. It was eerie. Shadowed columns of bark rose into the dark canopy, mist obscuring the spaces between them. The damp slicked his cheeks and hands, the droplets weighing on his feathers and drawing his curly hair into tighter ringlets. He toe-touched down on the patio of moss-rimmed slates at Lady Pina's log home.

Should he knock? Maybe dawn was *too* early.

He'd hunched into his black hoodie to wait when the round door creaked open. Lady Pina leaned out, her gray limb of a braid undone and falling in crimped locks. She blinked at him. "Pardon me for not setting a time. Come back in an hour, please."

No hardship, because she didn't say where to go in the meantime. He flew among the massive trunks, just him and the birds. At every turn, tree corridors beckoned, the now-bluish mist tickling the tops of young trees and shrouding bunches of brushy needles. Cor's heart swelled and sang in place of his pocketed earbuds.

This. This was a place he could endlessly explore, a forest like no other, the magical forest he'd yearned for. He might not be able to see much more than a hundred feet in any direction, but the sheer mass of the pines—trees upon trees—was a wonder that wouldn't grow old soon. And he'd not even gotten to revel yet in the shrubs and flowers and lichens and whatever creatures hid among the glorious trees. When the first splinters of light streaked between the upper limbs, he alighted on a limb to simply stare.

Too soon, the five-minute alarm chimed on his mobile and he headed back.

Lady Pina was waiting on the roof of her home in the hollowed log. She perched on a seat made from a curved branch that overlooked a patch of moss with several small, evergreen cowberry bushes and one three-foot-tall Scots pine, a spindly thing. It wouldn't be for long, so why was she risking the roots growing into her roof and weakening it?

She snapped a pocket watch closed. "Timely. I appreciate that," she murmured and gestured to a stump seat.

He kept his question to himself and sat.

A penny whistle appeared in her hand. She played, quite well, a pretty lilting tune he'd never heard. She lowered the instrument. "The first stanza. The words are"—she began singing— "Seed cracking. Cracking, cracking. Narrow crevice forming." Before she put the whistle to her lips again, she said, "Sing along to acquaint yourself with the tune."

"I, uh, don't sing."

She paused as if considering this. "Then you have wasted your time with that music device stuck in your ear." She stood up.

Spells, he was losing this. "Seed cracking, cracking," he sang. "Cracks, uh, forming."

She sat down again. "Seed cracking. Cracking, cracking.

Narrow crevice forming." She began playing, and he sang the inane song, something a toddler could pick up, over and over.

"Second stanza. Roots spreading. Spreading, spreading. Exploring through the soil."

The thing went on with the first shoot growing, the imaginary seedling reaching for the light, the roots finding water. If you had a primary-schooler's education in plant growth, you could remember it. By the seventh and last stanza Cor had grown bored.

Lady Pina asked him to sing the entire thing from start to finish. He did, and she lowered the penny whistle and it disappeared. "That's the base of it. In the version we use, and that you must master, some parts are drawn out, others peaked. It starts low and dark as a seed would, then rises to a crescendo of photosynthesizing interspersed with beats of rest representing night."

"What does singing this song do?"

She paused before answering, like this should be obvious. "It enables you to integrate your magic with that of the pinewoods. Each stanza is a magical act that we perform in caring for these trees, guiding the techniques going back generations in my family. Many of the pines on this isle were sprouted by my great-grandfather using this technique. It's what they know and through which they produce the bulk of the magic for Giuthas."

She was out of her tree, as his dad would say, making it this complicated, but he didn't argue. He'd learn the song, sing it and do what he always did to boost his saplings and protect mature trees. The last stanza about the dying ones returning to the ground wasn't anything they did at the estate, but likely it'd be like siphoning off energy from any plant. Cor nodded his supposed agreement.

This time when she sang, she extended the lines with droning and pitched her voice deep enough that he could hardly make out that the words were the same.

"Could you repeat that?" he asked. "I can't get the…" Words? Tune?

"Listen with your magic instead of your ears."

How the heck would he do that? He repeated what she sang the best he could, and she corrected him every few syllables. He tried tapping to figure out how long to hold the words *cracking* and *spreading*. They repeated the first stanza over and over, and the repetitive droning resounded like a drumbeat in his head.

Finally, they moved on to the root-spreading stanza and began again with the repetitions. This one flowed quicker.

He was getting the hang of it when she said, "Now apply your magic to it."

"Pardon me?"

"Magical intonations accompany the song." She flicked her hand, lighting her fingers aglow. "Or rather, they are a part of the song. Your magic should thrum like thus."

She. Had. To. Be. Kidding.

She wasn't. As Lady Pina began the song again, her energy flared over her. If she hadn't shown him the finger sparks, it would've been minutes before he noticed. The glow was dim at first, a mere flush over her skin, but with each repeat of the seed stanza, the glow grew. It was like watching the northern lights. You weren't sure if they were changing, because the changes flowed into and over one another. Cor gave up trying to sing along in his head, propped his chin on his hand and just watched.

After several singings, he noticed a dark divide in the glow over her hands. *Now* he could see the nut cracking open, the crevice, the creep of root tendrils, the spread of the magic. The tempo changed. She moved on to the second stanza. The color was brighter. Which went along with the pace and the slightly higher tone. Of course, as things progressed into the photosynthesis stanza, the song, and therefore the magic, should get lighter.

She didn't go that far. He had to perform it. And he botched it at every turn. He wanted to storm away, but couldn't with her watching. Blast, after feeling so confident yesterday, teaching Fern, today he was in her climbing shoes—and feeling he had no toehold. If he couldn't do this, the old lady's first lesson, then he'd fail and would be out of here.

A feeling of dread crept over him. *No, no, I can work the magic.* He'd done magic this complicated with the rowan trees.

Finally, he dropped his hands to his sides. "Can I just copy the magic without the song?"

She blinked. "Well…I suppose so. But it won't work without the song."

He closed his eyes and put that from his mind. This wasn't too different than directing the lighting of the rowans, just without a specific tree to direct it to.

He flared his magic and hummed. Lady Pina began the light sequence again, this time not singing. He copied her, making only two mistakes this time. They ran through it again, and she nodded appreciatively.

"That is enough for the day's lesson. Spend the afternoon practicing. Find me if you are truly stumped." She extended her closed hand. He automatically reached, and she dropped a handful of pine nuts into his palm. "Show me the roots you produce at the end of the day." She rose and fluttered off the roof.

He stared stupidly at them. "Uh, here?" he asked.

She waved a hand. "Anywhere you like. Best might be in the grove, for a beginner. Later, once you imbue the music with your magic and absorb it into your being, the technique will work anywhere you are, even off the isle." She smiled like she'd made a joke. "Though the saplings would likely not last long without our climes and the symbiotic fungi in our soil."

He ate his lunch, then flew until he found a pretty glade with light dappling the fallen needles and moss. Thank the Orb he looked before landing—the tiny white flowers lining the stalks were nearly invisible. He didn't dare damage the orchids Willow had pointed out, creeping lady's tresses, or the other pinewoods rarities. Cor settled carefully between the plants and dug his hands into the soil to commune with the habitat, as he'd told Fern she should do. His magic tingled with awareness of the trees. He sang the song to them. The entire thing first, so he was sure he remembered it, then just the first two stanzas in the droning version.

Ready to start, he flared his magic and hummed. It was still awkward.

I should use a pine nut. New magic always worked better if you had a thing to work it on. He held one in his open palm and sang the song. Everything came together better, but nothing happened. He did it again. Then again with his hand closed. He tried another pine nut. And another.

He couldn't get the damned things to sprout.

He went back to Lady Pina's home, where she had him sing the songs and perform the magic with them. Her only suggestion was, "Higher on the 'ing' of the second 'spreading.'"

He sang it through again, perfectly.

She tilted her head. "You would become acquainted quicker if you were staying in a grove."

His breath caught for a moment. "That would be brilliant," he said.

"Beri may be willing to make room for you. I shall ask him."

No freakin' way was he sharing a room with that bloke, but she didn't need to know that. He'd just hang his bivy sack again. When he arrived back at Lady Lark's hillside cottage, Beri was waiting, arms crossed, but he wasn't scowling.

"It was her idea," Cor said quickly. "I'm not gonna invade your space."

"My place, you mean? As *I* would also prefer you out of Lark's home and away from Fern's, I am willing to have you at the hollow. On one condition." He dug in his pocket and held up an orange glass rod.

Lady Pina's peregrinator.

Cor sucked his teeth. "If you think you can force me to go back, you have a bloody fight on your hands."

Beri shook his head. "You wish. This was my request in exchange for Lady Pina's. Living in a Pines grove will assist your trial. I'm willing to have you in my grove, but the moment you finish with that trial, or that Lady Pina dismisses you, you are to release Fern from the pledge and return to Bonterra. Agreed?"

He didn't plan to get dismissed, and once the trial was over on Saturday—bloody freakin' pine pitch. He had to be back in Bonterra by noon on Friday to be with Hazel. "Agreed," he snapped.

"Get your things."

In Fern's gran's spare room, he stuffed his clothes and the food Fern had provided into his pack and followed Beri on a flight across Lower Meadows to a grove of a few dozen ancient pines. Weaving through the treetops, they came to a giant tree blackened by an old lightning strike.

Beri glided down to it, and as Cor followed, the shadows resolved into a tree cave in the burnt core. Ah, right, Beri had said a hollow. Beri landed on a wide limb almost even with the hollow and walked to the entrance. The opening was over eight feet high, and as Cor landed, his mouth fell open. This was a room, furnished with two cots.

Beri was at one, stripping the sheets. "The other is clean, but I'm due to wash these anyway. Extras are in the bottom drawer if you prefer this bed." He gestured to a chest of drawers. He stuffed the sheets and pillowcase into a bag and cleared a drawer for Cor's use.

"There. It's all yours for the duration of your stay."

For freakin' bloody real? "Where will you sleep?"

Beri gestured westward. "I have a cabin at the edge of this grove."

He ought to leave it at that, but his curiosity got the better of him. "Why don't you live here full time?" He certainly would.

"Raven and I did for years, once we earned the right by apprenticing in the Pines. When we went on to trials, his took him to other habitats. I remained here for one with the Pines, and this grove became my responsibility. This tree cave is now mine, but it takes more energy to keep warm in the winter and has no water. He lifted a waterskin hanging by a shoulder strap from a hook and tossed it to Cor. "You should fill this from my well."

They flew back down, got the water at a one-room cabin, hand-hewn from local oaks. That would have been a cool house, if not for the tree hollow. He thanked Beri and left, eager to settle into the tree.

He landed in the doorway. *Brilliant.* The trial and now this. He rehung the waterskin and circled the room, touching the walls, feeling the tree beyond the dead heartwood. Chunks of it covered the floor, but someone had smoothed the ceiling long ago, and the growth rings spread overhead.

Cor flew up and found the center with the tip of his finger. A shiver ran through him. This was where the tree had begun its life, the sprouting of a pine nut, the first year of the sapling's growth. For its first few years, it had grown well, the rings wide, then the bands narrowed, showing slower growth. He counted them. Five hundred and seventy-eight before reaching the wall. There had to be another two hundred within the wall, judging by the thickness.

He squeezed the pine nuts in his pocket. Time to work on another generation.

The second day, Cor didn't arrive at Lady Pina's until an hour after dawn. She was closing her door as he flew up. She gestured to the roof and fluttered up, flushing a flock of black grouse. He let them fly off before he joined her on his stump.

"Sing the first two stanzas for me." He did, and she nodded. "Now we shall go on to the next."

"But I still couldn't—" Bloody hell, this sounded like pitiful pine pitch. He paused to collect himself. "I still couldn't get a nut to sprout," he admitted. "Can we review those stanzas and figure out what I'm doing wrong?"

"Sing them." He did, and she corrected a little inflection that was different than the one he'd missed last night, and then she began the third stanza.

His gut clenched, but he put up a hand to stop her. "Can't we spend more time on the first two until I have them down?"

"Seven stanzas, and you have six days to learn them, so if we don't move on, then you won't be able to complete a test on the last day of the week I agreed to." She said this in one breathless sentence, nearly the longest thing she'd said to him other than the songs.

"Right, then," he said.

She taught him the growing stanza and showed him the accompanying magic. Well after the sun was straight overhead, she pronounced that he had it and handed him another set of pine nuts.

"Once you get them to sprout, move through to the growing stanza as well."

Again, the magic didn't take. After trying over and over, he flew among the trees.

His mistake yesterday might have been feeling only the soil, not the trees. He brushed their needles, stroked their bark, rolled pinecones between his palms. He didn't actually intend to take magic from them—no doubt, Lady Pina would disapprove—but it flowed through his channels and returned.

Right, I know the trees. I know the soil. He sat cross-legged on the ground, his back to an orange-barked trunk, facing a two-year-old tree in a clearing, and held a pine nut. He began singing.

It glowed.

He broke off in surprise. "Ah, shoot." He began the song again. The nut glowed up immediately this time. The casing split. He sang that stanza twice more until the nut was pulled well apart, and then he moved on to the root-spreading lines. A root peeked out. It stopped. He had to repeat the stanza several times, but he had it. The root came out like a sneaky little worm, spiraled over his palm and laced through his fingers, but nothing he did got a sprout to form.

He raked his fingers into his hair and pulled. "Argh, I know I'm communing. But something is now wrong with the third part." If he couldn't keep up, how would he be able to get ahead so he could get back to Bonterra on Friday?

It had to be the song. Either he wasn't singing it correctly, or the magic was wrong. Why wasn't she correcting him? He thudded his head back against the trunk.

"Hallo there," came a soft call.

Cor startled, his gaze darting across the clearing to a light spot—Oyster's sandy hair against the tree he sat in.

"I take it I'm not interrupting now."

Cor shook his head, too tired to care that he'd been spotted floundering.

Oyster rose and came to squat before him, elbows propped on his bent knees, long, slender fingers hanging loosely. "Not going well enough?"

"No. I've gotten to lesson two, but to keep up, I have to master lesson three." He explained how he must still not have a part of the song correct.

"She's not much of a teacher," Oyster said almost apologetically, so polite that you'd never take it for an insult. "Never has done it much. When I've helped her, she always seems to forget a step."

"You don't think she's intentionally tripping me up?"

"Great Orb, no." Oyster looked aghast that he'd even suggested it. "She has too much honor to do that. In fact, it's likely a matter of pride to teach you properly. She admires parents and well-raised children."

Cor tossed a hunk of shed bark. "You must be a favorite."

A laugh hiccupped from Oyster. "Thank goodness, or I'd have quite a complex. According to my mother, I have considerable failings. There must be some trick you can use to remember precisely how she sings the songs?"

He'd rather delve into this brilliant bloke's life—which Cor doubted had any faults—but Oy was trying to help. Cor blew out a breath. "Listening to her sing them over and over should do it. That's how I've managed the start. But she's not willing to sing them again once she believes I have it right."

"Unfortunately, I know nothing about growing terrestrial plants," Oyster said. "In the Estuary, we focus our magic on the nutrient combinations carried by the mix of sea and land water." He gave a shy grin. "Different from most of the isle's magic, so I don't dare suggest a thing. I have to get back, but Lady Pina did ask me to tell you, if I saw you, to check in with her, regardless of how far you've gotten."

Instead of getting up after Oy left, Cor shuffled around until he could lie back without crushing any of the ground plants. He stared at the canopy. The big trees swayed against a bright sky. He'd like a nap before he flew back over Mount Lookout, but he'd also like to sprout a nut. He needed a moment before finding Lady Pina…

When he blinked his eyes open, the sky had dimmed. He felt better. He'd slept…and tree magic had looped through his channels. None remained, but the trees seemed closer now, more familiar. He smiled and pointed a finger at the sapling in the clearing. It lit up as bright as his rowans. He outlined the branches in magic, thinking of his failed pine nut. Perhaps he should try to sprout it his way—

"What are you doing?" demanded Lady Pina.

The magic snapped out. Cor shoved himself to sitting and practically levitated to his feet. His mobile fell from his pocket to the ground. He snatched it up. "I connected to its magic. I was, uh, just playing."

"The only magic you may work here is what I have instructed you in. Show me the pine nuts."

He thrust out his hand. But his mobile was in it, not the nuts he'd been holding for hours.

Lady Pina harrumphed. "If that is how you're spending your practice—"

"It's not, honest, I—" He shoved the mobile into his pocket and pulled out the pine nuts. He centered one on his palm and raised it to eye level between them and sang. The tune was now rote on his blundering tongue, thank the Orb. Her frown faded as the nut split, but after the root propelled its way out and dove down through his fingers, nothing.

She frowned again. "You've started the third on the wrong notes." She sang the line.

Bloody hell, he had. She sang it again, and he sang along with her, then repeated it correctly alone.

"Practice," she said, and with a dismissive nod, she left.

Darn it all, he had. Just the wrong tune. He started to shove his fisted pine nuts into his pocket, but the mobile blocked it. He pulled it out, staring between the two, an idea occurring to him. She wouldn't like it if she caught him, but he had to try if he was going to get these songs right.

19

STUMBLING BLOCKS

Over the weekend, Fern didn't see Beri much. Between their homework, her college essays, and Beri's work on the rip, neither had free time. Or didn't make time. She got that he didn't consider her rock-climbing lesson as a substitute for a lesson in flying. Or that he didn't think much of Cor.

She decided to talk about Cor as little as possible. He had the trial he wanted, and now it was up to him to convince Lady Pina. One way or another, Fern would be free of him in a week. She had the peregrinator to take him back, and Mom promised to help her.

Before bed on Sunday—dusk in Giuthas—she crossed over to see if Beri and Gran had finished for the day. Hillux was quiet. Cor had moved out, and Hilda was sleeping off her extra feedings. Fern walked into the Meadows and dug her fingers into the soil while she hung out for a few minutes. Without magic, she hadn't bothered to come and touch her land, but today she'd really missed the feel of new energy in her channels.

She called to her habitat's energy, but Cor's magic acted just like a quash.

"Well, well, well," echoed a voice around her. "Finally decided to put in an appearance?"

Fee. The security sessions. Fern slapped a hand to her mouth. "I forgot!"

His glow fluttered around her in erratic loops.

Fern backed toward Hillux. "I'm sorry."

"Do nae try to escape to Lady Heather for help. This is your responsibility."

She stopped. Yeah, she wasn't five. "I know. Can we schedule again for tomorrow?"

He jerked to a stop yards away, the tall grass coming to his waist. "Or now?"

Dang, she should. Guilt pinged at her. "I…" She wanted to go to bed. If she didn't get to sleep by eleven, she would miss the bus and Mom would get mad because she had to drive her… now there was a good reason. "I can't," she said firmly. "It's late where I live, and if I miss school, Mom—Lady Heather—will have a fit."

Fee's eyes narrowed. "A fit? Like that performance she underwent when I—*when you* returned from Bonterra?"

"Exactly."

He scowled and pointed a glowing finger. Fern held her ground. She had him and he knew it. Fee swirled away. "Tomorrow, then," he echoed. "Do nae forget."

The next morning at breakfast, Dad said, "I see the bees have had regular feedings, but I do nae see you working with them, lass."

She bit her lip. "I, uh, turned the feedings over to Cor and, honestly, forgot about them. Has he done anything wrong?"

Dad tilted his head. "Nay, but…"

"What?"

"I thought after we talked, you'd take a more hands-on attitude. Establish a routine for after your pledge is resolved."

Fern scooped the last of her granola from her bowl, rose and put her dishes in the sink. She hadn't heard Beri come in yet, but she didn't want to discuss this before school. "Cor will be gone soon. I'll do it then," she said. "Thanks for breakfast." She grabbed her pack and was out the front door and across the bridge before the door slammed again. She slowed enough for Beri to catch up.

He passed her a bag. "You forgot your lunch, and Merlin didn't look happy."

"Me either," she muttered. "He's on me about the bees." And Fee was on her about the security thing. And Amanda… "Listen, I've got to tell Amanda what we're doing. She told me I better arrange *something* with you so we'd be dating before you leave."

"That girl is smarter than she looks."

"Beri!"

"Ach, I did nae mean it quite in that way. Your friend spends so much time primping her hair and clothes, I did nae think she'd notice anything beyond her looks."

"It's what she lives for."

He raised a brow. "And what about you?"

Was this a comment on her looks? She eyed him, trying to decide how to answer and not get into a deeper disagreement. Then one thing went right—the bus rumbled up the road. They slid into seats next to each other near the door. As the bus began the winding descent down the canyon to Boulder, Beri stuffed a piece of paper into her hand and turned to ask the guy behind them, "Think state election procedures will be on Thompson's test, or just the national ones?"

She unfolded the note.

I can't do this without discussing it. I haven't seen you all weekend. I hope you understand.

He'd had this ready? Or done it magically? Fern folded the note and slid it into her jeans pocket. Yeah, hard to argue with that. Her problems rolled through her mind all the way down the mountain: How would she discuss this without bringing up Cor? What if Beri didn't want to acknowledge that they were together at school? And how could she avoid Amanda until they got home again to talk?

She didn't meet Amanda's gaze when she got on the bus. Beri continued to talk and laugh with the guys, so Fern got up as soon as the bus arrived and, head down, strode into the school alone.

Amanda caught up at Fern's locker. "So how did it go with Beri this weekend?"

"It didn't."

"Oh no! He doesn't want to—"

"No, I mean I didn't say anything to him."

"Why not? You know you like—"

"Chickened out."

"But Fern, if you don't tell him, how's he ever going—"

"Can't."

"But don't you want to—"

"No." Fern slammed her locker shut and glared down at Amanda. "Not now."

"Okay already, I get it. Subject dropped. When do you want to get together on our French actualities presentation?"

Until she appeased Fee and Dad, she wasn't free the next few afternoons. "Thursday? At my place?" The first bell rang, and they joined the rush down the hall.

"That works. See you at lunch."

Putting Amanda off hadn't been as hard as she'd thought it would be. If only Beri would be as agreeable.

Cor's third day of lessons was dismal. The fourth stanza encouraged the seedling to grow—*Tree reaching. Reaching needles for the light, roots seeking water. Reaching, flowing, growing*—and…well, he hadn't even gotten one to sprout leaves. Yet the song looped repetitively, and he was sure he had it.

Ha. He'd been sure he'd known the last one, too.

"You've caught on," Lady Pina said. "Go practice yesterday's sprouting lesson and see if you can add today's."

Flights, no…not…

She stood. He didn't. He stuffed his hand into his pocket, clicked on his mobile as he half turned away, withdrew it and hit the record button he'd cued up before he'd arrived. "I'm not sure," he blustered, and she turned back.

"Pardon me?"

"Can you sing it from the top—the entire thing for another review?"

She eyed him, then sat again.

He glanced at the mobile held awkwardly behind his leg. It was recording. He magicked it down among the glossy leaves of the cowberries, the microphone aimed toward her. "Thank you," he said. *Please, please let this work.*

She sang it all.

He nodded. "I-I think I have it."

"Very well," she said.

He thanked her again—*oh, please let it be clear enough*—and said goodbye. An awkward moment passed as she stood, waiting for him to go, but he quickly gestured her ahead of him. The instant she turned, he snatched up the mobile and fluttered off the roof with her.

"It's a brilliant house," he said. "Both yours and Lady Lark's. Every Windborne would value their surroundings more if they lived as part of them instead of *on* them."

She glanced over, seemingly studying him. "Well said. A week ago, I wouldn't have understood, except my visit to Bonterra reminded me that a good many of our people don't have that privilege. How do they keep their warding, I wonder?"

"The foundation struggles with explaining it to them as

well," he said. A second after the words left his mouth, he realized he'd slipped.

"What foundation?"

Bloody brilliant, Cor. "At the Gruen Estate. Where I-I work in the greenhouses."

She nodded. The knot forming in his gut relaxed. "They have a tree foundation to support energy requirements in the more developed enclaves," he said. "Bonterra has energy problems, too—not enough resources to balance the population who wish to live there."

"Surely the Gruen arboretum covers the energy requirements for Bonterra."

"Not completely," he said. "Not anymore." Heck, had she not paid attention on the city tour? "The streets are lined with trees. The academy campus and public parks are fully planted. We have no vacant land. Individual homes are now required to have one tree for every thirty square feet of land. Rooftops are being structurally reinforced to support landscaping, and every vertical surface has been analyzed for more plantings. We're long past ignoring any possible growing surface."

Lady Pina clasped her hands before her. "We have an imbalance here as well," she said quietly.

"How? All these huge—"

"Indeed, isn't it time to practice?" She opened the door to her house and closed it behind her with a solid thud.

Blast. Had he insulted her in some way? He'd taken wing before it came to him. Duh, she didn't have an apprentice. Her habitat—the biggest trees on the island—was probably lacking in magical output. And he'd pointed it out. *Brilliant move, Cor. She probably thinks you were angling for the apprenticeship.*

He flew through the Pines, as far away from Lady Pina's house as he could get and still be in the grove. A midlevel branch had as clear a view as possible in her direction, so he settled on it and hit play on his mobile.

"I'm not sure," said his own voice, loud and clear. Then the next bit of conversation was muffled. *No.* He turned up the volume. "Thank you," his voice said, clear enough, and Lady Pina began singing. The breath whooshed out of Cor. He leaned back with a smile and listened. After several more listens while eating his lunch, he began singing.

By midafternoon, he had five pine seedlings lined up beside him, bare root, each with a second ring of needle tufts. After congratulating himself, then studying their magic, he gathered up the trees and flew them to Lady Pina's home. He arranged the seedlings on her little round patio table before knocking.

She was surprised, and pleased, though she tried to hide it. "I'm sorry I don't have the time to go on to the next lesson today."

Darn. He'd hoped they could get ahead. "Do you have time to hear me out on something bothering me?" he asked slowly, brushing his hand over the tips of the trees. His magic flared in them, reaching for more.

She nodded and sat in one of the chairs, gesturing for him to do the same.

Ha, so this was what it took to impress her. Well, hopefully, she'd listen to what he saw as a problem. "These seedlings grew, but only my magic is in them."

"Theirs is in it, too." Lady Pina waved her hand over the small trees, and they flared again, this time in the blue-green of the Scots pine needles.

He leaned forward. "But there is nothing in them of this habitat, of the soil. When we plant at the estate, we take soil from the grounds to plant our bare root seedlings in. When they..." What was the word for it?

"Know it?"

"Yes, when they know it and attach to the microorganisms, the bacteria and fungi in the soil"—that came straight from Master Harold—"then they have an easier transition when we plant them on the grounds or around town. Not one has failed."

"I have no need of more trees to plant in the pinewoods."

"Wait a second here." He started to suck his teeth, stopped himself and stood up. "You're not going to just…*waste* my seedlings?" He waved at them. "They're perfectly good trees. You can plant them *somewhere*."

"I have a hundred *perfectly good trees* already imbued with this habitat's magic in my nursery. Why would I need more?"

Because they're mine, he wanted to say. But he got it now. They weren't of value without the magic of this land.

He stretched his fingers. *Magic I don't have.* And likely wouldn't.

He let out a breath. "Right. Whatever." He turned and took a few steps. Eh, he ought to confirm tomorrow, make sure she knew he wasn't quitting.

"I see your point," she said before he could speak.

He turned back.

Lips pursed, she was staring at the trees. "Or I see *a* point. You have put your energy into learning to do this. Only the second apprentice to succeed. Right," she said, oddly echoing his dismissive comment. She stood up. "Bring them along."

They flew to her nursery. At one end lay a sizable hunk of log that came even with his head when they landed next to it. Lady Pina opened a hatch on its side and gestured to the tools inside. "Here is everything you need, other than pots. Look around and see if you can scrounge up some, but stay to this half of the beds. I haven't had time to repair the damage suffered in our last thunderstorm." She pointed to the trees above the far end, where several damaged limbs hung. "Take your soil from anywhere in the habitat. Be judicious. No holes."

Just like on the estate. "I could heel them in, in the meantime," he suggested.

"I'd rather they were in pots," she said. "Tomorrow, bring a tree with you for your lesson."

He selected a trowel, then a question he'd had earlier came back to him. "Who was the other person that got the trees to grow?" he asked as she turned to go.

"Beri of the Moors."

Figured.

20

ACCESSING MAGICAL PROTECTION

Mondays were hard anyway, and on top of today's quizzes, Fern had to hurry after coming home on the bus to meet Fee. How long would this session take? Would she get her homework done later, and what about dinner? If they were going to Mount Lookout, it'd be cold. She got her coat and hat, then her gloves. She'd better pack a snack. For the first time in weeks, she wished she had a pop, or a Snickers, her favorites, which hampered her energy flow. She dug around in the back of the pantry, then ran upstairs to her room to check the places she used to stash them. She found a candy bar, peeled back the wrapper and...ended up staring at it. Her magic already sucked. The additives would make it worse. With a groan, she threw it on her dresser and stomped downstairs.

"Fern?" Beri poked his head out of the bathroom. "I thought you were on your way. Fee will nae let me leave Hillux until you come over."

"I'm hungry," she snapped and immediately regretted it.

He frowned and put out his hand. One of Dad's homemade granola cakes appeared in it, and he handed it to her.

She felt like crying.

"Do you need something else?" he asked.

"How come you can be so nice when everything is going wrong?" It didn't come out too whiny.

He shrugged one shoulder. "I do nae feel so nice, actually. I have to get to work."

She sighed. "Okay."

"And we can never talk."

"I know," she whispered.

He held the bathroom door and gestured her inside. The portal was activated, the edges of its doughnut-shaped entrance spinning in the energy colors of her magic and the rest of her family's. She was about to step through, then hesitated and turned around.

"I live for growing flowers because it's brought my family together—and you into my life. I can't drop everything I've grown up with, but knowing you all will be safe is just as important to me as wildflowers."

Beri looked at her blankly.

"You asked me what I live for this morning," Fern explained. "The elders think I was careless, and Fee thinks I purposely endangered everyone. I'm not sure what you think, but *I* think you feel I betrayed you. What really happened was I saw a kid like me who wants his dream and needs someone like I needed you helping me when I was on trial. Gran had the pull to make it happen, like Lady Pina has for the Pines, but I got boosts from you and Willow and Raven—friends—and that got me through. I'm gonna get Cor his dream, and maybe someday, he'll…I have no idea what he'll do, but that's his business and I have mine." She stopped for a breath. "And right now, I bet Fee is so buzzed that I'll be sick in the pereport."

Fern stepped through the portal. She kept walking across Gran's bathroom, because if Beri told her she was nuts, she'd probably turn around and crawl under her covers.

Down the hallway, Gran's living room flickered. Fern's steps faltered, but she pushed forward. "I'm here," she announced to the glow whirling from window to window.

"About time," Fee boomed like a crack of thunder.

Fern covered her ears, but the combination was dizzying.

"Save the granola bar for after that pereport," Beri whispered and slunk out the front door.

She went after him. Beri strode through the tall grass, his wings unfurling. A flash of light blinded her, and a whine filled her ears. The wind sucked at her coat and jeans, pulling her out of the light. She'd caught up to Beri, who was flapping his red wings and rising—

Ohmigod! *She was rising with him.* She passed him…

Her feet hit a rough surface, and Fern stumbled—on rocks. She threw out her hands, bounced against an invisible barrier and regained her balance.

The magic disappeared. Before her stood Fee, this time fully formed with his huge ears and crazy red hair, dusting his hands together dramatically as the wind buffeted her. Fern zipped her coat and stuffed her hands in the pockets.

"*That* took an unwarranted amount of effort," he said in a normal voice, "but you are here."

Here was the top of Mount Lookout, a barren mountaintop scattered with stones. She'd guessed right about where they'd go and needing her coat. Beri had been right about the granola bar. Her queasy stomach wouldn't have managed it.

She pulled out her hat and tugged it on. "Was that a pereport?" It hadn't felt like one.

"Nae precisely, but I have no time for side lessons. Security of the Isle of Giuthas. Observe." He gestured overhead. "The shield, comprised of the energies of each habitat and the wizards dwelling upon the isle, extends the length of the twenty-nine-mile-long land and out to sea an additional five miles at either end." He extended his arms in a scarecrowlike position, fingers pointing toward the ends of the island.

Fern scanned northward over the forested ridges to the wide, grassy cliff top of the Gathering Place and south to the low shoals of the isle's oyster beds.

Fee wind-milled his arms. "The isle is eleven miles at its widest. Its shield extends westward to encompass Lady Soila's islet and continues another five miles beyond. Eastward, our shield meets that of our nearest enclave neighbor, Tern Bay, on the coast of Scotland. As you see, the various energies do nae *exactly* delineate the habitat boundaries they rise from, but 'tis a close approximation of where they lie."

Fern tore her gaze from the mainland on the horizon. "Hold on a second. Are you saying I should be *seeing* the shield, those energies?"

"Is that nae why we have scheduled this session?" Fee snapped. "For you to become familiar with our protection, the rules and methods of accessing the enclave?" He made it sound like she was an idiot for asking. "I did assume to start with the basics for you."

"Yeah—yes. Not a bad idea, but—"

"Moving on, as you should have gleaned by now, the main access is here, where security processes visitors. Each habitat has an access cipher tied to the energy of its manager and designated family. Your Meadows access rises when you call it up, at Hillux's porch…"

When they called it up? He continued saying something about the shimmer indicating passage granted—

"Hold on again. I don't see a shield. Or shimmers. I don't see *anything.*"

Fee blinked—his eyes at first, then his entire body winked in and out, brightening with each blink until Fern wanted to put her finger on him like Mom had. Doubt it would work for her.

"You are from here," he said, the words cutting in and out with him. "Your kin…maternal for hundreds of years, paternal for less, but two hundred fifty is naught to dismiss."

She gritted her teeth, refusing to remind someone yet again that she was pretty much unskilled. "Perhaps…you can teach me how to find it."

"F-find it?" he stuttered in outrage. "It is there."

"Doesn't mean I can see it."

Fee fisted his hands, becoming steadily visible again, but his high-pitched whine rose over the mountaintop. "She is from Giuthas," he said insistently and argued for a few minutes with someone she couldn't see. Then he stuck out his hand. "Magic."

She put out her hand. "Because of the pledge, you'll have to get it yourself."

He did. The ball of energy disappeared, and Fee turned bright green. He twinkled for a moment, then the energy reappeared and he handed it back.

"It works."

"I know it does," she said through clenched teeth. "That's not the same as 'I know how to work it for *this*.'"

The wind kicked up, knocking Fern off-balance. She crouched. Fee whirled away in a magical tornado of light. The wind left with him—or he became the wind, she wasn't sure. She scampered to the protection of a large rock and sat. Her phone was in her hand before she realized it, her finger hovering over Mom's name.

Shoot, I can't call Mom. I don't want to be here, but I don't want to act like a wimp either. Her parents knew where she was. If Fee abandoned her, they'd realize it…eventually.

Fee's light reappeared before her, and he came into view, his red hair whipping around his face. "Very well," he muttered. "Teach the lass how to see it." He scowled.

He was so short, Fern decided to stay seated so they were looking eye to eye. "Thanks, that'll be great," she said, hoping he'd be nicer if she was grateful.

"Actually, I canna teach you that," he said, and her excitement fell. "Only where Windborne access the magic." Extending a finger, he offered her a pea-sized ball of energy.

Fern pinched it between her thumb and finger. It shimmered in no defined color, but in all colors, the same as Fee's energy.

"If you allow this tracer into your channels, I can show you where to direct your magic."

"How do I get it in?"

Confusion crossed his face. "Just…allow it."

Okay? She imagined pulling it. *Absorb?* It disappeared. A hologram of a body appeared in her vision—her body. Instead of blue and red for arteries and veins, this showed lines of bright green…and a lot of dark areas. The image shifted to a close-up of one of the dark areas, showing hollow tubes.

Fee tutted. "Well, no wonder. You have nae activated all of your channels." He flipped through images without context within the hologram, so she had no idea where in the hologram they were. He muttered, "Flight, empty. Communication, empty. Defense, empty. Conjuring, weak."

Well, that might explain why her magic was poor "Can you show me where these are?"

"Magical Protection—aha! This is why that lad could take advantage of you—with no self-protection, you left yourself vulnerable. Here." He pointed to the image. "Magical Protection, empty. Push energy to it."

"Where?"

He admitted—grumpily—that he didn't know where Magical Protection was located in the body.

Would it be like physical protection, like she used for wrestling? "Like, is it in my hands?" They played with the hologram, and it *sort* of looked like it was in a Windborne's skin— which meant all over the body. "That might make sense. Skin, protection…" She snapped her fingers. "Hey. I made a protection for myself. A seed."

With a lift of his chin, Fee's eyes narrowed. "You could nae without magic in these channels."

"Did so. Watch." She thought of a hickory seed, but no green shell encased her. "Crap. This pledge is—"

"Not possible!" he barked. "That activated magic in your hair. Not a place that has channels."

Okaaay, her magic was trying, even though it wouldn't work. "You must have seen wrong. Just a sec." She collected her long hair and wrapped a band around it, then tried the hickory spell again.

Fee crossed his arms and frowned with a stoic look. "Hair."

Ohmigod, did this mean she couldn't cut her hair? Fern pressed her fingertips to her temples. *Just calm down. My magic isn't where it's supposed to be.* No one had ever thought to check that. *So maybe I can do the same stuff as every other wizard.* Her head popped up. "If I fix where my magic is supposed to be—"

"Likely not repairable," he said in the most uninterested way imaginable.

She frowned back. "What if I get magic into the empty channels? Would I be able to fly? Or thought-speak or these other things I can't do now?"

He waved a hand. "That is nae my concern. Only a session in accessing the isle properly."

She. Could. Just. Scream. He was so stuck on his stupid rules.

"Push magic into the proper channels, and we will proceed."

She tried, flushing magic under her skin, through it, over it. Fee affirmed that those channels did open, but she still couldn't see the shield.

"I canna review security with a wizard who does nae have the magic to see it, and I canna show you where to activate it if your channels are…irregular." He held out his hand. "Magic."

This time, he meant he wanted his back. It'd be handy to have this view of her channels so she could explore more, but she was tired of arguing. Plus, she had homework. She sequestered the blob of multicolored magic and drew it into her palm. "Hey. I've never done that before."

Fee flickered irritably. "Then you activated *something*."

She eyed him. He'd actually helped her. "When shall I come back for my next session?"

He huffed. "There is nae point if you canna see what we are talking about. Contact me when you can."

"Will you be reporting this to the council?"

His hair flipped wildly, and she caught a fleeting expression. He was worried.

"You came to the session," he said. "Naught else to report."

Well, that got her off the hook for the rest, though she wasn't about to admit any of this to anyone. Once she got home, she'd try to corral Cor's magic and get rid of it. It'd probably be futile, but she could still try.

21

DAY FOUR OF SEVEN

Tuesday morning, Cor collected one of his seedlings—not the largest, a midsize one. He wanted to save the largest for when he got better at this. Lady Pina was waiting on her roof. She sang the fourth stanza alone and then with her magic. He listened, impatient to begin, then sang them perfectly the first time alone, the beats of the tune and his energy flowing in perfect harmony.

She looked at him curiously, then to the tree.

An additional ring of branches circled the top.

Brilliant! He started to raise his fist, then stopped.

"You've been practicing."

"But not with a tree," he said defiantly. "I left them in the nursery so they could get acquainted with their habitat. Thought that was a good idea," he couldn't resist adding.

"Apparently, it was." With a little sigh, Lady Pina leaned back to study him. "You have good instincts for this," she finally said.

"Thank you. I told you I love trees. Working here would be a dream come true."

To his surprise, Lady Pina burst out laughing. She wiped her eyes. "I cannot tell you how many times I have heard that phrase used to persuade me. Please, don't say it again."

Cor leaned his forearms on his knees, head bent. He wasn't like any of those other wizards, he was sure of it. Yet he had no way to convince her of that. "I won't."

"You must complete my requirements."

He nodded.

"Back to this tree. Again."

Within two more rounds of the stanza, he'd hit a flowing rhythm, which made sense because growing was a continuous phase for trees.

She put up her hand. "You have this mastered. I rarely use it, actually, preferring to let the trees mature on their own. Come along."

That was it? No congratulations? She didn't like using it, so this must be it for this lesson. They returned his tree to the nursery. Then Lady Pina gestured to an eight-foot tree in the back row.

"Give the stanza a try on this one."

Right-o—*this* was her congratulations. Cor drew a breath, flared up his energy and sang, strong and clear. The needles twitched at his first round. He pushed harder in the second, and when he hit the last note of *growing*, Lady Pina put a hand on his arm.

"The roots extended," she said. "On a tree this large, branches are harder to—"

Bright blue needles flushed over the branches—new needles on stubby orange twigs.

A crazy thrill ran through him, and Lady Pina gasped.

"That is…" She blinked. "Quite remarkable." She looked him over, and for a beat, Cor didn't think he should be grinning. She nodded. "Well done. Shall we move to the repair stanza?"

His grin faltered. "Does this mean I need to break one of my trees?"

"Well…" She seemed to weigh the question, then looked beyond him. "There are those." The storm-damaged pines she'd pointed out alongside the nursery.

They retrieved a pruning saw and loppers and flew up. Landing in an adjacent pine, he surveyed the broken limbs criss-crossing each other. On one tree, a fallen limb had carved off all the lower limbs on the outside.

Cor whistled. "This is a lot of widow-makers, as they'd say on the estate."

"They bore the brunt of the storm a fortnight ago, protecting the interior from worse. I should be taking better care of their health, seeing as how they are the grove's line of defense on our windward side."

Heck, she'd admitted it, so he couldn't resist gently suggesting, "And perhaps plant additional trees that might protect them for a few more decades before taking their places?"

She sighed, her defenses down for once. "In good time. I must stabilize the giant you saw a few days ago." She gestured for him to follow. "Because the storm was several weeks ago, some have begun to heal over."

In one of the damaged treetops where they could both stand, Lady Pina pointed to a break in a two-inch-diameter branch that had left the end hanging. "Did the estate train you in arborist techniques as well?"

"Yes," he said. "Here, I'd remove the hanging piece near the break. Then I'd make a second cut back at the intersection of the next branch. Angled to an oval so the bark can heal over quickly."

"That's what I wanted to hear. By singing the repair stanza in addition, you'll heal it immediately."

He ran through this song in his head. The words could have that meaning. "I see." He could think of another, easier method to heal a broken limb, but this was how she wanted it done. He'd learned that lesson fast.

She nodded to the hanging branch. "Make the cuts. Then we will start."

Gripping the pruning saw handle, he eased the blade's teeth back and forth to start the cut, then sawed through the branch. The teeth were dull, but with the wood half dried, it didn't take much muscle to trim.

She sang the song, "Breaks sealing. Sealing, healing. Protective coat reforming," and demonstrated the accompanying energy.

He copied her, but couldn't heal it. *Why didn't I practice more last night?* After two more tries, Lady Pina healed it, a brush of her hand that he would have sworn was just ordinary magic if it hadn't been for the song and flare of orange. He had no time to think on it before she pointed to a hanging twig the size of a straw. "Lop off that one and try again."

Flights. This was like being issued a pencil when he couldn't write his name in pen, and one of those fat pencils at that. So much for getting in two lessons today and being home in time to meet Hazel. Cor pressed his mouth shut and removed the twig. The cut was a pea-sized blond spot on the branch. Great Orb, he'd die of embarrassment if he failed this one.

He gripped the branch and sang the song. Nothing happened. He repeated the stanza, no pause in the hum of his magic. The tune and energy lifted and fell in all the right places, he was sure, since she hadn't interrupted. The branch vibrated with the smallest twinge in his hand. He faltered.

She *tutted*.

He kept singing, concentrating on the twinge. It felt like the cambium rising. Blast, it *was* the cambium rising. At his urging, the living layers of bark flowed from all around the cut and sealed it off, accelerated by song and tree magic.

"Excellent," Lady Pina said.

"Thanks." Should he tell her? Yes. "We must have missed a step. I have to connect to this tree's magic to do a repair. Not sure why I didn't think of it myself, because it's like second nature when doing magic. I was too focused on getting the song right to think of it."

"I didn't review that?" She tilted her head. "But you were holding the branch before."

"I was only holding it."

"I was too focused on the song to notice. I'm sorry."

He grinned. "Let's try another."

It worked. He healed a two-inch and a five-inch, and following a bunch of arm-sized branches, they approached an eight-inch limb. After healing it, he wanted to try something bigger, but no larger branches on these trees were accessible except by flying. To use hand tools while bobbing on flapping wings wasn't a safe idea. If he'd had his climbing equipment, he could have done it safely. He debated asking to go home to get it. She had promised a trial, and now he'd had enough success that he didn't think she'd block his return. He asked.

"We have that equipment on the isle," she said in a way that he wasn't sure if she was impressed or didn't approve of tree climbing. "You know how to use it?"

He took out his red card certifications from various climbing centers, including Bonterra's, and the Windborne Arborists Association certification. "I've trained in arboriculture and this summer worked with the enclave's crew to maintain the city's trees." He'd also worked in other enclaves, but that would take more explanation than he was willing to give.

After a careful study of each card, she handed them back. "I will make the inquiries. You have a good head on your shoulders, and I'm willing to allow you to continue working alone if you'd like to attend to these smaller limbs adjacent to stable platforms."

Work on these giants alone? *She trusts me.* For the first time, Cor felt he'd made real progress with *her*, not just his magic or the training. "Ma'am, once I finish these, can I work on others in the grove?"

She thought for a moment. "Work with the pines will draw your magic and theirs closer. A good plan, but before I release you to do that, I wish to check over your work here."

It was past noon, so he took a break and reconnected his energy with the grove's. These healings had to be perfect. He performed each with care, double-checked them and fetched her.

"Well done," she said. "Your perseverance is admirable. In fact, I don't mind telling you that you have passed my first requirement. You work as hard as one of our own on Giuthas."

He was hot, sweaty and coated with itchy bits of sawdust, but after four days of working with her, he'd swung over one hurdle. "Thank you, ma'am. It's not work when it comes to trees." Then, realizing what he'd said, he put up his hands. "Not just saying that either. I mean it."

"I believe you do." She smiled, the first smile she'd given him. "I'm glad we started on this lesson today. It's one of the most used and most important for the health of trees that live hundreds of years. Tomorrow, we shall continue it."

Blast it, was there any hope of finishing before Friday? "Not move on to the next?"

"No need. We have our schedule set out."

They had three days and only two lessons left. Dare he ask to speed things up and take the test a day early so he could meet Hazel?

She tilted her head. "As we agreed to, correct?"

He didn't dare.

With a sigh, Fern closed her text, shoved her books to the coffee table and sank her head to the back of the couch. "I hate calculus," she muttered.

Beri shifted beside her. "You do nae have—"

"Don't say it," she said. "Keeping my options open, remember?"

"Then push magic through your channels so you have *more* options, you ken?"

She rolled to face him. It'd felt terrible keeping secrets from Beri, so she'd told him what had happened with Fee, that he'd been helping her move her energy into the empty spots. It didn't like staying there.

He scooted closer and lightly touched her temples, his face inches from hers. Magic loosened from her core and raced to her head, making her light-headed.

"I feel it." He dropped his hands over her shoulders, and she ran magic there. Then to fingers and knees and on and on until he returned his hands to her temples. He stared intently into her eyes. After thirty seconds, he sighed and dropped his hands. "You did nae hear that, then?"

She groaned and flopped back.

Beri grunted in disgust. "This blasted pledge. I canna wait until Saturday and his test."

"You can't blame Cor. Nothing I did before the pledge worked either," she said halfheartedly, her mind on the newly flushed channels instead. Her heart leaped—something new had appeared. Gold—oh. Cor's energy was visible, looking *and* feeling like honey, too sticky to collect and get rid of.

"Would you prefer I blame you?" Beri asked. "You've stopped even going to the Meadows. If you did only the bee chores, 'twould keep up appearances with the elders."

Crossing her arms with balled fists, Fern huffed out a breath. *Quit being a jerk,* she thought at him, shoving the jab with as much magic and anger as possible.

Of course he didn't hear her.

"His help was a trade-off for mine," she ground out. "If we had more trade-offs like that, maybe you wouldn't be stuck on the isle every afternoon so we could do things together. Like normal, dating people do."

"If you hadn't gotten your magic bound up in his, maybe we could do things together like normal, wizard people do.'

"It's not like that."

"Then what is it like? Because I am nae sure that chap will release you even after his trial with Lady Pina is complete. Have you thought about what you will do come Saturday?"

I am so over fighting with you. Fern stood up. "What happened to your philosophy of trusting that what happens will be right?"

She stomped up to her room and locked the door.

2 2

CLIMBING AND CONNECTING

The next morning, Cor arrived to find another wizard knocking on Lady Pina's door. Other than wire spectacles, the thin man was nondescript, fluttering back when Lady Pina answered the door, like he'd blow away at the first gust of wind.

"Pina? I'm making rounds," he boomed, his voice carrying to Cor. "Storm coming from the southwest, four days from now. More than rain. Near-gale to gale winds, thirty-three knots. Batten your hatches, as the Seas would say. It'll pass quickly, though."

She nodded, like receiving a personal weather report was normal. "Thank you, Chinook. The Pines' trimming will be completed by…Saturday, did you say?"

"At nightfall," he called over his shoulder.

Lady Pina smiled at Cor. "Your progress with the healing lesson is timely, then. You've allowed me more time with my ailing giant."

That did seem to be where her mind was as she checked his healing songs on larger limbs and declared he could continue alone.

"I have not forgotten about the climbing equipment," she

said. "Ash said he would try to make it over. In the meantime, please practice by cutting and sealing any limbs that you can safely manage within the grove. Ignore my giant. We don't need to confuse its magic, but the others will bear a newcomer's touch." She nodded, then put up a finger. "Mind you, none of your other fancy magic."

"None, ma'am. Thank you."

Pitifully few damaged limbs needed healing in her grove. It felt like a waste of his practice, yet he had permission to be in this incredible forest. He flew lazily around the various trees, earbuds in, the tree magic stanzas playing in a continuous loop. He listened to the last two in particular, made sure the variances were what he thought they were and belted out the songs.

He'd just ended a set, when a shockball of pink energy crossed the clearing before him.

Cor pulled up, yanking the earbud cords—nearly swiping his arm with the teeth of the saw blade—and spun, tracking the energy's trajectory back to the source.

Laughter rang out, and Oyster waved to him from where he held to the leader of the nearest pine, wings outstretched and his foot pressed to a too-small limb in the uppermost branches. "Didn't want to interrupt, but after two rounds of this lovely ballad, I determined it has no ending. I detected a pattern to your flight"—he spiraled a finger upward—"so I came up here to wait."

Cor's face warmed. "Get off the tree before I have to fix that limb as well," he said gruffly.

Oy fluttered his wings gracefully and lifted off. The branch didn't even sway. "No weight. This might not be my habitat, but I'm respectful." He glided to a decent-sized limb and perched again. "Ash sent the equipment you're looking for." He tapped the canvas duffle strapped to his chest. "Want to check it out?"

Damn, could he have shoved his own foot deeper down his throat? Cor landed on a branch that drooped under his weight, adding to his embarrassment. He flapped into a hover. "Sorry. Didn't mean to snap, but you scared the hell out of me. Suppose it's not safe to fly like this." He swung an earbud cord.

"You're safe enough on the isle, and if you always sing while flying, everyone can find you as well." Oyster chuckled.

"Just make it more embarrassing," he muttered. "How about we land?"

The gear Oyster pulled from the duffle was exactly what Cor needed to hang from one limb and brace to cut another.

"Shall we head to the damaged trees?" Oyster asked. "Ash will meet us to check your methods."

Weren't his certifications enough? It was a freakin' pain being the newcomer *and* keeping his mouth shut about it, but it was their time. Cor helped stuff the gear back in the bag, saving out the coil of rope to help carry things, then led the way to the grove's edge. They set up in one of the damaged trees, Oyster handing out the gear Cor requested and watching without comment, while Cor hung the lines and got into a heavier climbing saddle than his own climbing harness.

Ash arrived and greeted him with a smile and another pruning saw. He reviewed the lines and Cor's saddle, approving the layout and connections, then he glanced over the limb. "Did you do a wildlife review?"

Cor shook his head. "Lady Pina didn't seem concerned. Would anything have had time to move in since the damage happened only a few weeks ago?"

Oy snorted, and Ash pressed his knuckles to his chin. "Pina never concerns herself with the lesser creatures, just her giants. You know how to do a magical scan for life?"

He did, he'd just never thought of doing it on dead limbs. He touched the break in the limb and swept magic outward to the tips of each dried needle bundle. Little pricks of glow lit on anything alive.

His breath caught. There were so many—insects, salamanders, and even a mouse. As his dad had to remind folks, a forest wasn't just trees. Every organism interacted and produced energy for the habitat. "I'm embarrassed I didn't consider doing this earlier. I've surveyed insect populations to determine if a tree has an infestation, but we only ever found insects and maybe a squirrel or bird we overlooked."

Ash laughed. "Welcome to the big-tree habitat. 'Tis different than even our Forest management, but Mimosa believes everyone should consider their whole habitat. Leave the insects," he instructed. "They'll hold on well enough or fly off."

He and Oy tossed pellets of magic, dotting the damaged limb in yellow and pink. Cor added his own honey-gold pellet to one nearby, pleased to capture a young salamander. He brushed a two-inch moth into flight—it'd been camouflaged only a foot from his hand. They collected the wiggling magic balls and carried them to nearby trees.

"Clear," Ash confirmed at last. "May I suggest tying this limb so once it's cut, it can't fall on anything below?"

Er, right. After that check, it was clear a falling limb had a good chance of hitting wildlife, or bouncing onto the nursery trees. *Suppose I'm not as up on everything as I thought.* Cor tied it off, then rolled the lock on his saddle's carabiner and secured himself to the climbing line. He looked along the limb one last time. "Did those creatures come all the way up from the ground after the storm, or were they in the tree all along?"

"Salamanders are so slow-moving they had to move locally," Ash answered. "Who knows with the flying insects?" He handed Cor the saw he'd brought. "New blade. Have one for Pina's saw as well. She never changes them."

The sharper teeth made the sawing quick, and soon the limb was swinging on its line. Ash instructed him to spread the cut limbs out in this section of the pinewoods so the dead wood could continue to be used by the insects.

He nodded when Cor returned to the tree. "Good to finally

have this grove's care underway. Pina usually keeps her trees pristine, but for months she's been immersed in healing her ailing giant. It'll be a boon for the enclave if she pulls it off."

If his sister, Hazel, were here, they could know for sure. "You don't think she will?"

He shook his head. "Her will is strong, but that tree has suffered much in the storms following a lightning strike decades ago. Looks like you're set, but these are some large limbs to be hauling around." He looked at Oyster. "I have a bit of time to help with the largest, and frankly, I'd like another set of eyes here for the heavy work."

That echoed the safety procedure for the Bonterra crew he'd worked with.

"I'm also free for a few hours," Oyster replied. "Do you mind some company, Cor?"

"Not at all." Because they were treating him like an equal. "You climb, too?"

"Ash trained all of us teens, and I get in a lot of climbing because Lady Pina needs the help." Oyster tossed back his curls. "I'll head home and collect my gear." He fluttered into a shaft of sunlight and took off, the afternoon light forming a halo in his swaying hair and glinting brilliantly off his pale wings, creating an image as delightful as an ash tree in bloom.

Cor cleared his head with a shake and bent to disconnect his saddle. He hadn't given it much thought, but Oyster must live close-by since he'd turned up several times this week. He and Ash set up for another limb and were ready when Oyster returned fifteen minutes later.

Not far at all, then. Oyster tied his knots and set up his gear as proficiently as Cor did himself. He looked up at one point and caught Cor watching.

"Habit to double-check your skills," Cor said quickly to cover his stare. "I took Fern for her first lesson Friday and had to be on my toes."

"How do our skills compare with what you're used to?" Oy asked.

"Everything is set up by the book."

He nodded. "I did my own verification of your skills."

"And?"

"You pass."

Cor swallowed. In just climbing or…anything else? Heck, he could read so much into that…or not. This perfectly polite bloke had probably meant nothing by the comment. Cor nodded dismissively, hefted the saw and began climbing.

Together, they took down the limb, making cuts from either side, while Ash monitored from above and held the limb's rope so it wouldn't sway. It took the three of them to fly it through the forest and lower it.

"Which next?" Ash asked when they returned.

Cor grinned. "Is this a trick question? It means moving to another tree, but I'd say that large one while we're all here."

"Good choice."

After they'd removed the limb, Ash had to leave. "If you aren't too tired this evening, might you have time to give Kory another lesson?" he asked. "And stay for dinner?"

"Sure," Cor agreed, and they set a time.

He and Oy worked on the remaining limbs, talking as they did. Cor learned more about the estuary at the mouth of the river that flowed across the island, and he shared some about his work on the estate and with Bonterra's trees. He shared only what he wouldn't mind getting back to Lady Pina or the other Forest folks here.

"So you have a family?" Oy asked.

"Just one older sister," he said carefully. "You have any siblings?"

"No, it's just me." He gave a sad sort of smile.

"Then, from what you've told me about Giuthas' system of

passing down habitats, you're the automatic heir of the Estuary?"

"Maybe." Oy shrugged. "Maybe not."

"You're not meeting your family's expectations? Or the enclave's?"

"Ouch," Oyster said with a grin, but Cor could tell the question had hurt.

"Poor question, sorry. Actually, you come across as a brilliantly polite bloke who rather has it together, no matter if it's for yourself or for your work."

"I do fine with the habitat. Mother has delayed appointing me heir because I'm gay and potentially won't produce another heir for the Estuary."

Heck, he is *gay.* Cor couldn't think of what to say that wouldn't sound completely flabbergasted at the easy reveal, or selfish.

Oy shrugged again. "You asked. It's not a secret."

"Potentially?"

"Her words, not mine. She refuses to acknowledge I'm gay, because the ridiculously outdated Windborne rules require a partnered heir who will produce an heir. I won't be. She threatens my cousin might be a better choice, but she's still holding out hope I'll find a girl I like. Fern was her latest push."

Cinching up his climbing rope and checking his knots and carabiner lock, Cor wrestled with what to say to this pretty chap who was living his preppy appearance and had no freakin' fear in stating his sexuality. He could say anything. *Me, too.* Or, *Glad my parents aren't dumping that on me.* But he couldn't get the words out.

The pause in the conversation reached the awkward point. Oyster waved his saw at the branch. "I do have duties, though, and must be back in an hour for low tide to check the beds."

That was bloody easier to answer. "Right. Let's do it."

They finished carrying away the last of the branches.

"They're distributed widely enough," Oyster said. "Yet Lady Pina will double-check the placements when the woodpeckers start in."

"Let's hope I'm long gone by then," Cor replied. "Or…" What was he saying?

"Really?" Oy asked. "You're working like you want this. All that singing and such."

"Heck, that was more of an automatic thought." Cor snorted. "I do want this, but I've learned not to count on things, much as I hate it." A cloistered enclave wasn't likely to accept him… Light-skinned Oy might not understand that, but he'd definitely get not being accepted for being gay.

"Then you're not inheriting any role in your family?"

"Flights, let's hope not," he blurted before remembering he still had to be careful with how much he said. "Er, that all goes to my older sister, if she chooses."

Oyster began undoing his climbing knots. "Ash says he'll be here soon, and it's time for me to head home," he said. "Lucky you with no family duties to keep you from singing your little heart out."

No family duties—that was bloody funny. It was Wednesday. He had two days to finish this trial and be back in Bonterra by noon on Friday. If he wasn't, there'd be hell to pay.

"You remembered something?" Oyster asked.

Cor grunted. "Just thinking of completing Lady Pina's training and her test."

"Your songs are coming along fine."

"She passed me on her first hurdle—hard work—but I have some spiritual thing to pass."

"Communing with the habitat? I think singing to the trees qualifies." Oyster smiled as he coiled the rope.

"Drop it with the singing already," he said firmly. "Isn't that something every one of you do?"

Oy shook his head. "I swim in my habitat. Every day, regardless of the temperature. My magic stirs the sediments over the beds."

"Huh." He'd love to dish with Oy about magic, and if he asked to go with him to see the Estuary, he'd likely be invited. But Cor did have family duties. As much as he wanted to complete this trial, he had to be home for Hazel, which meant he had to arrange a way home with Fern. And, if he had to, confess to Lady Pina that he had responsibilities at home.

He arrived at the Meadows by five, hours before Fern had ever appeared after school, but he'd still hoped she might. Lady Lark wasn't around. It wasn't enough of an emergency—yet—so he didn't dare cross the portal and approach Fern's mum. He left Fern a note saying he'd be at the Forests' and he had to talk to her ASAP, though he knew she couldn't get there unless Lady Lark happened to return.

He gave Kory a lesson, trying to expand on what the boy could do. "You've drawn out the energy, so let's try inviting the tree to take it back in again."

With that simple way of establishing a connection, Kory managed both. It was a success for both of them. After dinner with the Forest family, Cor excused himself on the pretext that he was tired. He was, but he had to recheck the Meadows for Fern.

At the hillside cottage, the guinea pig greeted him like a long-lost friend—clearly no one else had been there. He petted and fed Hilda, thinking of Toots. He missed her, making it easy to give in to two carrots with Hilda's greens. "Abandoned, just like me, huh?" While he'd enjoyed the work with the fellows today, it made his solitude here even more acute. Everyone else on this island was connected by thought-speaking in some way, or used a peregrinator to go where they wanted. He was at Fern's mercy, and it'd been days since he'd seen her.

And she was at his mercy.

Since his pledge affected her magic, he'd have thought she'd be after him for regular reports on his progress. Now that he *had* to talk to her, it was frustrating. Like the others, she had a family to go home to and talk to. And could. That he might let down his sister made him feel trapped.

"You chose this, mate," he muttered, feeling stupid and helpless at the same time.

With the guinea pig eating, he placed a magical trip over the doors so he'd know if anyone arrived, went out and fed the bees, made more sugar syrup and played his stanza recordings, carefully singing the upcoming harvest one. Though he hung around for hours after dark, Fern didn't turn up. Neither did Lady Lark or even the scowling Beri.

He had another day to catch Fern. He flew back to the tree cave, not wanting to think about what would happen at home if he didn't arrive as promised.

23

CHALLENGES AND COMPROMISES

The harvesting stanza flowed well through Cor's magic and made sense in his mind. He could feel the loosening of the tree's energy as he tugged with his, but it wouldn't let go of the tree. "It's like it needs it still," he finally complained to Lady Pina.

"This small amount? No. Try again."

He did, but it felt as if tentacles held it in different locations. "This is the animals!"

"Yes, yes, their interactions bind up energy." She waved a hand. "Ignore them. Pull harder."

Just as Ash had said, she thought only of the trees. "Ma'am, don't you think they need it?" Without asking, he flushed magic over the branches with the worst pulls. "See? Salamanders are living here and"—what was the bigger blob?—"a family of red squirrels," he said in exasperation.

Lady Pina crossed her arms. "What do you propose?"

Cor bit his lip. "Select another tree?"

"How many of these trees do you suppose have *no* wildlife living in them? How much time do you think I can spend sorting out individual trees to harvest that have few or easily moved creatures?"

He snorted. "You can't fool me. You know each of these trees *personally* and can recall which shelter wildlife."

She stared a moment. "Point to you," she said, "for paying attention. This tree didn't have squirrels in it last year."

"Wait a second. Do you have favorites that you use all the time?"

She sniffed. "It is easier. When you work alone and are as old as I am, and your habitat's energy is in demand, you must find ways to work efficiently."

"That's not logic for taking on an apprentice? Or maybe three?" He recognized the warning in the tightening of her jaw, but kept on. "This grove is huge! Its energy potential is phenomenal. You should be making the time to get help. If you don't think so, can I show you what I trimmed yesterday?"

"I viewed each tree you visited yesterday," she said through clenched teeth. "Following the trace of another's magic here is child's play to me."

"So how long would it have taken you to do that work?"

"As long as it took you."

Argh, she was a stubborn old biddy. "I mean, what did you accomplish in the meantime?" he asked, but he could tell he wasn't getting anywhere. "Right, then, how about this? We work around the squirrels. Only harvest from one side of the tree, not where they're depending on those branches that secure their nest. Same for the birds."

She put up a hand. "Do not suggest we avoid every salamander."

Yes! He was getting somewhere. "A compromise, then. The salamanders can move."

Without a word, Lady Pina outlined a section of the tree in orange magic. "Attempt this portion of the tree."

It perfectly excluded the red squirrels.

"You could do this all along?"

"Of course."

He rolled his eyes at her.

"What exactly does that mean, young man?" she asked in a tone reminiscent of the way she'd spoken to him at the conference.

"It means that I know that you know exactly how to do this to work around the wildlife," he said, his tone sliding to exasperated again.

She sniffed. "I was simply giving you the exercise to think through the process."

"But the animals—"

"Fine." She threw up her hands. "I should take their needs into account, at least while production is going well."

That was likely as close as he would get to her admitting the wildlife was important. He sang, "Magic loosening. Breaking holds, collected, come to me," and pulled at the tree's energy.

This time, it slid out with no effort. "That was much easier," he said over his shoulder.

"Either way is easy for me."

"But is it easy for the habitat?" His parents had always encouraged foundation applicants to consider the whole habitat —and wouldn't award them grant assistance until they did. Since Ash had said that's what the other woodland managers believed should be Giuthas' method, he would push Lady Pina to honor the Pines' wildlife, too. "What if there had been a woodpecker cavity?"

"I said I would exclude birds."

"But woodpeckers? They tap holes in trees."

"To feed on wood-boring insects. Surely they taught you that in the city…oh. You think you're being clever?"

"Making a point."

"Which is?"

"You know these animals, and you know the Pines need them."

"Cor?" she huffed. "Do your work. See how long it takes you to scan a tree's wildlife and energy and exclude their needs."

Two hours later, he had to admit it was harder than she'd made it look.

But she let it slip that in the last two days, together they had harvested half of the energy she was expected to provide the Isle of Giuthas each week.

That made his efforts worthwhile.

The second afternoon Fern had been dreading this week arrived —Amanda coming to her house. By the end of school, she'd come up with the perfect maneuver to get Beri to the cabin and through the portal before Amanda made it inside. Then, on the bus, Amanda insisted on sitting in front of Fern and Beri's seats. She talked to him the entire way home. She wouldn't stop for ice cream at the general store, because Beri had—cluelessly— refused Amanda's invite to join them. Even with her shorter legs, she'd kept up so they could all walk together.

Ugh, if only they had mastered thought-speaking, Fern could have explained he only had to let them order first and then come up with a reason to leave without them.

Instead, they walked up the road, and Beri had to approach the neighboring cabin where they claimed he lived. Then Fern had to pull Amanda along, nodding and giggling at her gossip when she just wanted to apologize to Beri.

A backup plan was coming to Fern as she got Amanda into the cabin. "Hey, Mand? Can you grab us juice and chips while I take these orders to my mom? I forgot to give them to her this—"

The bathroom door opened, and Cor burst into the hallway. "Fern! Thank the—"

Amanda shrieked and backed into Fern, who blurted, "Cor! What the hell?" *Crap.* Would nothing go right?

Eyes wide, Cor swallowed, his face shifting from eager to wary. "Fern," he said firmly. "I've been waiting. I need to talk to you."

No way. He had to get out of here. She shook her head, but Amanda was looking from her to Cor…and kept looking at Cor. Her head tilted, a look Fern recognized.

Great, just great. Things were going to get even worse if she didn't get rid of him and quick. "I'm not…I don't have…my mom will—" OMG, he'd come from the *bathroom*! What kind of reason could she give for that? "The leak," she said with sudden inspiration. "We aren't sure where it's coming from. You'll just have to look." She turned Amanda by the arm, but Cor looked confused. "We've got homework."

Amanda dragged against her. "You know him?" With a smile, she pulled loose and closed in on Cor. "Introduce me."

"He's a guy from town fixing the plumbing. Cor, you're not finished, are you?" Crap, he was not taking the hint to go back into the bathroom. No, instead, he aimed a stony scowl at her before turning a smile on Amanda.

Double crap.

She flipped a hand at Fern. "I thought you wanted snacks. Go take the papers to your mom, while—Cor, is it?"

"Right-o, luv." Cor slouched against the wall, slyly grinning at her.

"While Cor and I raid your kitchen," she cooed at him. "You're British, aren't you?"

"No," Fern snapped at the same time that Cor said, "Fancy that, you recognize a Brit? Been across the pond, have you?"

No, no, no. Fern wanted to smack him as he eyed Amanda and laid on his accent thicker than she'd ever heard from him.

"You don't look like a plumber," Amanda said. "Where are your tools?"

Fern froze. Cor met her gaze, a slow grin spreading over his face, and her blood raced like a raging river in her ears.

He pushed off the wall, gesturing to the powder room, and she wanted to deflect Amanda's steps forward, but she couldn't move. *She'll find out I lied. I'll have to tell another lie and another, and who does that and keeps friends?*

"Huh." Amanda screwed up her nose. "You know how to use them? To fix leaks and stuff?"

"Nah." Cor shot her a sincere smile. "I just know how to make them look good. How about I help you in the kitchen, luv?" He held out a crooked elbow as if to escort her. "Until Fern has a bloody spare minute—"

"I do." Fern stumbled into action and stepped between them. "Got one right now, Cor. Unless you'd prefer to speak with my mom?" She cut a frown at him and jerked her head toward the front door.

Cor tossed Amanda a winning smile. "Later, luv." he said over his shoulder as he crossed to the door.

"God, Fern," Amanda erupted when he'd left. "Do you have to be such an ass around cute guys?"

Fern shoved her toward the kitchen with a hissed, "This is not the guy for you, believe me."

She got Amanda into the kitchen and that door closed before storming back toward the bathroom. She poked her head inside to see a red canvas tool bag sitting open on the toilet seat. Scattered across the floor were wrenches, pliers and a huge flashlight. Fern chewed her lip. Instead of stomping outside, she let herself out and closed the door quietly behind her.

Cor was leaning against the rounded log siding, no longer grinning. "A plumber?" he snapped. "Do I look like a plumber? Or is that your default career for black chaps?"

"It was the first excuse I could think of for someone being in our bathroom," she ground out.

"You couldn't introduce me as a mate, a *friend*, as Americans say?" He huffed. "A friend using your bathroom, like everyone does!" he said, voice escalating.

"*Shh!*" she hissed, then furiously added, "Amanda knows you don't go to school here. How was I supposed to explain that? Then it'd be, how do I know you? Where do you live? It'd add one lie to another."

Cor raised his hands to the sky. "Does every human attend school? No. You and I both know that. After climbing together, I thought we *were* friends." Scowling, he waved a finger at her. "Instead, you lie about me being a plumber."

Clearly, she'd hurt his feelings, but she wasn't about to apologize when he'd broken Mom's rules—which would get *her* in trouble. "Look, you know you aren't supposed to come over here without Mom's permission. So exactly this kind of stuff doesn't happen." Her voice was rising now. She lowered it. "And what the crap was that with calling Amanda *luv*? The British way to pick up girls?"

"Everyone says it." He sucked his teeth. "Just not me. It was to get your attention. I said I'd been waiting for you, and I meant it. It's been days since I've seen you, and I wasn't gonna blow any chance I had."

"You couldn't wait another half hour?" This time, Fern flipped her hands skyward. "I would have come down as soon as I got her upstairs. You can't interact with regular people that way."

"What way? Flirting? She started it, not me." He stuffed his hands into his pockets. "And I am regular people. So are you. At least I'm not regular people wasting time like you are."

He had a point. She blew out her breath and stretched her clenched fingers. "Fine. Why do you need to talk to me?"

"I need the peregrina—"

"*Shh!*"

They both looked around, and Cor rolled his eyes. "Now you're making me nervous. It's a *real person* word. No need to get your panties in a twist. I have to get to Bon—to get back."

"Why?"

He scowled again and pulled at his ear. "I'm not justifying my reasons. I need to fetch some…something tomorrow, midday, and you won't be around, so I need the…the *stick* now."

"I can't just hand it off. Crap, what would happen if you lost it? I'd be in more trouble with Fee than for forgetting…" Uh oh, shouldn't have admitted that.

He pointed at her. "Trouble with Fee is your fault. Need I point out that I've been pere…*doing this* longer than you have? I wouldn't ask unless I absolutely had to get back. I do. Please, give it to me."

Oh geez, she should ask Gran, or Mom, first. But any moment, Amanda was likely to come looking for her, and then she'd have to get alone with Cor again, and that would take even more explanation. Plus, he'd magicked her lie into reality.

Cor slid to the door and grasped the handle. "If you'd rather, I can talk to your friend again while you decide." He thickened his accent again, exaggerating *raw-ther* and *tawlk*.

She batted his hand from the door. "You're trying to ruin everything for me," she said in exasperation.

He shook his head. "Fernie, Fernie, Fernie. I've been dragged around to human towns and cities my whole life. I know how to handle myself right proper with *girls*. Unless you want a demonstration—which probably wouldn't hurt your continuing education with Beri, by the way—I suggest you hand over the stick."

Darn it, he had her. Huffing a breath, she pulled out her pouch and gave him the peregrinator. "I want this back tomorrow when I get home from school. *I'll* meet you at my gran's. Now wait until we go upstairs before you sneak back in."

He grinned broadly. "Got it, luv."

Rolling her eyes, Fern put her hand on the knob, then hesitated. "We are friends. Sorry for calling you a plumber, and thanks for covering my lie. You produced a convincing setup."

"Only because I know exactly where the estate keeps those tools."

24

HAZEL

On Friday, Cor tried to cut the morning's lesson short, which did not please Lady Pina.

"This is the most difficult of the songs," she explained yet again. "You do nae have the harvest magic correct for a massive energy release of an ancient. Sing it again." Then she pointed out a lag in his magic.

He corrected it. And another spot in which the note fell instead of rising. A third—

"I can't focus," he finally just blurted—the truth. "I need a break."

"You're progressing well," she said. "Take fifteen minutes."

"A longer break." He grabbed at the excuse, though Lady Pina was frowning. His plan might work, if Hazel could be coerced. And if he could get her past Fee's security. He had to try. "I'll return midafternoon to continue practicing."

Lady Pina threw up her hands. "'Tis your lesson."

Flying off, he felt bad. At least he hadn't lied to her, he told himself as he landed before the porch of the hillside house and took out the peregrinator. As much as he'd blustered Fern, he wasn't sure if the device would work anywhere else on the isle, so he returned to the only spot he knew where everyone else came and went. It worked. The pereport took him to Bonterra without any hitches—except that he was thirty minutes late because of his delay with Lady Pina.

He dodged out the station doorway and ran along the sidewalk. It was too slow. He stopped and magicked his longboard into his hands. He threw it down and shoved off with his foot, pushing until he'd picked up speed. Weaving between cyclists on the left side of the road, he skimmed through the business section a mite faster than everyone else, getting dirty looks and wishing he could open his wings to speed things up. He turned onto the quieter residential road. The estate gate was a block ahead. It was only thirty minutes. How worried could Hazel get in thirty minutes?

Barnaby, the gate guard, watched as he drew closer. The clacking of his wheels could probably be heard all the way to the manor house.

Cor let the board slow as he approached. "Is she—"

"Calling every five minutes to check if I've seen you," Barnaby answered.

Blast. Cor picked up speed, kicking as far as the cobble drive, then leaping off and running, barely remembering to magic the board back to his room. Under the rowan arch. A shortcut across a section of lawn. Through the birch stand, breaking out onto the path—

Two old ladies squealed at his appearance.

"Sorry!" he gasped, holding the stitch in his side. He jogged around a large spruce.

A shadow burst from the boughs, screeching.

Cor threw up his hands and ducked automatically, but he knew that call. "Toots!" He raised his arm, and the owlet circled, extended her feet and landed on him. He cuddled her to his chest, walking fast while she alternately cooed and hissed. "I know! I missed you, too!"

He sprinted past the house, past the conservatory, headed for Aunt Syl's cottage.

"Corylus!" a girl shouted.

Toots took wing as he spun back to the greenhouse. Hazel, a curvy girl in paint-splotched white overalls and a faded tie-dyed T-shirt, clung to the door. She clutched a drawing pad to her chest, her brown knuckles lightening, her face twisted to keep from crying.

Cor sucked a breath. "Hazel."

Master Harold came up behind Hazel and put a hand on her shoulder. "I told you he wouldn't forget," he said soothingly. "Though I can't say the same for reporting in."

Drawing another breath, Cor crossed to her. Her hair was still French-braided into the pigtails she kept it in while painting. Pieces had come loose, and with her round face, the frizzing made her look fourteen instead of seventeen, a year older than he was.

"I didn't leave soon enough," he said. "I didn't forget. Sorry. Of course I didn't forget." He opened his arms. She fell into them, and he hugged her, trying to pat away the tremors coursing her shoulders as he bit down on telling her this wasn't a major catastrophe, because it was in her scheduled world.

He was working up to announcing he had to go back, that *she* had to go back with him, when she pushed out of his hold and whacked his arm. "The one weekend Aunt Syl has to be gone," she hissed. "Just the one and you weren't here!"

He scowled at her. "Right, I deserved that, but hit me again and I'll punch you back."

She scowled.

Master Harold raised a finger. "Not in public."

"Come on." With Toots fluttering overhead, Cor wrapped an arm around Hazel's shoulders and urged her along the path. The cottage door was open, her duffle and art backpack on the floor inside. Toots flew inside and landed on the refrigerator.

"You couldn't wait here?" he asked, then didn't listen to her rant about being alone. They were never alone on the estate, but it made no difference to tell her that. She knew and still wanted family around her. Orb forbid he ever got an actual internship and moved away. He threw together two peanut butter and jelly sandwiches, poured them each a glass of milk, then waved her to the table. "Eat. You'll feel better."

"Don't pretend to be Mum."

"Not. I'm pretending you remember our agreement." He ran some frozen meat under the hot tap for Toots.

Hazel opened her mouth, closed it, then picked up the sandwich and began to eat.

He let her finish half before attempting to say more. "I got an internship of sorts last week."

Her eyes narrowed. "Where?"

"You can come with."

"I don't like the sound of this."

He put up a hand. "The family agreed that I—" *Have the right to pursue...* He stopped to rephrase the words. "I should think about what I want to do. At the arboriculture conference two weeks ago, I met a witch who manages big trees." He told her the rest, ending with, "You can bunk with me in the tree hollow I've been assigned. Two cots, rad view, lots to draw. Hardly any people."

"Where?"

"An island in the Irish Sea."

She pointed. "I knew this couldn't be perfect."

"It is for me." He pushed back from the table. "It's a peregrinator trip, faster and easier than taking the train down south, which you bloody hate and do anyway to go to this art program."

"What about Toots?"

He shrugged. He'd like to bring her, but *he* didn't have a spot yet. Hazel continued to scowl, and he began to clean up. "Get some camping clothes for the weekend. I'll bring you back Monday morning in time to catch your train."

He let her rant while he packed the peanut butter and jelly supplies and some snacks Aunt Syl had left for the weekend. Then he shouldered his pack and crossed to the front door. "Suit yourself. Aunt Syl will be back Sunday night, right? I'm here, I offered to take you with me. I'll let Master Harold know you'll be holed up—"

"Give me a minute," she spat and grabbed her duffle.

Fifteen minutes later, he returned a sleepy Toots to her nest, and they left the estate, Hazel's arm rubbing against his as they walked to the station. "Hey." He dropped an arm around her shoulders. "It'll be a fun change. You'll—"

I said, don't pretend to be Mum, she sent him, her features frozen into that look she got when coping. But she didn't pull away, so he kept his protective grip around her shoulders. *I know it's fair to give you these opportunities, but you could have at least sent me a note.*

Didn't think of it, he admitted. Luckily, they came to the station then. It was freakin' backed up this time. They shuffled through, Cor worrying Hazel would change her mind, same as he had with Fern the last time leaving for Giuthas. When they were finally in their stall, he knew she wouldn't be able to leave, even with him dropping this:

"Hey," he said as he clasped her arm and activated the pereport. "I'm sorry, but there's gonna be a commotion when we arrive."

Hazel stiffened. "What?"

Their pereport filled with magic. "Isle security is a bit...*touchy* about visitors."

You are so quashed when Mum and Dad get home, Hazel shouted at him.

A rush of color whirled by them, then the world stopped moving. The wisps of magic cleared from their travel globe moments before it dissolved, only to be replaced by the multi-colored cage. "Just hold on," he said to Hazel. "This bloke takes his job seriously, but he's no meaner than Barnaby."

Unfortunately, his whisper was amplified.

"Trainee Corylus!" Fee boomed across the cool mountaintop. "Breaking and entering *is* serious business. State your intentions."

"I am returning to my training with Lady Pina," he gasped as Hazel clutched him in a near stranglehold. Her heart thudded against his shoulder.

"You know what I mean." Fee's magic hummed in a rising growl all around them.

"Please, call Lady Pina for me," Cor said. "She is expecting me back."

It seemed like forever before a woman called, "Why am I here?" Lady Lark picked her way around several rocks. From her drawn brow, he wasn't sure if she'd help them, but his energy ratcheted down a notch.

Fee landed before Lady Lark. "Trainee Corylus is technically still designated as a Meadows visitor, and Mistress Fern is nae available."

Frowning at him, she waved a hand at the cage. "Please dispense with this first."

Fee did, then flitted around Cor and Hazel in its place. "State your intentions."

Freakin' bloody hell. Lady Lark had been nothing but kind to him. She didn't deserve the trouble he was putting her through. Neither did Hazel. All he'd had to do was tell Fern the truth, and he could have avoided this. "Sorry for the trouble, ma'am. I had to fetch her back. She's supposed to spend the weekend with me, and I couldn't just leave her hanging."

"What?" Fee asked. "Speak plainly."

Hazel looked upward in the direction of Fee's voice, her grip loosening. "He's not allowed to abandon me," she said. "He promised."

Fee snorted. "This lad and his promises will be the death of us."

"This one he has to keep."

If it was one thing Hazel knew how to do, it was advocate for her needs—which sometimes made him think she didn't feel as nervous as she claimed. Fee's flitting slowed. The security wizard came to a shuddering halt before them, his clipboard and pen in hand. "Guest's full name?"

"Hazel Avellana," answered Cor.

Hazel side-glanced at him.

Sort of your name, Cor sent. *I didn't do anything that Dad wouldn't like.*

Fee ran through the other questions, arriving at, "Wizard responsible for guest?"

"Me, Corylus Avellana."

Lady Lark put a hand on Fee's clipboard. "I take responsibility."

Fee huffed. "Location where the guest will reside during the visit?"

"The hollow in Beri's pine grove," Cor said firmly.

Fee's magic hummed in a disgruntled murmur.

"Decide," Lady Lark grumbled. "The others are waiting for me to return. We're testing a way to remove the roots and reconnect the rip without Pines magic."

Heck, he'd interrupted her work and other people's.

"Harmless," Fee snapped. "But I insist she meet Lady Pina."

Oh brilliant. Cor could feel the smirk in Fee's energy. However the little wizard did it, he was good—Fee knew they were van Gruens. He must have followed up Cor's prior answers.

Lady Lark put out her hand. "The peregrinator."

Cor closed his fingers over it. "I need it again on Monday to take her back."

"I will return it to Lady Pina. Following your test, you will see her about travel to Bonterra."

Blast. He'd blown it.

"We will discuss chores for you to repay my time interceding on your behalf when Fern arrives this evening. Meet me at Hillux at seven."

"Yes, ma'am," he said quietly.

As soon as they were out of earshot, Hazel began railing on him. He apologized again and again.

"Is that all you have to say for yourself? I'm sorry?" she demanded in exasperation.

Bloody… "No. I made a mistake by not telling anyone I had a responsibility to you. I'm telling the truth from now on. Lying is not worth it."

Despite the freakin' feeling Fee was watching to make sure that they went to Lady Pina's, Cor made a detour so they could stash Hazel's bag in the tree cave.

"You didn't tell me how cool this place is!" She opened her sketch pad.

He had to drag her off to the main grove. Lady Pina wasn't at home—another place he had to drag Hazel from. Hazel wanted to walk, and he knew where Lady Pina's ailing giant was, so they did. The massive trunks rose around them. Hazel turned, admiring them, and reached out to brush the nearest.

"No magic," he said. "She doesn't like others to work anything in her habitat."

She ran her fingers over the bark, then patted it. They continued on, Hazel touching the little trees and the big ones. "I can understand why," she whispered. "It's like being in a cathedral. How did you get so lucky?"

"I'm not in yet. It's been work, and I still have another lesson to master."

"For a test, that witch said." Hazel poked his shoulder. "Get practicing as soon as this meeting is done. You can tell me more about it later."

"As if you won't be dogging me all the while I'm at it."

She looked up again, her gaze transfixed by the shafts of light cutting through the canopy. "I want to draw. I might be able to wander this place by myself. It has good energy."

He poked her back. "The best."

When they reached the giant, Lady Pina was waiting for them, hands folded before her. Cor immediately began apologizing.

She put up her hand. "Shouldn't you be practicing instead of running off to Bonterra?"

"Yes, ma'am. As soon as I make introductions. Lady Pina, this is Hazel. Hazel, Lady Pina of the Pines."

Lady Pina looked her up and down. "Pray, tell me why Fee said I would be particularly interested in meeting you?"

Cor's gut twisted and he closed his eyes. He'd wanted to earn this himself, which wouldn't happen if they revealed Hazel's birthright. That's why he hadn't used their real surname.

Don't worry, Hazel sent and flipped through her sketchbook pages.

His eyes flashed open. She held up one of the few colored-pencil drawings among the inked pages. At a glance, it looked like a rainbow tornado, but any wizard would recognize what it really was. Hazel didn't tell many people. Their gazes met and she shrugged.

By the Orb, he loved his sister.

"I can predict the future energy flow of trees," she told Lady Pina.

25

THE GIFT

Lady Pina looked at Hazel, then down to the drawing again, her eyes widening. Her gaze shot to Cor.

He lifted his hands. "I only feel it in current time."

"Is it any species? Trees you have worked with or any you see? How specific can you identify the flow—a large area or down to the branch or twig?"

Cor leaned between them. "Mind if I get to my practice?" *You can find me?* he added to Hazel.

I doubt I'll need to.

Lady Pina put a hand on Hazel's arm. "Would you mind terribly if I asked you to look at a giant in decline?"

"I might not be able to absorb it immediately to show its path," Hazel said. "For a large tree, it might take several hours to record it. It's cumulative. Like growth rings."

Lady Pina nodded.

Cor wanted to laugh. They were talking the same language. "Could you hear out my harvesting stanza once more?" She was willing, so he sang it through, with magic.

Lady Pina nodded. "Much improved from earlier. Sing it until you have no hesitation between the notes and flow." She glanced at Hazel. "Your distraction, I gather."

Uh oh. The lady's closed-off look from days ago had resettled on her face.

"Corylus, do you understand that to *earn* this position, you must also earn the trust of this community?" He nodded. "You do? Describe to me what that looks like."

He rubbed his earringless earlobe. This wasn't an easy answer for him. "I would live here. See to the trees—but you don't mean that, do you?"

"No."

He drew a breath. "Folks would need to...know that I'm taking care of things, not running off when I want to. I'd need to promise to..." The enormity of it hit him. "I'd be promising to always be here."

"Not only promise, but to be here *without fail*," she said. "That doesn't mean you're barricaded here. You can take trips. Reasonable ones. But the purpose of an apprenticeship is to mentor wizards who intend to spend their whole lives tending a habitat."

She held up a finger, so he didn't dare speak.

"The decision doesn't need to be made right now," Lady Pina said. "But before you attempt your test tomorrow, you should determine if it's even a possibility. This is a very different enclave than the one you have come from."

That was the truth. "I'll be going off to practice, then," he said. "Thank you for welcoming another guest to your habitat."

She frowned at him. "Is that sarcasm, young man? Because if you weren't such a hard worker and progressing extraordinarily fast in your lessons, I might be miffed."

"Actually, I'm serious. Hazel doesn't take to everyone either, so you have something in common."

Hazel put up a hand. "I'd like to make it clear that I'm not interested in an apprentice position here. I have my own stuff going on. I'll try to help you with your tree, but I'm not in competition with Cor."

Cor left, listened to the recording again and sang until he could sing it with assurance. Releasing the energy from the dead limbs took more out of him than he'd expected it would. He ate all the snacks that he'd packed and was rather hungry when he returned to get Hazel. Only Lady Pina was in sight when he flew up. She was studying a page torn from Hazel's book.

When he landed, she dropped her arm and, if he wasn't mistaken, sighed.

"Everything all right, ma'am?"

She offered him the page. He took it and studied it. A few areas swirled in orange, but for the most part, the colors were dull, the lines broken. He knew what that meant.

"This type of gift…is she ever wrong?"

He shook his head. "I'm sorry." He shoved his fingers into his hair. This was a rather bloody blow. He didn't know what to say.

"How was your practice?" Lady Pina asked politely.

"Uh, good, actually." He held out his cupped hands and produced an energy ball the size of a beach ball. Inside, his honey magic swirled the pine's blue-green energy. "I collected it for you in case you wanted to apply it to…"

Lady Pina was already shaking her head. "A nice thought. I doubt it will work, but go ahead."

After he pushed it to the ailing tree's bark, she gestured for him to follow her around the broad trunk. Hazel was curled up, asleep, in a hollow among the roots. "I suppose this takes a lot out of a wizard."

"When it's struggling, I gather so." He stooped and gently shook Hazel's shoulder. "Hey, time to wake up. I owe Lady Lark chores for rescuing us."

When they flew to the Meadows, Fern was pacing back and

forth in front of the hobbit house. She stormed up to them, casting a glare in Hazel's direction.

Hazel moved behind him.

"How dare you lie to me?" Fern spat. "Again! Something you needed? Ha! You didn't have permission to bring back your girlfriend." She prodded him in the shoulder. "Thanks to you, Sir Humus assigned me more community service."

"Sorry." He couldn't make himself look her in the eye. "On the bright side, my test is tomorrow. That should release the pledge."

"What pledge?" Hazel asked.

"Tell you later," he said at the same time that Fern huffed.

"Oh man," she snarled, "I'd get a load of things straight before you go any further with him. Here." She thrust a note at him. "Gran's chore list, but if you get booted off the island tomorrow, forget it and just go. I'll gladly do them to be rid of you."

She strode inside and slammed the door.

Hazel started laughing. "Don't tell me you let that witch think you like girls. Did you make her a promise, and she now thinks I'm—"

"It was the return of a favor I did for her, and she has a prebond. No interest in me. No trickery on that front."

Hazel eyed him. "Knowing you, it was a favor you pushed, and you skipped telling her you're gay. Is this what you meant when you said you'd tell the truth after this? Why didn't you start with her?"

He shrugged. Why did he sabotage it every time he had something going well? He read the list Fern had given him. "How do you feel about helping me add quilt boxes to the beehives? And pulling oak sprouts on the eastern property boundary?"

With two of them, the winter insulation boxes were installed in minutes. They searched the woods' line until he found the spot Fern had sketched out. Cor used the time pulling sprouts to pop in his earbuds and sing through his stanzas. At sunset, he looked around for Hazel and found her sitting in the tall grass, drawing.

"You weren't helping!"

"I was." She ripped out the page and handed it to him.

The page was divided into seven panels like a comic. The images showed a pine nut sprouting and growing through the panels until the last showed the pine he'd just worked on. Then over each, she'd drawn starbursts, swirls and sparkles in gold—his energy. Lines of gold and blue-green spiraled from the last panel to reconnect back to the first panel's seed. Cor lowered the drawing to stare at Hazel.

"Isn't it clear?" She cocked her head. "It's you, singing tree energy."

He pointed to the last panel. "This makes it look like I've sent my energy through the Pines doing other stuff. Doing"—Lady Pina's words came back—"*fancy* magic. She made it clear I'm to work only the magic she's instructing me in."

Hazel frowned. "You've touched so many of her pines that I'm not sure." She tapped her pencil to the paper, lighting a staccato of gold sparks. "That's the way it came out. You must have…*inspired* them more than lesson work."

"I bloody freakin' hope not. If she sees that in the test, she'll be angry."

Back at the tree hollow, a figure sat on the opening's edge in the dusk's shadows. Oyster.

"Cor?" Hazel's voice broke, and she stopped behind some upper branches.

Damn, this had been going so well. What would he do if Hazel refused to sleep here tonight?

Cor landed on the branch leading in and confirmed the

folded sandy wings as the bloke rose. "Oy," he called cautiously. "What are you doing here?"

He raked his fingers through his curly hair, making Cor's stomach drop. "Stopped by to see how your last practice went."

It was an obvious lie, and Cor's mood shifted from longing to run his fingers through that hair to wary. "Not exactly within your proper manners to simply stop by." Cor tilted his chin toward Hazel. "Here to ask about her?"

"Your sister?"

He *was* fishing for information. The chap who'd already volunteered he was gay wanted to know whether the witch Cor had "brought home" was—or wasn't—a romantic interest. It would be so easy to say yes. And so hard to explain everything else: *She's my sister, our parents are away, they travel for an energy foundation, yes, we own it, and if folks here find out, my dad will assume they'll show me favoritism and I won't have earned a position here on my own and I'll have to start again. Somewhere else, where you aren't. Right, by the way, I like you.*

"Are you asking because we're both black?" Cor stepped forward, intending to spout off about people making assumptions, but he couldn't. Not to Oy. He lifted both hands helplessly. "I'm in trouble, I know it. Everyone makes stupid decisions sometimes."

"Like now," shouted Hazel from wherever she was behind and above him.

The cot with the rumpled blanket was visible behind Oyster, and Cor wished he were in it. "Right." He rubbed his face and pulled at his earlobe. "This has been a long day, and I'm gonna have another tomorrow."

Oy waved a hand. He stepped onto the branch leading from the hollow and spread his wings, but then turned back. "I'm here because I heard the rumor that you'd brought another person to the isle. The council has postponed deciding what to do since Lady Lark insisted Fern has to be present for the deliberations, but I wanted to hear for myself why you'd jeopardize your trial here."

"Because he loves me," Hazel yelled down. "That's why."

"You're only making this worse," he shouted back to her. The weight of his secrets settled over him, but he still couldn't reveal them when so many of his hopes were at stake. "I doubt anyone will believe me if I did explain."

"I'm here as a friend," Oy said. "I believe you've got a shot at convincing Lady Pina."

"Thanks."

"Forget the rumors and give it your best." He jumped off into a spread-winged glide, and that curly hair disappeared into the distance.

Hazel landed on the branch beside Cor. "Nice wizard. Seen much of him?"

"Tree work. Climbing."

"Cute."

Cor turned and walked into the hollow, forming up an energy ball to light the dark interior.

"He doesn't know you're gay, does he?"

"Good to meet you, my name is Cor and I'm gay," he said in a singsong voice.

"Oh for Orb's sake, you could find a way to work it into the conversation when the fellow is clearly gay also and a darling on top of it. He likes you, Cor!"

The damnedest thing was, there had been an opening and he hadn't managed to take it. He spun around. "I can't. It's no easier than you telling people you have debilitating anxiety and may never be able to fulfill the expectations others have for you. People see you differently."

They glared at each other for a moment, then Hazel rolled her eyes. "You're welcome, by the way."

"Thanks for not telling," he said.

They made peanut butter and jelly sandwiches again for

dinner, then Cor crawled into his cot and pulled the blanket over his head like a hood. Hazel's panel drawing danced through his mind, so he took it from his nightstand and lit his fingers. His magic and the swirling lines connected, one of Hazel's indications that the magic was strong.

"You'll do fine," she whispered from her cot.

He closed his hand over the glow. "Thanks for coming."

TRIAL BY TREE MAGIC

Cor woke before dawn. His sleep had been solid, but it was two hours before he'd set his mobile alarm to go off. He sat up. Hazel's cot was empty—she was already sitting at the hollow's entrance and sketching.

"Morning," he said as he flew off to pee in private. He washed up in the creek, then flew out some of his nerves before returning.

She had two peanut butter and jelly sandwiches made and her art backpack packed and was waiting while she sketched. He lowered beside her, and she shoved the food closer without even lifting her pencil. Her sketch was the tree line on the horizon, visible through an opening in the branches.

They ate in silence. He paced restlessly until she slapped her book closed. "Let's get over there."

The sun was rising over the ocean when they topped the ridge at Mount Lookout. *Nice.* His gaze traveled down the coast to where the river emptied into the sea. The Estuary. He'd kept thinking he'd go over and have a look, visit Oy and check out where he lived. But he'd been waiting to be invited. Now he might not have—yes, he would. He'd make the time before he left—if he left.

As he studied the Estuary, it began to glow pink. Cor laughed, and Hazel tossed him such a perplexed lock that he tried to stifle it—unsuccessfully.

She'd followed his gaze. "Wow," she breathed. "That warlock?"

"Suppose." Tucking his wings, he dropped into a dive down the mountain. Why couldn't he even share this with his sister, who knew him better than anyone?

They landed within the grove and began walking to Lady Pina's house. She'd still know they were there, but it was better than landing on her roof before she was even out of bed. They didn't talk while passing through the wakening forest. The trees enveloped them in the moist richness of building soil and growing pine, bird calls and the wind, the pure energy of a well-aged habitat.

An hour later—at what had become his usual arrival time—Lady Pina met them with a welcoming smile. "Good morning. I assume you are ready, and I admit, I am curious how you will fare today."

Did that mean she was rooting for him? A pleased sense of fellowship settled on him, strengthened when Hazel gave him a thumbs-up.

"Do you mind if I start?" he asked.

"Not at all. It will take several hours, I expect. Several of the others plan to stop by to view your efforts. I've asked no one to interrupt, and I doubt any of them will stay for the entire test."

"Except me," said Lady Mimosa. She glided down through the branches on gold-burnished wings. She folded them, said, "Good morning," and was introduced to Hazel before she turned back to Lady Pina. "I should like to monitor the entire test."

With a nod, Lady Pina led the way to a clearing ringed by

ancient pines. Her small patio table and a chair were set in the center. On the table was a bowl filled with pine nuts.

Was he going to have to grow them all? Cor stuffed his hands into his jeans pockets to keep from fidgeting.

"I have already determined that you are a hard worker," Lady Pina said, "the first of my requirements. I have witnessed that you have learned the traditional Energy Songs needed to integrate your energy with that of Giuthas' ancient pines, my second requirement. That leaves my third requirement, your spiritual presence being fully joined to the pinewoods. This is how you execute the energy methods on your own, the decisions you make and your success in carrying out your energy work in this habitat. Today's test will be in three sections. The first is to grow a Scots' pine of at least thirty feet in height."

Whew. He nodded.

"I hope I have given you enough choice." Lady Pina gestured to the bowl. "If not, ask for more. Pick one to sprout—or sprout several—and determine which you'd like to grow."

He nodded again. That sounded reasonable.

"It must be viable."

He looked around the clearing. "This spot has plenty of space for another tree. Do you mean it could stay here?"

"Exactly. It must be connected to this habitat. Not isolated within your energy."

"Got it."

"Then, because I understand it goes against your values, I won't ask you to harm this tree. I've saved another for the second part of your test, sustaining living trees." Lady Pina gestured beyond the clearing. "For the final section," she said, "I have removed my energy from a dead tree and ask that you remove its energy so it may be used at another place on the island. Any questions?"

"How long do I have?"

"As long as you need." She smiled. "Yet I should like to be

done by dinnertime. Now we shall withdraw. Let me know when you feel you have completed your first part."

He sat at the table, sang and sprouted several of the pine nuts, letting their roots trail over his fingers before setting them down. None felt right. He closed his eyes. What was different? He'd done this before with better results. It was clear that she expected him to stay within this clearing. He glanced around—oh, right. She hadn't told him he *had to sit at the table.* He gathered up the bowl and lowered himself to sit cross-legged on the ground.

Immediately, Cor felt the energy of the roots running beneath his thighs. He anchored himself, grounding his magic with the trees' and began singing.

The first pine nut he sprouted sent a root past his knee, reaching for the soil.

This is the one.

Still singing, he dug a hollow in the soil, gently set the pine nut in it and sang until the root tip dove deeper. He repeated the second stanza, keeping one finger to the nut until it felt secure, then he transitioned to the third stanza. The hum of his energy escalated with the switch, rising, rising...the shoot emerged.

Bless the Orb.

He hadn't realized he'd been holding his breath. He repeated, "Shoot sprouting. Growing, growing. Needles in their pockets twisting forth." The wrapped needle bundle wiggled upward, and he brushed the soil lightly over the seed and around the tender stalk, planting the seed. In another round of verses, the paperlike covering of the needle bundle burst open, and the three needles spread in a blue-green fan.

Cor smiled and slowed the song, though he kept his energy flowing around the sprout. His fingers in the soil told him the roots were spreading. His other palm above its needle tips indicated the tree wasn't quite ready. He allowed the tree—and himself—a pause in the song. He magicked over his water bottle from his pack and took a drink. Now for the hard work.

The growing took hours. The first tiny branches were easy, requiring less energy from him and less for the seedling to gather. But as he added more, the lower branches kept growing, and each new ring added five to six branches for him and the tree to fuel. Singing and with his energy humming, Cor rose to his knees, then to his feet and unfurled his wings and hovered alongside the tree. After each new ring of growth, he stopped to allow the tree to pull in the needed nutrients and water from the soil. And to rest himself.

His world became the tree, its energy, his energy and their spreading connection to the soil within this clearing, the sunlight falling on them, the droplets of water underground, the other trees wound around them. He couldn't steal from their resources, so increasingly he searched to send the roots to find supplies that weren't already being used, to balance the needs of all the individuals. His throat began to rasp from constant singing.

Following a particularly difficult search for nutrients, he flew backward from his tree to clear its lower branches and landed. Someone cupped his elbow. Lady Mimosa kept him from stumbling, and beside her, Lady Pina's lips were moving. He couldn't hear her. He shook his head to clear it, and like coming up from an underwater swim in murky green algae, he dropped his singing to a whisper, let his energy fade and emerged from his magical immersion.

"You have completed this part of the trial," Lady Pina said. "Had you not noticed your pine is an ambitious fifty feet tall?"

"No." Was that a problem that it wanted to grow more?

"It's pulling too much from you now," said Lady Mimosa. "Come sit."

They towed him to the table, and he slumped in the chair.

They handed him his water bottle, then put a piece of jerky in his hand. As he ate, his senses came back to him.

"Cor, do you know where are you?" Lady Pina asked.

He startled. Lady Mimosa, Lady Lark, Sir Humus and several others stood in a semicircle watching him.

"Uh, the Isle of Giuthas."

Lady Pina sat across from him. "I shall revise this trial if I have anyone else attempt it. I had no idea anyone could become so fully immersed so as not to notice the tree had taken over."

"It…" Cor looked up at his tree and swallowed. "It did?"

The elders glanced among themselves and, at Lady Mimosa's gesture, walked a distance off and huddled to talk. At the perimeter of the clearing, a crowd—council elders, some of Fern's fan club and a few residents he'd never seen—was standing in the shafts of light and shadow.

Freakin' flights. He didn't see his sister. He tried to call to her, but had no energy left to do so. "Where is Hazel?" he croaked.

"Safe." Lady Pina smiled and pointed upward and back a few trees into the grove.

He spotted Hazel's white cargo pants against the bark on a limb high in the air.

Lady Mimosa took a seat at the table, too—though there hadn't been extra chairs earlier—and leaned in. "She confided in me that people make her nervous and asked to wait out of sight until you have finished."

Lady Pina cleared her throat. "Also, I admit that I didn't believe this vigorous growth could result from the energy of one wizard and suspected she was helping you in some manner. She agreed to leave for a few growth rounds until Lady Mimosa and I ran checks to verify yours was the only magic in the glade."

That was good news, right? Cor rubbed his hands together, then through his hair, removing an errant pine needle. He automatically grabbed his ear to twist his earring, but dropped his hands to his lap. He wanted to ask, *Beri didn't do this?* "Something isn't right, is it? That's why everyone is sticking around."

"It is unusual to see a tree grown so rapidly…" Lady Mimosa started, then looked at Lady Pina.

"It took a few tries before we could get your attention," she said gently. "I believe you so completely integrated your energy with the tree's that it was pulling more energy from you than what most wizards would deem *balanced* in a habitat."

Oh. That was bad.

Lady Mimosa pushed a bowl of nutty granola and a stack of jerky across to him. "You must be more aware of your energy flow during the remaining test sections," she said. "Please, eat and rest before you continue."

Lady Pina stood. "We will ask the others to withdraw to give you time to refresh. Tap the ground with your magic to signal me when you are ready to resume."

They left to talk to his audience, and Cor took a handful of granola, feeling self-conscious. As they started to leave, he glanced around to see if he knew anyone. Right, who was he kidding? He was checking to see if Oy was here.

He was.

Oyster caught his gaze and held it a moment, two fingers rising in a salute. Cor lifted a hand to return the wave as a woman in a ruffled blouse walked in front of Oyster. She spoke to him, and he fell into step with her. They left with the others.

Cor sighed and picked a few nuts from the mix to eat. Fern was there, Lady Lark, too. Also, Fern's brother alongside Willow. Beri was missing. Cor resumed eating and drinking. Once the woods had fallen silent, he set the alarm on his mobile for forty minutes, lay down on the ground and closed his eyes.

How badly would this count against him that the tree had taken over his magic?

HARDER TESTS

When his alarm chirped, Cor turned it off and lay staring at the faraway canopy. The sky had clouded over while he'd rested—or maybe earlier, he hadn't noticed. It wasn't even noon yet, but he'd dozed. He checked his cores and flushed energy through his channels to check his reserves. His magic was restored, likely by his contact with the habitat.

I hope Lady Pina doesn't disqualify me for that.

It was generous that they'd let him rest, but then, tree growing wasn't a race. It was the long haul. He got up, had more water and a handful of nuts. He ran through the repair stanza. Ready to begin, he touched his magic to the ground. Lady Pina sent back an echoing response of her magic.

She came and took him to her declining giant, the only Scots' pine left with dead limbs, and reviewed the tools and climbing gear Ash had brought. Cor had what he needed. Then she showed him which branches to work on. Two of the giant's branches were truly dead. A third was damaged but not dead.

That made the test not as clear-cut. On the estate, they'd have already repaired the limb. On a fresh break, they could reconnect the cambium layers and have them regrow. In fact, humans had a growth chemical that Master Harold sometimes used. It would even bind together in a graft two different species of branch stock. Cor would rather do the magical version here, and support the limb with ropes or cable until the healed spot had a few years' more growth.

Giving himself some time to determine exactly where he'd anchor the supports, he set up to remove the first dead limb. After he'd gotten into the climbing gear, he remembered Ash's policy about checking for wildlife. Spells, that would have been a mistake. He unlinked his saddle, fastened the pruning saw into it instead and flared his magic over the dead wood.

A gazillion pricks of light flared, and he laughed. This was a setup. At least he hadn't forgotten. Cor threw out pellets to catch the animals, including too many salamanders for a single limb, a mouse—suspiciously the size and species of the one they had removed last week—and a small snake.

Bloody lucky he wasn't afraid of them.

He loaded several of the suspended creatures into his palms and scanned for places to put them. His gaze landed on his new tree far below, and a grin spread over his face. What better way to get it immersed in this habitat? He ferried the animals, then returned and grabbed up all the insects he could find. His tree needed those, or none of the others would stick around. He performed the same "rescue" on the second dead branch.

Singing with extra gusto, he cut and healed over both branches and carried them to the ground beneath his pine. If the animals decided to abandon ship, perhaps they'd take refuge in their old home spots and return to his tree later.

At last, Cor returned to the living, but damaged, branch. Using a rope he'd found in the gear duffle, he hauled the branch back to its predamaged position and secured it there. He placed his hands on either side of the break, reached for the tree's magic, flowed his energy to the tree and began to sing the repair stanza. He repeated the song over and over, but the cambium layers weren't growing. He stopped and flexed his fingers. He had magic enough. The tree had connected to his. Just…this wasn't working.

Setting his hands on the break again, he poked about inside with his magic. Duh. The cambium cells in the old break had healed over, so of course they weren't growing. With a bit of magic, he scraped away the scar tissue and began the repair stanza again. Still, it didn't seem to be working.

He hated to spend any more time on it. He looked around the clearing. Only four figures sat outside the perimeter, and they didn't seem to be looking up at him.

Cor tugged at his earlobe.

No one said he had to get things perfect. *This is how you execute the energy methods on your own*, Lady Pina had said, *the decisions you make…* He blew out a breath. Just how good did his decisions need to be?

Well, he knew what Master Harold would have him do—treat this branch as if it was going to live, then wait to see if the tree reclaimed it. He took a pair of pruners from his back pocket, gave himself more line on the rope, unfurled his wings and swung out into a hover. He pruned the dead portions off the branch and sealed over the cuts. It looked pathetic when he was done, but the needles remaining were very green.

Moving on.

He stowed the climbing gear. Lady Pina appeared at his side and, without saying a thing, led him to a dead tree. "Your third section of the test. Remove the energy from the tree and hold it for transfer."

He surveyed the dead tree from the base. Flying, he circled it, then landed on the branch of another tree and looked down on it. Not a living needle on the thing, and very few dead ones at that. The dead pine wasn't that big, only fifteen feet taller than the tree he'd just grown. Was it someone else's attempt? He didn't like that thought. He dropped to the ground again and put his palm to the bark. No thrum of life in it—meaning no xylem and phloem were moving up and down it.

Still, it had plenty of magic tied up in it. The pinewoods as a whole. Traces from the surrounding individuals. Wildlife... He should remove them. He flashed his magic over the tree. Hundreds lit up. He'd have to go branch by branch, and that would take...too long.

Why do it? Lady Pina hadn't said anything about felling this tree. Ash had said that in the Forest they left standing snags for wildlife. Cor pushed his energy into the trunk and down into the roots. They were stable. This dead pine could stand in place for years as a shelter for wildlife.

He pressed his lips together. That would be his decision, if it were his to make—it was. That's what she'd told him to do. He began humming to himself. He ran through the first six stanzas, working his energy with the song, but not applying it to the tree until he got to the seventh stanza. Then he sang aloud. His energy rose and fell just as it should, went into the tree and collected up the pine's energy.

Yet, each time he tried to corral the last bit in the heartwood, it threw him off.

How could it? It was dead. He worked around it, trying to figure out the puzzle. As Lady Pina had promised, she'd removed her energy. It had to be the pinewoods themselves, the habitat.

Every time he started again, even in a different location, it did the same thing. A few times he kept pressing through, singing the stanza over and over. Once, he sang for twenty minutes straight, knowing it wasn't working. He tried to separate the pine's energy into sections, as he had with removing a branch. That didn't work either...and now he knew full well that Lady Pina didn't mean for him to take this tree apart limb by limb.

He dropped his hands and rested his forehead against the

rough bark, hoping some insight would come to him. It didn't. What she'd said was true—handling the energy of an ancient tree was difficult. Finally, he lifted his head, and beneath a gray sky that made him feel even sadder about this, he walked across the clearing.

Lady Pina and Lady Mimosa came to meet him.

He waited a distance from the other wizards milling at the edge. When the witches stopped before him, he said, "I can't do it."

IF AT FIRST YOU FAIL...

While Cor waited, Lady Mimosa veered to the dead tree and put her hand to it. Lady Pina watched her for a moment, then turned back to him.

She held out her hands in a helpless gesture. "It's a start," she said quietly. "A very nice start. I'm confused as to why it won't complete."

Damn, he'd expected her to have an answer, to give him the next step...if she thought he'd done well enough so far.

Instead, she looked from him, to the tree and back again. "I suspect you are not...settled enough in yourself. If your spiritual identity is strong, then your magic follows suit."

Lady Mimosa walked over, her golden magic dimming. "A brilliant effort. I'm afraid I agree with Lady Pina's theory. You show a good deal of confidence during your lessons with Kory, but is there some other area of your being that you feel you haven't mastered yet?"

He snorted and turned it to a cough while shaking his head. How the heck was he supposed to answer that? *No, I rely on blah-blah-blah?* The damned irony of it was, Hazel relied on *him* for confidence. "Can't think of anything."

Lady Mimosa tapped a finger to her lips. "Until you identify this area, your magic won't be mature enough to complete the spell. It's something I've seen my own children grow into."

"Are you suggesting he try again in a year or so?" Lady Pina asked.

A year? Cor swallowed, trying to form some sort of response…or question.

"Magical maturity takes time. Be patient." Lady Mimosa patted his arm.

Patient? She expected him to just go back to the city like this was a game he'd get better at once he developed more muscles?

Cor spun on his heel and stormed away, ignoring their calls to wait. What was there to wait for? Them to kick him out? His wings unfurled, and with a spring of his knees, he launched himself airborne, his rapid wing beats carrying him up and among the branches. He could have landed on any branch and been hidden from view, but he kept flying. He broke through the outer edge of the grove. A ridge lay before him, its stones protecting the Pines from the sea's winds. He flew over it and arched his wings, letting the current take him.

Damn.

The land below was so dense, so brimming with life and magic, that he could feel its energy into his cores. He'd dipped his magic into the soil and pulled its magic out. He combined it to sprout seeds and grow trees, to repair them and protect their wildlife. In the Pines, in the Meadows and in the Forest. He'd built so many links to this isle in so many ways…

How could they say that he didn't have whatever it took? Oh. For freakin' starters, he'd run off rather than wait to hear what they had to say next. *Bloody mature, Cor.*

He should go back, but the damage was already done. The wind lifted him higher and higher, until the entire island was laid out below, and he touched overhead clouds as dark as his soul felt. He passed above the rocks on Mount Lookout, leaving the ancient pinewoods looking like the treetops on the estate. A warning light flashed up at him, like lightning from the ground instead of the clouds.

Too high, Trainee Corylus. Either return or call someone to catch your falling body.

Cor glared in Fee's direction, but he didn't dare challenge him.

He dropped out of the current, but took his time spiraling down. He couldn't return to the grove—Lady Pina would know—so he glided seaward and landed on a large rock, one of a line surrounded by the incoming waves.

For a while, he stared. Then he closed his eyes. The rhythmic drawing back and crashing of waves calmed him after his day of applying Energy Songs. Between, he heard the sound of the wind rushing through the pine boughs, carrying a lullaby he wouldn't get to hear again. He wiped the start of a tear. Only a start, because he wasn't going to cry about this. A year to mature. That sounded like it could mean a chance at another trial—if he could convince his dad there was still no favoritism.

Ugh, the only way to find out was to go to Lady Pina and ask. He wasn't ready for that yet. He needed an idea to offer of what he'd try differently next time, and right now, he didn't have a clue.

"Hallo," called a soft voice.

Cor's eyes flashed open just as Oyster stretched a foot to a rock several over and landed. Cor didn't move as the other boy nodded to him. His wings disappeared, and he removed the climbing gear duffle he had slung over his front and draped it over one shoulder. He slipped his hands into the pockets of his khakis and strolled across the rocks, making the leaps between them with more grace and assurance than anyone else Cor knew.

Cor scowled at Oy's pressed trousers, the unwrinkled pale blue shirt that managed to come off as dressy despite it being homespun and the cuffs rolled back to his elbows. At this fellow who could stay here when he couldn't. At least he wasn't Beri.

"Are you here to wrestle me back to Bonterra?" he asked.

Oyster's thin lips quirked for a moment. "No."

"Here to tell me I can stay and try again?"

The perfectly polite wizard looked away. "No one has offered that. Sorry."

"Then clear off, so I can…" *Be pissy in peace.* What was he doing here? *Feeling sorry for myself* wasn't what he wanted to say to this fellow. "Avoid the trees I'm banned from."

Instead of leaving, Oyster sank down, his shoulder inches from Cor's.

"Maybe I can help you," Oyster said quietly. "I'm not a terrestrial wizard, but I know a few things the isle elders routinely teach their apprentices. Perhaps you haven't been here long enough to really do what some call communing with your habitat."

Cor stared off. He'd done that. "You don't understand. I'm supposed to be able to do this."

"Because you want it so bad?"

Telling even one person on this island could garner him favoritism, but Oyster wouldn't tell anyone if Cor asked him not to. He needed new ideas if he wanted to stay here, and Oyster couldn't give him any if Cor kept the chap clueless. Plus, he wanted to confide in him, more than he'd ever wanted to tell someone his secrets before. "Because I'm a descendant of Clarence the Courageous."

"Who's that?"

Really? Cor pressed his hand to his forehead. "Clarence van Gruen. A seventeenth-century wizard who settled Bonterra and forged a magical sword that heals trees."

"Does it?"

"Yes." Cor looked up. "It does. I've done it." Over and over, for the street trees, the estate trees and planting his new bare root stock—kind of stupid to do with an eighteen-inch broadsword and six-inch pots, but he wanted his trees to have every chance they could. Cor took a breath. "If he could give it lasting magic like that, and I can learn these songs to grow a fifty-foot pine, then why can't I do the reverse to release one's magic?"

Oy shook his sandy curls. "Believe me, I understand all about expectations and having your parents' hopes for the future pinned on you, and in ways you are not the least interested in. Some days, it seems more than you can bear, and *you* can't be there. They had a debate about your magic after you stalked off. Some think it failed because you aren't fully yourself."

"Then who am I?" Cor snapped.

"A fellow relying on Clarence's sword?"

Oh. Cor hit his fist against his knee. "I'm not believing I can do it myself."

"Exactly. Being fully confident in yourself and your magic is a huge part of it working for you."

"I don't use the sword for everything. Kind of hard to get it out of the armory."

"Were those non-sword experiences successful?"

"Of course. But I didn't have anyone watching me for a test." Could that be it? "I do great at stuff I study, like these tree songs. I excel at growing woody plants. I shouldn't have any problems."

"Ever fight anyone? Physically or magically?"

"Yep. I'm badass at both of those, too. Not so much with routine spells, but I've never been laid out or fried. I get by with everything."

Oyster laughed and rapped his thigh. "You don't sound like a fellow who lacks confidence, so maybe that's not it."

Cor laughed, too, but purely from nervousness. Spells, this chap was so comfortable. If only he could get to the same nonchalance around fellows he liked as he could with girls he didn't. For a moment, he closed his eyes, thinking of the way he'd boldly talked to Amanda, teased and jostled Fern or touched the elbows of any of those witches at the conference. Then he let himself picture tossing an arm around Oyster.

But when he opened his eyes, all he could actually manage was flicking a brown finger against Oy's lighter pinkie. He did it again, and their gazes met. He cleared his throat. "You've helped me a lot here. Been a real friend. Appreciate it."

"About time you two got together," called a faint voice.

Cor scrambled to stand up. Oyster did, too.

Hazel glided down and landed next to Cor. "Well, this is a different choice of moping spots. I'm happy to see you've found the right company."

"Thanks, blabbermouth," he said in warning.

Hazel looked from him to Oyster and back again.

Spells, she was going to say something, something he wanted to say himself.

"It wasn't a horrible failure, for a first try," Oy said helpfully.

Cor didn't want to hear it. *Hazel, just leave.*

Why? He'd expect your girlfriend to hunt you down. She whacked his arm. "Tell the damned truth for once."

Oyster stepped back, eyes darting.

"Riiight," Cor stalled. If he didn't, she would, and then he'd seem like the wimp he was. "Hazel is my sister," he said instead. "She has anxiety and didn't want to stay the weekend alone while our aunt is gone. I needed to be here, so I brought her back with me."

Hazel whacked him again, and both he and Oy stepped back.

"Ow," Cor grunted. "Do you have to do that?"

"The other truth."

"Spells, just leave me alone."

She pointed at him, her finger sparkling. "Since you outed

me, you…you better be back at that tree by sunset, or I'll do worse." She spread her wings and leaped off the rock.

Once she disappeared between the trees, Cor turned, met Oyster's curious gaze, then dropped his. "I-I'm gay. And I like you. Though why the hell you would like me when I can't pull myself together to tell the—"

Oy shoved him. Cor teetered on the wet rock, and Oy slammed him again, his face twisted in fury.

Cor tumbled into the sea. A wave caught him and tumbled him under. He kicked and came up sputtering, mouth full of nasty salt water and eyes stinging. Oyster turned his back on him, his fists balled in pinkish magic that also blazed over his upper back. His wings burst forth. He flapped hard, leaped from the rock and flew off.

Cor bobbed in the roll of the surf before drifting to the rock and crawling up onto it.

At least he watched to make sure I could swim. But Oy had rejected him. Cor hadn't expected that, not after Oy had tracked him down. He'd blown it.

Cor lay on the rock for some time before drying his clothes. The sun wasn't going to do it—bulging clouds completely covered the sky. He magicked out his wings. Once he was airborne, he didn't know where to go. He certainly didn't want to spend any more time than he had to with Hazel. He flew up the coast, trying to tire himself out so he could just fall into bed when he got back to the tree hollow. But he couldn't keep his gaze from the Pines, and, finally, flew among the treetops.

The thought of not being able to stay nearly made him cry.

He flapped harder, flying upward to return to the tree hollow. He broke from the needled boughs. Another wizard was flying over the grove—Oyster, dammit. Cor tucked his wings to dive back into the cover, but the bloke spotted him.

"Cor. Wait," he called.

Cor didn't.

"...sorry."

Bloody hell, you've got to be kidding. Cor squeezed his eyes shut, then blinked them open again, spreading his wings to slow his drop among the branches. Maybe Oy was apologizing? He glanced up. Oyster was hovering overhead uncertainly. Cor waved him down and glided to the first broad branch.

Oyster landed a safe distance away. He gripped the leather harness he wore to carry the gear duffle. "I, uh... I'm sorry. You said I'm too proper? Well, that was the most improper thing I've ever done. I was angry that you'd ignored me after I'd asked in all the discreet ways."

"Don't feel too special about that. I've ignored or lied to most everyone about it."

"Will you stop already?" Oyster snapped. "You're even lying to yourself."

Cor crossed his arms. "Fine. I like you."

"I like you, too. I wish you could earn a place here so we might find out where that like may lead."

"What if I can't?"

Oy shrugged. "I can't leave. Our energy balance is so delicate. One departure would put the entire island in a downward spiral. Besides, all I know is estuaries. All I love is estuaries. There isn't much call for that on the mainland. So I don't want to start anything with you unless you are here."

Another ache ripped through Cor's gut. He ducked his face. "I get it."

"Now that that's said, I'll point out *again* that you can't stay unless you give this another try. I told you that I commune with my habitat by swimming through it." He patted the duffle. "Do you wish to climb?"

Cor gestured to the cloudy sky. "Not a lot of time with the storm coming up."

"Couple of hours." Oyster wrinkled his nose. "We'll have

more climbing time if we fly the line up. I'm crap at aiming the throwing weight."

Cor extended his hand. "Give it here."

With a lightweight throwing line knotted to the weight, he carried them out as far as he could stand on the branch. The next limb up was a good fifty feet up, and he wasn't quite far enough back for the right throwing angle. To prove he could— fine, *show off*, because he felt like crap—Cor toe-balanced-hovered farther out on a branch too thin to actually hold him. He swung the weight like a pendulum, checked his aim and let go. With a whoosh, it flew—the line uncoiling with it—up and over the branch. The weight fell, and Cor caught it with a stream of magic.

"You magicked that over," Oyster shouted.

"Did not, you blimey chap." He laughed as he glided over. "Well, maybe."

They pulled the climbing line over that limb, and then Oyster magicked the weight over another. They set up so they could climb side by side and ascended, careful not to touch the growths of lichen. The old pine had so much to see. They hung in their saddles to admire miniature trees, poked at leaves and captured salamanders with their magic. At a patch of late blae-berries, Cor snatched a huge one from under Oyster's nose. When he laughed at Oy's pretend outrage, the fellow swung across and knocked into him. Then, with a laugh, Oy pulled himself over the next branch.

"Race you," he called back.

Cor followed, climbing in earnest, ignoring the salamander cavities and looking only for handholds and toeholds. Ten feet, twenty, forty. Sweat beaded on his brow and rolled down his temples. His muscles began to make themselves known, but in a good way.

Their only stops were to pull up the ropes and send the throwing line over higher limbs. The trunk narrowed and swayed in wider and wider circles, and they had to search out creative holds to protect the thinner growth. Two hours later, Cor heaved himself up between two branches to find only clouds overhead. Before him lay a jagged platform, the broken-off top of the pine.

It wasn't one of the nicer treetops, either unbroken or where a new leader had taken over. But over the yards of bare wood, the spiky breaks had caught windblown needles, leaves and even dirt, because a few scraggly grasses were growing. While Cor waited for Oyster, he gathered a few loose leaves and wedged them into a gap to better support one clump of wind-tossed blades. He flushed magic to his fingertips and, humming, reached for the tree's magic to secure them.

It flashed blue-green.

Wow. That was—wow. He'd been humming the growing stanza, not thinking about the rightness of that song for this task. He stroked the grass blades. These grasses would grow, and eventually this exposed wood would be covered in the wild-flowers they'd seen on the way up. Other species would find their way here, too, the lichens, moss, the various shrubs, as well as animals. This broken tree could fuel new life, still have a productive place in the pinewoods.

Oyster's head popped over the top, and he pulled himself up with a grin.

Cor grinned back and waved him over. "Come look at this." He touched the leaves again, before Oy was close, because he wanted to know if it was as bright as he thought.

Oy stopped, so it was. Cor could feel the pine's hum in every spot his body touched it.

"Nice, mate." Oy came to kneel beside him, their shoulders brushing. "You know this tree like you were born here. What are you going to do about it?"

"I, uh—" He'd left his test too soon, expecting Lady Pina to say no. He hadn't waited to hear what she thought, what options she might present, what chance he still had. Like this tree, he *did* still have a chance to grow, if he let himself. Cor met Oyster's gaze. "I'm going to go to Lady Pina and ask for another opportunity to prove that I have these connections. And ask for more time to grow into the position."

Oyster thumped his back, and for a while they looked over the treetops at the sky full of boiling blue and gray cumulous clouds. The air tingled with the coming storm, but Cor had never felt so calm, and that was entirely because he'd finally admitted to Oyster of the Estuary—and to himself—who he was.

29

STORMY NIGHT

When Cor told Hazel about his plan, she agreed with his decision to request a second chance, but not enough to fly with him at night to seek out Lady Pina, and not in the rain. Large drops had started hitting his wings moments before he landed in the tree cave, his timely arrival preventing another sibling fight. Distant thunder sounded as they climbed into their cots. Within minutes, it roared closer.

"Cor?" Hazel's voice wavered.

"Right," he said. "Let's get to the ground." But where? Hillux seemed too far to fly in a downpour. Arguing the risks, they collected their packs.

A glow appeared outside, distorted by the driving rain. "Hello?" someone shouted, and the magic expanded, lighting a torso and wings, but whose? The green figure loomed closer. Hazel clutched Cor's arm, both of them forming balls of magic—and Beri dashed inside, hair and clothes plastered to him.

"Sorry to intrude, but this storm is worsen—" He looked them over, and Cor elbowed Hazel and sucked his magic inside. "Aye, ready to leave. Smart. Follow me. Straight down and a bit westward to my place." He paced the edge while they put on their packs and unfurled wings, then lit his wing feathers green, arched them and stepped from the hollow.

Another crack of thunder sounded, this one closer. Cor began counting—to determine how close it was—then stopped himself. Beri was drifting slowly so they could follow.

"Go next," he urged Hazel. She jumped, also alighting her feathers.

A lightning's flash cut across the distant sky, spurring Cor's leap after her.

Darkness closed around their glowing wings. Below, the pine's needles provided more shelter from the rain. Beri's wings pivoted like a compass needle, and seconds behind, Hazel's did the same. Branches to avoid, Cor realized, making the twists himself as their descending lights silhouetted huge limbs.

Beri's green seemed to fall into a dark hole and race away. Hazel did the same. They'd reached the understory clearing. Raindrops pelted Cor's face. He put up a hand to shield his eyes and dove after them. Ahead, yellow lights flickered, and Beri was leveling, stopping. They'd landed.

Beri shouted, "Wings in. It's a squeeze!" They ran among the oak-birch forest surrounding the grove, shoving through bushes of dripping branches, and the yellow lights ahead resolving into the rectangular windows of a cabin. Beri raced for it, threw open the door and plowed inside, whipping around to gesture them in.

The three of them stood, dripping, in Beri's one-room cabin, the rain pounding on the tin roof above the sleeping loft. Beri pointed to the only door within the interior. "I have a shower if you'd like to use it."

Hazel took a breath. "Yes. Thank you." She disappeared into the bath with the click of its latch.

Cor looked everywhere except at Beri until he couldn't. Their gazes met. "Thanks for coming for us," he said, his voice rough. "Hazel was too frightened to trust me to lead her to Hillux."

Beri shrugged. "'Twas the decent thing to do. But do nae think I like you any more than I did." He flicked magic over his hair, drying it, then his clothes.

Staring at the floor, Cor magicked the wetness from himself. The place was tiny, and he had to share it with a bloke who hated him.

Beri headed for the ladder to the loft. "I'll toss down my extra winter blankets, but the only extra pillows are the sofa ones."

It was likely too late to make a difference, but Cor had to try, at least to get Hazel through this night. "My sister will be grateful."

Beri stopped on the first rung and looked over his shoulder. "Your sister? There has been some speculation, but—"

"I let it happen. I'm gay. I'm not interested in Fern."

"But she said Amanda…"

"Right, well…" He shrugged. "I can be a freakin' bloody ass if it gets me my way. Playing up to Amanda unnerved Fern until there was no way she wouldn't give me the peregrinator. I had to have that to fetch Hazel, because…" Blast, she'd already called him out for spilling her secrets once. "She was going to be alone this weekend, and who wouldn't have preferred coming here instead?"

Thanks, Hazel sent him. *These walls aren't that thick.*

Beri hesitated a moment, then his mouth twisted. "You've still got something dodgy going on, but my opinion about you is turning a bit." He climbed the ladder and tossed down the blankets.

Cor threw them and himself onto the sofa. "Meh, keep on the defensive. I'll still do whatever I can to stay on this island."

"Unfortunately for the rest of us, Lady Mimosa shares that wish for you," Beri said before disappearing into the loft's shadows.

Soon after they extinguished the lights, a howling wind

joined the thunderclaps. Cor stared up at the ceiling, unable to sleep on the rug in front of the fireplace. He blamed it on the hard floor, the patter of rain, being indebted to Beri, storming away from Lady Pina and how he would persuade her to give him another chance. But those weren't the real reasons.

Something else gnawed at him, something hyping his energy. He took his blanket and sat in the chair next to the sofa where Hazel tossed and turned.

"You all right?" she whispered.

"Yeah," he lied. He stood and paced the width of the cabin, eight stockinged footsteps each way.

Hazel sat up and beckoned him over. "You think we're far enough away that none of those pines can hit this cabin?"

His gut twisted. He dropped to squat beside her. "Why did you ask that?"

"We're within range," Beri said from the loft. "But they're stable. It was my habitat and hasn't been turned over to anyone else, so its energy is still with me."

Cor bit his lip. So, he wasn't the only one assessing the danger, but... "Why did you ask that?" he said to Hazel again.

She formed up an energy ball. Inside it, wisps of orange and flecks of blue-green magic whirled like a tornado in one of her drawings. "Something is wrong with the pine trees. You feel it, too, don't you?"

"Yes, I—"

Rumbling cut through the rain. Not close enough to drown it, distant. As Cor turned that direction, the cabin shook. The windows clattered, the dishes clinked and the table lamp swayed. Cor caught the lamp as the shaking started to die.

"Flights!" Beri leaped from the loft. He landed feet from them behind the sofa in the crouch of someone who wasn't sure whether to run or hide.

The rumbling surged twice more...then stopped.

The rain continued falling as if nothing had happened, but

the painful stretching in Cor's energy said something had. Something bad.

His gaze dropped to the magic still in Hazel's hand. The last bits of color fluttered to the bottom of the ball.

"A tree fell," she said sadly.

"No." He squeezed his eyes shut and scanned his energy, which he should have done before. "Three trees fell." His eyes flashed open. "Lady Pina!"

30

LOSS…AND GAIN

How he managed the flight in the rain, Cor didn't know. Beri had argued that they go somewhere to pereport, but Cor didn't wait. Battered and soaked, he skimmed the treetops as low as he could, cringing each time lightning zigged between the banks of clouds. Even with the flashes, the downpour obscured his view. Instead, a new sense in his energy drew Cor. The ancient pines loomed before him. He ducked among them, beneath a branch and over another automatically.

Then he lost the route. The intense scent of pine and wood engulfed him before his flight crossed a clearing—a clearing where there had been none before. A flash of lightning showed limbs and whole trees sticking up at odd angles from trunks bedded on a litter of broken debris that covered the ground.

The gap fell into darkness again, but the glimpse had been enough. A sickening feeling welled up within him. These giants had smashed everything in their path. A hundred-year-old log home wouldn't stand a chance.

Please let her be all right.

His magical connection to this habitat should have been able to tell, but now it was jumbled with adrenaline and dread. He wasn't sure which way to go. Cor lit his wings as he'd done earlier, and the magic tossed out enough light for him to avoid the shadows that resolved into trunks and branches.

In the slashed space, he alighted on a giant trunk imbedded in the ground. He closed his eyes. He'd been headed…there. He turned and flew, following instinct again. Around a trunk, his gut wrenched again to find himself in another clearing—a smaller arm of destruction. He crossed it, knowing Lady Pina's grandfather's log home should be—had to be—somewhere ahead…

Another glowing figure was descending through the forest— a pink one.

"Oyster," he yelled and shot forward.

"Her house is still standing," he yelled back.

They practically collided at the door, wrenched it open and tumbled inside. It was dark, quiet after the rain and rush of wind.

"Lady Pina?" Oy strode through the front room and disappeared into the next. Cor followed. It was a library. Oy stood at the far doorway, staring.

"Thank the Blessed Orb," he spat as Cor joined him. "What are you still doing here?"

"The turmoil," she answered weakly from her bed. "It paralyzed me."

"You should have left," Oy said flatly. "We were setting out to fetch you when they fell. Mother decided she had to go back to make sure you didn't come to the house in our absence, and I had to make sure she got in the door. Then I lost my way because my usual landmarks are gone."

"The ailing giant." She sighed. "And two others."

"Countless more on the perimeter damaged as well." Cor cleared his throat. "I am so sorry."

She closed her eyes. "Actually, they can be counted. Twenty-three pines are broken." She blinked away tears. "Thank you for coming. For…your concern."

He lifted his hands helplessly. "I had to."

"A good thing he did," Oyster said. "Get up, ma'am. We'll need his help to fly you home with me."

"Oh, I don't think I need—"

"Mother insists," Oy said. "You know what that is like. I daresay she's called the council and will have the lot of them here if I don't report back that you're on your way."

"Um." Cor put up a finger. "Likely they're on their way anyway. Beri was headed for Lady Lark's to get here via pere-porting."

"How exactly did Beri know I was in danger—or you, for that matter?" Lady Pina asked as she sat up in bed, something of her regular spark igniting. "Did you hear the trees fall all the way over at the Meadows?"

"Yes, distantly. But…" Cor touched his abdominal core. "I felt it."

"You felt…" She shook her head.

"Hello?" came multiple calls from the front room, and footsteps sounded across the stone floor.

"I suppose there is no getting around leaving," Lady Pina grumbled.

The next morning, Cor woke again before dawn in the room with twin beds that he'd shared with Hazel in Lady Sedge's home. As he got up, he scuffed his foot on the rug and was pleased that Hazel turned over on the first try.

"What are you doing?" she asked.

"Going to check on the Pines." He squatted beside her, a déjà vu of last night coming over him of discussing the same trees. "I'd like to do more. Three trees lost and twenty-three more damaged. That's some pretty big limbs to trim."

Hazel groaned.

He eyed her, and when she didn't speak, he said, "If I had—"

"Please." She put up a hand. "Just…I want to go back to sleep, not go there. Please?" She rolled her back to him.

"Do you mind if I do?"

For a moment, she didn't respond, and he was afraid she'd gone back to sleep. Then Hazel sighed. "You have my blessing. Go ahead."

One new hurdle jumped. He hugged her, though she squealed. "You're the best, Hazel."

He slipped from the room and walked past the other bedroom doors on the upper level. The one that was Lady Pina's was open, her room empty, as he'd halfway expected. Now to find her in the grove. He let himself out of the stone house nestled at the edge of a wood and unfurled his wings, about to fly. One of the chairs on the edge of the cliff above the river was occupied.

After a moment's consideration, he walked over. "Good morning, ma'am."

"Good morning," Lady Pina answered wearily, her gaze on the estuary below.

He sank into the second chair. "I didn't expect to see you *here* this morning."

It was some time before she answered. "I cannot face seeing it."

The breath rushed out of him. "I can help," he said. "If you'll let me."

"It's not just my decision."

He knew she meant the outcome of the trial, not repairing the pines. "I know. I want to heal them anyway. Might I borrow the peregrinator for a quick trip to Bonterra?"

After a moment, she sighed. "Don't get Fern in any more trouble than you already have." She extended the device without looking at him.

Two new hurdles jumped.

He took the peregrinator and started to leave. Then he slid his mobile from his pocket and clicked a few buttons, bringing up his nocturnal playlist.

"Lady Pina? You might hate technology, but sometimes a bit of music can be comforting. I'll leave this open, and if you'd like some company, you can click the arrow to try a set of songs that are favorites of mine." He set the mobile on the arm of her chair and left.

Forty minutes later—and his third new hurdle jumped—he stood on the trunk of the ailing giant, a scabbard slung around his hips, surrounded by meters-deep slash. The tree Lady Pina had worked so hard to heal had taken down a neighboring tree with it. Debris thrown against a third had felled it at an angle that had created the second clearing he'd crossed last night. The trunk had broken, leaving it precariously balanced against another tree. Cor could feel the strain of its roots gripping the ground. He needed help for that one, so turned his back on it. Plenty to do before others arrived, which they were sure to do… just not so soon after dawn.

He eyed a broken three-foot-diameter limb. No, not a good choice for the first cut of the day. First cut of a couple of years, in fact. He scanned the trees and settled on a midsize tree with no broken branches over six inches. That was the one to start with.

He flexed his fingers around the hilt and pulled the sword from the scabbard. The metal rang with a high note, the magic pushing to be free. Cor's energy soared instinctively to meet it. Golden magic flowed down the brown skin of his arm as green energy rose upward from the tip of the blade. The energies surged into a ball of light where Cor's fingers wrapped the hilt, then spread over the engraved metal, filling the lines until the twining branches and leaves glowed.

Leafbringer, the sword forged by Clarence the Courageous, was ready to work.

Cor bent his knees and sprang into flight. In the chosen tree-top, he hovered steadily, assisted by the power of the sword. Two-handed, he swung at a one-inch dangling limb. It fell, cleanly cut, but the stub brightened with magic that flickered angrily.

Hmm, out of practice. He aimed again and swung, this time making the cut flush with the trunk. The cut shone with the hue of his family's magic. The cambium layers drew together over the raw wood, then hardened to a new layer of bark in the blink of an eye.

The next swing was accurate. Two more and he no longer bothered checking. Leafbringer guided his aim.

Cor hovered over the tree, swinging Leafbringer, trimming out the damaged limbs. In a half hour, he'd finished. A touch of Leafbringer to the trunk assured him of that. He sought the next tree with the least amount of damage and attended to it, then completed another easy one before moving to one of the more damaged. Time to try a two-foot-diameter limb.

He selected one that had a nearby branch to brace against. He set his feet, raised the sword and brought it cleanly down.

The magical ringing echoed, followed by a long whistle. Cor turned.

Oyster was standing in a tree on the far side of the new clearing. "Spells upon us. That was... I have no idea what that was."

"Magic." Cor grinned, and when Oy came over, he told him how he'd gotten Leafbringer and showed how the sword worked.

"So...you're just letting the limbs crash down?"

Cor bit his lip. *The animals.* "In the interest of time, I thought... I guess I didn't think." He stared at the mess covering the forest floor.

Oy rapped his shoulder. "Admit it, you got drunk with power at the chance to use this amazing thing." He grinned.

"I did," Cor admitted. "This is what the sword was designed for, and believe me, it doesn't get used enough for it."

"In truth, I doubt the wildlife remained after the winds shook them, but I can remove any."

Oyster checked over an entire tree while Cor finished up smaller limbs that he could quickly check himself. Then they switched trees. It might have been that Cor's select-hover-and-aim technique was improving, but it seemed that the more Leafbringer cut, the easier the cuts became and the faster they healed.

Cor didn't know. His only other experience with a devastated area had been when he was eight and Hazel was nine. Their dad had been asked to bring Leafbringer after a storm in the Sherwood enclave, and they'd gone along. Dad had let them trim some of the easier hazels. Cor had barely been able to lift the sword. The sparkle in the handle hadn't been as bright as it had been for Hazel, and it'd taken him two swings to manage cuts of one-inch branches.

Those seemed like twigs in comparison to the branches he was dealing with now.

Cor paused to wait for Oy. They'd finished eight pines so far, a third of the damaged trees. Arms loaded with glowing pellets, Oy fluttered back, surveying the pretty pink magic coating a dangling bough before siphoning it off. He noticed Cor watching and winked.

Heat flushed Cor's chest and neck, and his hover faltered. A lot had changed since he was eight.

He flapped to regain his height, chose a limb and swung Leafbringer. They worked their way around the clearing as the sun rose and lit the center. It was an awful mess of woody debris. Hazardous, too. They avoided the leaning pine and anything else propped until they could talk to Ash. Cor tried not to think about the time and labor it would take for the area to be plantable again. He didn't know where to start—or even if Lady Pina would want it cleared. If she took a natural approach, it would all be left. Perhaps the logs could be nurse logs to host some of her many saplings? Regardless, he was starting to feel better—which meant the pines felt better.

"Where did you get that?" The shout of a high-pitched voice echoed after the ringing of the last healing, followed by the crash of the severed limb.

Cor lowered Leafbringer to his side and turned.

A mousy little witch with her hair pulled into a bun fluttered down with the fiercest expression Cor had ever been the recipient of. He wiped the sweat from his brow and pushed down his magic that was rising with his nervousness.

Two more frowning wizards backed her, a tall, middle-aged white warlock with graying hair and the thin man who had come to Lady Pina's house with the warning about the weather.

Oyster flew up, joining Cor before they completely closed in on him. "Sir Humus, I don't believe you've met Corylus. Cor, this is—"

"I know who he is," the tall wizard, Sir Humus, snapped. "I also know what this is." He pointed. "How did you steal the sword of Clarence the Courageous?"

Of course they'd assume theft when I—a black kid—have something valuable. "I didn't exactly steal it," he said, because he *had* snuck into the armory this morning.

Sir Humus looked both smug and horrified—like it was the answer he'd expected, but had been afraid of.

The mousy witch sniffed. "It's not yours, and you shouldn't have it here."

No, it wasn't his, and he supposed he should have filled out the tracer spells paperwork required to remove it from the armory. He'd conveniently skipped that in his excitement at being able to help Lady Pina. He'd figured he'd have it back before the estate opened for tours at one.

"I have permission to use it. Honest."

The two other wizards began countering this, but Sir Humus stopped them with, "Roda. Chinook." Alone, he hovered closer, landing on the same branch as Oy and Cor. "I canna allow our enclave," he said quietly, "or our magic to be complicit with deceit."

"But Lady Pina also gave me permission to help her."

Sir Humus waved a hand. "You told her of your complete plan? That you would trim her trees with Leafbringer?"

"No, I—"

"Then she didn't actually give you permission to do what you're doing."

Hell, if he wasn't allowed to speak—and his parents' rules were not to argue with elders—he saw no point in continuing. Cor plunged his hand into his pocket, grabbed the peregrinator and visualized Hillux. In three seconds, he was on the porch. He sheathed Leafbringer, twisting the hilt in the scabbard in toward his hip. The sword, scabbard and belt disappeared from view. He held out the peregrinator and brought up the link to the station in Bonterra. A backup of travelers delayed him enough that Sir Humus appeared, but Cor pereported before the elder could say anything.

Most of the station's travelers were making their way outgoing through the styles, likely for a day in the country. Cor nodded to the gatekeeper and strode from the building. At the estate, Barnaby hailed him. "Hazel forget something else?"

"I did this time." *Like, what a fool I am to think I could help someone and not be judged by my skin color.* "Thanks," he said automatically. "Say, what time is it?"

"Busy morning, huh? It's quarter past ten. Maybe you should pick up some lunch. You're looking a mite tired."

Lunch. That made the perfect excuse to be in the house,

though no docent staff would have arrived yet to question him. As he had earlier, Cor avoided the conservatory side and entered by a side door closest to the armory. Two short corridors and he was keying in the armory code and replacing Leafbringer safely on the wall.

In the kitchen, he found leftover croissant sandwiches from some catered event. He'd eaten half of one when the back door opened, and Master Harold walked in.

"You're back a day early."

"I needed something and was hungry. Only so many peanut butter and jelly sandwiches you can eat."

"Hazel?"

"Still there. She wanted to sleep in." Giving an eye roll at Master Harold's frown, Cor picked up an apple, too. 'I'm going back."

Master Harold handed him a container and gestured to the platter.

Once at Hillux, he made a second pereport to the chair on the cliff where he'd seen Lady Pina this morning. Having that mature conversation with her was long overdue.

She wasn't in the chair, so he headed for Oyster's home. *Hazel?* he asked quietly. *You up yet?*

She snorted in return.

What's that supposed to mean?

I'm fine if that's what you're asking.

The sarcastic way she said it started an uncomfortable feeling churning in his stomach.

Wherever you are, stay there, she said. *There's some discussion going on downstairs about finding you.*

His hand froze in reaching for the door. He had time to back up a step when it opened, and Lady Lark came out. Her gaze landed on him, her eyes widening.

HOLDING PATTERN

C or lurched back, but the wiry Lady Lark was as quick as her daughter. She clasped Cor's arm. Before he could protest, the cliffs and sea spun in a pereport that shifted to mountains, forests and fields. They landed on the front porch of her cottage.

"Come in," she said. "Quickly."

He decided to trust her. She closed the door behind them and waved a hand of flickering yellow-green sparks at it.

"Hey!" Had she locked him in? The windows sparkled in yellow-green, too.

"Concealment," said Lady Lark. "I knew the moment you returned to my land and left as soon as I could get away. Under the guise of fetching Fern."

"I'd like to talk to Fern, too." He stepped toward the bathroom.

"'Tis"—she looked at the ceiling—"half past three in the morning in Colorado. We will wake neither Fern nor Heather at this hour. Wouldn't go well since Heather closed the portal until you leave Giuthas, to prevent you from pestering Fern's friends again. You've caused enough of a stir, young man. There and here."

Freakin' bloody brilliant. He'd never be allowed back.

Lady Lark gestured him into the living room and pointed to the sofa. He sat. She perched on the edge of a chair and leaned forward, her face beaming with some sort of delight that he just didn't get.

"Mimosa and I are thrilled at the quick help for the plants, as are Ash and Merlin, but they have no vote on the council. Among Giuthas' council members, Lady Roda is outraged and has drawn her usual cohorts to her side, Mr. Chinook and Mr. Grouse. Humus holds his opinion unless a tie-breaker is necessary, and this time Dolph and Snap have taken neither side. Water wizards rarely comment on the tree issues, though they are directly affected by their loss, so that's a stance I have never understood."

She had skipped one person from their council. "What does Lady Pina think?"

"Learning you wielded the sword of Clarence—your sister assured her that it was—piqued her interest, and she consented to view the devastation in her habitat." Lady Lark laid a hand on his arm. "Your repairs have helped, but the loss has still taken its toll. She is resting before the ceremony this afternoon."

"What ceremony?"

"The End-of-Life Ceremony to release the magic of the dying trees, of course. You made a fair start on the work, Mimosa is saying."

"Didn't the released magic go back into the Pines?"

Lady Lark shook her head. "Pina has it redirected right now. So much flooded the enclave's resources that it drew Lady Roda from her early morning wildlife survey. What, did you think she turned up because of an interest in the pinewoods?"

"I'd never seen that witch—er, lady before," he muttered. "How was I supposed to know?"

"You wouldn't." Lady Lark gleefully relayed how rattled Lady Roda was at the energy coming from the Pines and what the rest of the council proposed doing with it.

"It's up to Lady Pina, isn't it?"

"Ultimately. A few hoped to sway her while this is in turmoil, but Humus put a stop to that talk just before I felt you here."

"Tall, white man, graying hair? He's in charge, not the mousy witch?"

"Most definitely."

Thank the Blessed Orb. Cor sagged back into the sofa.

Lark stood up. "You should rest. Have you eaten after your work?"

"I did. Hope you don't mind that I put a box of extra food into your refrigerator."

"Fine." She looked him over. "Use the shower if you like. I'd recommend not leaving the cottage, though, unless you'd like company before we head to the ceremony. Where is the sword everyone is talking about?"

"Took it back."

She huffed. "Probably for the best."

He showered and magicked over clean clothes in the backpack he'd left on Beri's hearth. He lay down while Lady Lark did some gardening. He thought he'd go to sleep, since he'd had so little last night, but he didn't. Hazel didn't want to talk to him, and she definitely didn't want to know where he was.

I can't tell anyone I don't know where you are if you tell me, so don't. I have completed the most stunning drawings of the coast, the river and their house, and Oyster has promised to accompany me around this tip of the island, so I must get going. Can I meet you at this ceremony?

He agreed—because any of his ideas seemed dodgy next to Lady Lark being willing to protect him.

Fern woke up feeling terrible. Why? It was Sunday, no alarm, no school. Rolling over, she punched up her pillow and pulled her comforter over her head again. Nothing she could think of was too bad. Beri had acted somewhat normal during Cor's testing yesterday, even expressing regret that Cor hadn't succeeded at his last test. Stewing about it in bed was no fun, so she gave in to her growling stomach.

Mom looked up from her perch at the kitchen bar, pencils tucked over her ear and paperwork spread before her. "Ah, here you are. Good morning. Sleep well?"

Mom didn't think to ask that unless something was up.

"Yeah?" Fern got a glass and poured herself some juice.

When she turned, Mom had pushed everything into the file and stood up. She wore a green linen dress—not work jeans, clothes she'd wear to the isle.

Yep, something was up. Fern grabbed a jar of peanut butter and a spoon to quickly get food in her stomach.

"Last night, several trees fell in a storm on Giuthas," Mom said.

Was that it?

"Scots pines."

OMG. "Not Cor's fault. Please tell me it wasn't his fault," she begged.

Mom told her as much as she knew from Gran, and it wasn't Cor's fault—thank goodness. "But the lad did some trimming early this morning that no one expected, that Mum and others are trying to smooth over. So..." She smiled a sort of grimace. "We should attend the energy-release ceremony and do our best to help with that smoothing."

The ceremony sounded like a funeral. Fern went back upstairs and changed into the embroidered green dress Gran had made her for the Council Gathering this summer. She scooped out a last spoonful of peanut butter and went with Mom through the portal.

In Gran's kitchen, Cor was washing up a huge soup pot. Measuring cups and an empty bag of sugar sat on the counter with ten filled quart canning jars.

"Hi," he said carefully. "Thought it'd help to have bee syrup on hand. It's sealed so it won't spoil before you can use it."

"That should last a month," Fern said.

"I hope so." Cor put the pot in the rack and dried his hands. Then he extended a hand to Fern.

She rolled her eyes and ate her peanut butter, ignoring his offer of a handshake.

He dropped his hand. "I suppose I don't blame you. How much have you heard about last night and this morning?"

Fern glanced at her mother. "Everything Gran knows. What else is there?"

Cor drew a breath. "Right, here's the deal, nothing hidden."

Lady Heather raised a finger. "Let Mum get in the house first."

The door was already opening and quickly closing with a sparkle of Gran's magic.

Fern bit her lip. Gran must not trust that her smoothing had worked. Cor was just as nervous, alternately stuffing his hands into his pockets and scratching his ear. Gran took the spoon and placed it in the sink.

Straightening, Cor brushed his hands down his leather jacket and held them at his sides. "My father is a many-times great-grandson of Clarence van Gruen, better known in Bonterra as Clarence the Courageous. My older sister, Hazel, is the direct heir, so she'll inherit his sword when our dad is gone. I got her permission to use Leafbringer this morning. So the sword is not *mine*, but yes, I can use it. Any blood relative can. No, I didn't get the correct permission when I took it this morning, but yes, we're allowed to take it from the estate and use it.

"I did ask Lady Pina if I could help her. She said yes and gave me the peregrinator when I asked. She knew I would use it to go to Bonterra. I just didn't tell her what I was going to get, and she didn't bloody care at that point. She's gutted by this. I wanted to help. I bloody am a tree freak. After working with her all week, I feel strongly about those woods. This..." He put a hand to his stomach. "This hurts. Maybe not as much as it hurts her, but it I felt those trees go down. By removing the damaged limbs and healing the pines in the most efficient way I could—that I daresay no one else here can match—the healing began. I wanted to give her that, and I did. Sorry that the others didn't like it and want me to leave. I will. I won't stay where I'm not wanted."

Fern glanced at Mom and Gran, but they were looking at her. "Is that all?" she asked Cor.

"Uh, no. I'm not after your friend Amanda. I'm gay and would rather get to know Oyster, but that's pointless if I'm not on the island, because he's not leaving. I told Beri that last night when he came to get Hazel and me during the storm. He's a good bloke, even if he does hate me, and I'm sorry for anything I did that came between the two of you. I'd like to dissolve the pledge now, because you've done all you can to get me a trial here, and I've done all I can to pass it, and it just isn't happening. *Now* will you shake my hand?"

Fern filled her channels and clasped it.

Cor's magic flowed over her fingers once more, but this time it pulled rather than pushed. After Fee's help, she could feel *and* see it loosen. The wisps of foreign magic slipped from her as Cor withdrew his hand.

She wiggled her fingers and flushed her channels again, searching them—wait, she could do that now? Yes. Her internal vision was much clearer. "Nothing extra there." She looked past her green energy to Cor's glum face.

"Again, I'm sorry," he said. "That might not be enough to undo the damage. Walking away from Lady Pina would have been better than having you affected, too."

"Thanks," she said. "I'll try to explain it to Beri again."

Beside her, Mom made the grumbled sound she made when she was annoyed that Fern still had something wrong. Fern turned to her. "What? He can't guess what's going on here, and neither can I."

"If Beri is not able to get over this, then he is not worth having in your life."

Fern frowned. "That's harsh, Mom."

"Oh?" Mom raised a brow. "Because if he went to retrieve a boy he supposedly hates in the middle of a storm, then he's over it." She turned to Cor. "As for you, you have a logical and true explanation for having that sword, and you didn't give it to the others?"

Understanding flashed over Cor's face, and he dropped his gaze. "No, ma'am. I walked away."

"Is that what your parents have taught you to do?"

"If I'm going to get into a racial argument, yes. Better for me to not annoy anyone than defend myself to deaf ears."

Lady Lark put her hand on his shoulder. "What led you to believe this was a prejudice against you because of your skin color?"

"That white witch with her hair in a bun didn't let me talk."

"Lady Roda," Mom and Gran said in unison.

"Believe me," said Fern, "if it was Lady Roda, it's not about your skin color. Or at least not completely."

"It is prejudice, but not the kind you assumed." Lady Heather clenched her fist. "She doesn't like anyone who does not hail from Giuthas and fit her ideal of magical perfection. Maybe that's something you need to learn to assess, though in fairness, you could never have guessed Lady Roda's reasoning. In her eyes, you had a second strike against you for being a plant wizard rather than tuned to animal magic. Your third strike was helping a little boy with magic lessons."

"But they wanted me to help him. They *asked* me to help—oh, that lady doesn't want him to have the help?"

"Lady Roda doesn't believe he should receive extra help or time to mature. I suspect she's afraid of being proven wrong if he improves."

"That's ridiculous. He's from here."

"He's not wizard enough." Fern grimaced. "Neither am I, in her eyes. But I got approved. You can, too, if you stick it out."

"Does it help to know a few people are on your side?" Mom asked.

Cor nodded, but unenthusiastically.

"Are you willing to repeat this to Lady Mimosa?" Gran asked.

"To the council?" Fern asked, with a glance at Gran. She nodded.

"He-heck, all of it?" He looked horrified.

Fern smiled her mischievous smile. "Skipping the part about Beri and me. No one knows about Amanda either." She paused a moment to let him stew. "And you and Oyster, of course."

Cor gave her a wry grin. "I'll give it a try."

Gran patted his shoulder. "Then we shall leave for the ceremony." Lady Lark pulled at a chain around her neck and held up her glass globe peregrinator. "I recommend we all go together."

As they exited the cottage, Cor handed Fern Lady Pina's sticklike peregrinator. "Now I can honestly say I don't have it anymore, but please don't leave me stranded. Hazel and I would like to go home as soon as I've given the council my version." He tugged his ear. "I just hope I can get through it without being interrupted."

"Mom will make sure that happens." But somewhere between arriving at the ceremony and its start, she had to find Beri. Her excitement of no longer being bound by this pledge was growing. *He'll be as excited, too.*

Fern? Beri said from somewhere nearby.

She turned to search across the Meadows, but didn't see him.

That was you, was it nae? Beri asked.

"Ohmigod." Fern pressed her fingertips to her temples. "Beri? You can hear me?"

"You don't need to shout to thought-speak," Cor said.

I can. You do nae need to shout. Beri was laughing.

She could hear it in his voice as clearly as if he was right beside her. She wanted to laugh, too, but she started crying instead.

"Meadowsweet?" Mom hugged her.

"He can hear me," she sobbed. Stupid, but geez, she'd worked so hard for this to happen. When she wiped her face, Mom and Gran were grinning.

Cor rapped her arm. "First time for that, huh? Congrats, girl." He put up his hand, and she high-fived him.

Where are you? Beri was saying. *I want to hug you so bad my arms hurt.*

"We…" *We're about to go to Lady Pina's. Can you meet us there?*

Already here. Arms waiting.

THE END-OF-LIFE CEREMONY

Whatever he'd thought would happen at a ceremony at the Pines, Cor didn't expect the grove to be crowded. After they'd landed on Lady Pina's patio, a wiry, gruff wizard in a suit ushered them along the path of tree cross sections before another wizard pereported in.

Wizards waited in small groups between the giant tree trunks, care taken not to step on the orchids and children held by their hands. Most were talking quietly in the late afternoon shadows and watching the house. Everyone was dressed up, as Fern and her mother were. He hadn't seen Lady Lark *not* in a dress, so hadn't figured anything was up.

In a crowd like this, his first thought was for Hazel *Where are you?* he asked as Beri fluttered his way around a group blocking the path. He led Fern across the needled ground toward the end of the log house, and Lark also scurried off. Fern's mum put a hand on Cor's arm that held him in place and made others veer their gazes away.

Behind a tree somewhere, Hazel answered. *With Oyster. Because you told him about my problem, he asked if I wanted to wait away from the others. Suppose it's not so bad having some people know.*

At least not Oyster.

I want to watch them conduct it, but can you wait for me so we can follow the others over?

You wait for me, too. I'm supposed to tell the council something with Fern.

All right.

He had to suppress a laugh when Fern came back around the end of the house. "You want to talk to them while you're glowing like that?"

Fern's cheeks turned from green to red, and she backhanded Beri in the chest. "Why didn't you tell me?"

"Ach, you're always that color to me." He clapped Cor on the shoulder. "Thanks, mate. Seems the trouble you got Fern into prompted Fee to give her magic-opening lessons the rest of us didn't think about."

"Maybe they'll help with flying," Fern said excitedly.

"Come along," Lady Heather said. "Mum has gathered the council members."

The group with Lady Lark headed for Lady Pina's house and filed inside. Lady Pina must be there, but where was Lady Mimosa? She was on his side, so if she wasn't a part of the group, then he would demand they wait. Or *ask* that they wait. But Lady Heather was holding the door and gesturing for them to *come on*. Beri hung back, and he and Fern entered.

To his relief, Lady Mimosa was already in the front room, standing beside a chair where Lady Pina sat, looking less haggard than she had this morning. But not by much.

Lady Roda stood by the fireplace, her arms crossed and two stern-looking wizards flanking her, the wizard with the wire-rimmed glasses from this morning and a younger, rotund warlock. Apart from everyone stood the tall, graying wizard who had challenged him this morning…Sir Humus.

The door closed with a thud.

"Thank you for agreeing to meet," said Fern, and Cor couldn't have been more startled.

It sounded like she'd called this meeting—she had suggested it, so maybe she had.

"I want to give Cor a chance to explain himself. This morning, he was exhausted from hours of magical work and caught off guard. He wasn't sure who he was answering to, and that's not fair. Please hear him out."

He managed to stumble through the same points. No one interrupted. He could say more, he supposed, about his family or his training, but in the end, he just stopped.

Beats of silence followed.

Lady Pina lifted her hand. "I concur. I gave the permission and the peregrinator. After a week of introducing his magic to the grove and having successful results, I put my trust in the lad. In hindsight, I'm not surprised Corylus is from the esteemed van Gruen family. He has a way with tree magic that I've seen in few others. He surprised us, but the healing has begun, and I am grateful."

Lady Roda stepped forward. "But the released magic is—"

"That is not why we are here," said Sir Humus. "I doubt any of us wish to delay what has to be done today. Fern asked us to hear out Corylus' story and we have. Pina has suffered a grave loss, and we shall not trouble her more with this. The meeting is adjourned." He nodded toward Lady Pina. "We will await your lead outside."

Lady Roda stormed out first, causing Cor to edge over and bump Fern. She rolled her eyes. He made sure to exit with her, and she led the way to Beri and another tall man who could only be Fern's father. People weren't saying much, so Cor didn't either.

Shadows had grown by the time Lady Pina opened her door and came out. Silence fell around the grove. She closed the door behind her and walked across her patio, looking neither left nor right. Lady Mimosa and Ash fell into step behind her, then their family. Kory saw him and gave a small wave. Cor waved back. People began to file in behind them, taking the stepping cross sections and then a winding path among the giant trunks.

Fern nudged Cor. "Gran wants to go."

"I need to wait for Hazel. She's with Oy, but I'm not sure where."

Beri looked around. Then lifted his chin. "Yonder. Walk with us, and I'll show you where."

Lady Roda had entered the procession earlier, so he went with them. *I'm headed your way,* he sent to Hazel.

At the rise, almost to the new clearing, Oyster and Hazel came out of the woods and joined them. Cor took Hazel's hand as he'd done since they were children and squeezed it reassuringly. He shot Oy a grateful smile. Maybe someday he'd be holding the hand of a fellow like Oyster.

Ahead, people filled in a wide viewing arc that had been cleared at the side of the ailing giant. He assumed Lady Pina must be in the center, closest to the tree, but he wasn't tall enough to see. The sun had dropped below the treetops, leaving the clearing in shadow. Dusk, the perfect time for an End-of-Life Ceremony.

Everyone became still, waiting.

"Now the time has come." Lady Pina sang the familiar stanza. "To let lifetimes of building free." She drew a breath before continuing. "Let loose, release, set free your burdens, tree."

A glow of energy shot up the pine's trunk, met the branches and split, flying to the smaller limbs and dividing more and more until each needle was alight.

It was an awesome sight.

Lady Pina began the stanza again, and this time the energy rose and fell, twisted and turned with her words. Cor had heard her sing this release stanza in person only a few times. If those had been the only times he'd heard it, he might not have noticed the nuances that created the releases. Because one of those renditions had been for his recording, the tune seemed etched into his soul. Yet, hearing it now as she mourned the loss of her giant, emotion filled the tune in a way that had been missing when she'd sung it simply as a lesson.

He had to confirm how her energy came from her hands, to see exactly which wiggles went with which words. Pulling Hazel along, he edged around folks and came to one side of the semi-circle. Lady Pina stood in clear view, her eyes closed, her hands raised as she began another round.

She sang. He joined her in his head, studying the mournful, swaying flow of her energy. She ended the stanza and started again. He caught on to it by the end. By the third time, he knew what he'd done wrong in his test yesterday. He'd lacked the depth of emotion, but also the intent. This was the opposite of the growing stanza that depicted energy going in. This was energy loosening and leaving, just as the words said.

"Now the time has come," Lady Pina sang again.

The tree was alight with her bark-orange magic, and the sky had darkened enough that the light could be seen withdrawing from the needles. They looked like candles extinguishing. Then the twigs began to pull in their light, and the clearing dimmed noticeably.

"Now the time—" The song broke on a sob.

Cor held his breath as others gasped. Lady Pina pressed a hand to her forehead and shook with silent sobs. Lady Mimosa put an arm around her.

"Ach, this is nae good," said a wiry wizard beside them. The older man who had met them on the patio was speaking to a middle-aged man who was a younger version of himself. "If she canna sing it together, the magic 'twill be stuck."

The energy had stilled over the tree, the light in the twigs frozen. She had time to regain her composure and start again.

That would be hard. He felt awful for her. Should he help? He did know the song.

A small girl tugged at the older wizard's hand. "You do it, Grandpap Snap. You sing the song."

"I dinnae know the song, lassie. 'Tis a Pines song."

Lady Mimosa would know it—but when Cor pivoted toward her, she was in a whispered huddle with Sir Humus and Lady Pina, and Lady Pina didn't seem to be answering them.

He glanced up the length of the tree. The energy was holding…he thought? A twinkling seemed to have started—

"*Somebody* needs to do *something*," the little girl said.

Right, somebody did. He looked at Lady Mimosa, at Ash, at Willow. Why weren't the Forests stepping in?

Dry needles crunched behind him. Oy had come over, and Fern with Beri. They stood beside Hazel, looking at him expectantly.

Kory pushed between them and tugged at his arm. "Lady Pina has trained you, Mam said. You need to sing the song for the pine."

He shook his head. "I didn't succeed in my test, so I won't be able to loosen the magic."

"Did you invite it out?"

Kory's innocent question made Cor hesitate. No, he'd been trying to *take* the magic from the tree. "Good point, little man. I have not been inviting the magic out." He'd helped Kory work through his problems, and here the boy was returning the favor and boosting his confidence.

"Often, the magic is somewhat stuck in its ways," Beri said, "looping old habits. But if the opportunity to try something new presents itself, we can direct wayward magic to new roles."

Cor narrowed his eyes at him. "You must know this song. You apprenticed in the Pines."

Beri shrugged one shoulder.

Oyster nudged Cor. "You worked with the habitat the most recently. You're the one who should do it."

He'd said *do it*, not *try*. That Oyster believed he could surged Cor's confidence further.

Beri gave a nod of agreement. Fern, gripping his hand, nodded, too.

Cor squatted down to face Kory. "Will you do it with me?"

Mouth parting, Kory turned toward the fallen pine "I can't do that."

"But you'll ask with me, when it's time?"

Kory swallowed and nodded.

Cor straightened. *Sorry,* he said to Hazel. *Could you guard my back if this turns ugly?*

He didn't wait for her answer, but took Kory's hand. This time, they boldly walked in front of folks. He put his hands to the trunk. Kory copied him, scrunching up his face. Cor's hands flushed with gold energy and his magic found the blue-green within the trunk.

"Now—" Cor's first note wavered in the silence. He closed his eyes against people's stares and started again. "Now the time has come, to let lifetimes of building free. Let loose, release, set free your burdens, tree."

33

HOLDING TREE ENERGY

By the third round of stanza singing, Cor had touched every bit of power in the giant, just as he had with his test pine. But unlike that smaller tree, the energy in this giant was freakin' incredible. He felt like a toddler at the petting zoo who had asked to hold a python, then couldn't keep all the moving parts from slipping from his grasp.

No one had pulled him off or yelled, so he plowed ahead. He'd collected the energy from the twigs, the smaller branches and finally the large limbs, even those spiked into the ground. The root energy was there. Everything roiled around the heartwood, the exact position where he'd been stymied yesterday—and this one contained a hundredfold the amount of energy.

He blinked his eyes open. Time to make this his best bloody effort. Cor looked down, and Kory met his gaze.

"It's time to invite the energy to go on?" asked Kory.

Without halting the Energy Song, Cor nodded.

"Tree?" Kory said. "We have new work for you on the isle. Would you please let Cor show you where that is?"

That was a fair enough invitation. Cor had decided to echo the message when the magic in the heartwood flared.

"Ohhh," Kory said. "I think—did you do that?" he asked accusingly.

Cor shook his head.

Kory smiled. "Then it agreed."

He thought so, too, but Cor sang another stanza, adding his own, "Come along, please."

The magic snapped to his. He had no other way to describe the feeling of it being on its own, then completely within the control of his energy—his *meager* energy in comparison.

At some point, he'd known that Hazel had come to stand behind him, but more rustling sounded, and someone whispered. Hazel moved, and someone tall shifted closer to Cor. He didn't like taking his attention from the energy, but a stolen glance confirmed it was Fern.

With his acknowledgment, she leaned in. "Lady Pina is making her way over. She asks that you wait for her before continuing."

Fern disappeared. A stanza later, the rustling sounded again.

She is here, Hazel sent him.

He stumbled over a word and dropped a note, but managed to continue without breaking the flow. The magic sat complacently within his grasp.

"This one I wish to release to the grove," Lady Pina whispered. "I will help you let it loose."

Of course she wanted it here. She'd worked so long with it. Understanding, he nodded and continued the song. He automatically began another stanza. It seemed to be echoing, then Lady Pina's voice grew stronger with his.

Her hand closed over one of his and one of Kory's, then her magic joined his in holding the collected energy. She nudged him to lift it from the trunk.

The pine's magic streamed through the heartwood and burst from the crown like fire. People gasped, its light shining on their faces and casting the farther trees and debris into shadows. At first, it was thrilling, majestic to watch…and then it became rather daunting. The magic was tumbling, boiling and seemed barely contained. Were they actually controlling that massive energy?

They'd never talked about this. What next?

She sang, so he sang, and the tree magic took the shape of the standing tree as it had been, replicating the branch angles and the lightning scar. Then Lady Pina squeezed his hand, and they slowed the tempo of a stanza, ending on a melancholy, "…set free your burdens, tree." She drew their hands from the trunk as their last notes faded.

The cloud of energy hovered, its silhouette bright and still. The clearing was silent, everyone watching. A slight contraction shuddered through the magic, and it broke into twinkling bits that hung in the sky.

The beauty of it took his breath away. The spectacle became even more enchanting as the bits began spinning in lazy spirals. Beside him, Hazel gasped and Lady Pina sighed. Kory laughed. The sparks floated outward and downward, landing in the tree-tops and flaring with long flashes before disappearing like a drawn-out firework.

Then they were gone.

"Thank you," Lady Pina whispered. "If you would be so kind as to release the other trees, I would appreciate it." She patted Kory's shoulder, then hugged Cor before she turned him toward the elders from the council now standing behind them.

Lady Roda's jaw was slack with awe. Cor nearly cheered.

"Someone may collect the energy of the other pines for the isle's shielding," Lady Pina said. "The difference is you keep singing until they have it under their direction." She handed him his mobile. "Interesting recordings you have here. Especially the one you made this week."

Bloody blast it—she'd heard herself singing the Energy Songs?

Before he could ask, she walked away through the dark pinewoods.

———

Standing hand in hand with Beri, Fern watched the awesome power of Cor singing the magic from the second fallen pine into another dazzling tree cloud. Lady Mimosa accepted the energy cloud and flew, pushing it before her, up out of the clearing and westward. A number of wizards accompanied her, and Gran kept those remaining from interrupting or intimidating Cor, while Dad fed him and Kory warm spinach-and-cheese pasties.

As the last pine began to drain of energy, Fern leaned into Beri and whispered, "Could you have done this?"

"Maybe." He grinned without looking at her. "But is it nae more impressive to have a new fellow, one you brought to the isle, have the honor?"

"Well, yeah… Hey, was that in your head all along, to get the elders impressed by Cor so they'll like him?"

"I have known them much longer than you have." He shrugged one shoulder. "Lady Pina needs the help that I no longer have time to give. And you do nae exactly have the time or skills to be tutoring Kory. Not this year, at least, with your insistence on us attending your school."

She swatted him in the belly with a splash of green sparks. "You made your own choice to come to Boulder High." *But I'm glad you did,* she added.

Me, too. His hand tightened around hers.

"Beri?" Gran bustled up to them. "Mimosa and the Forests have enough to do directing the application of the first energy to the rip. Would you be willing to ferry this cloud to them?"

He smiled. "Only if you make sure Fern can get there to see it arrive and be used."

Gran thought for a moment, then produced Lady Pina's peregrinator from her pocket. "Heather will have to take her."

"But, Gran…" Fern leaned down to her ear. "Mom has been in a stare-off with Lady Roda, the only reason she hasn't tried to bypass you to bug Cor."

"I ken, but as soon as Beri moves the energy, Lady Roda will follow, none too pleased that I have selected a *youth* to do this." Gran winked. "Just in case, take Cor and Hazel with you as soon as Beri leaves. And Kory. I promised Mimosa we'd watch the boy."

It happened just as Gran said. As soon as the tree cloud had formed, her tiny grandmother slid up to Cor, had a word with him, and Beri took her place before anyone noticed. He shifted the energy into his control as fast as Lady Mimosa had, from what Fern could tell, and took flight with it. He was at the level of the treetops before Lady Roda realized what had happened and took off after him. Mom started giggling like a middle schooler, despite Dad hushing her.

Fern leaped over and around several downed branches and took her arm. "You're taking me and the others," she said and guided Mom toward Gran, who had Kory by the hand and was shepherding him, Cor and Hazel to meet them.

"How long have they been at this game anyway?" she muttered to Mom.

"I canna say." Still smiling, Mom wiped away her tears. "But it sure makes returning to the isle interesting."

They landed in the woods at the same rip Dad had taken her to two weeks ago. She'd known the wizards were still trying to close it, but geez, this was taking forever. As before, the yellow magic of the Forests held the sides, and the ice-blue magic of the Streams covered the tumbling water. But now, the section of mismatched broken boulders, where the boundary had been ripped, undulated with a blue-green glow. The opening was shorter—hooray—perhaps a dozen feet long.

The islanders crowded the rip, stationed around it, hands held to the magic and waiting. Kory joined his family, and so did Gran and Mom. She might not want to practice magic, but she'd never refuse her friend—and the exhausted Lady Mimosa had clearly beckoned her over. Fern waited back at the tree line with Cor and Hazel, holding to her own magic as the electric snap in the air grew.

The energy cloud appeared like an alien ship above the tree-tops. It came to a stop, hovering...with Beri at one end. Using both hands, he shook the energy, just as she'd done with a huge parachute in gym class. It lengthened and narrowed, the magic flowing upward to make it taller—ah, he was reshaping it so it would fit down among the trees. When Beri stopped, seemingly satisfied with the shape, it looked like a...round-cornered cereal box?

Cor leaned toward her. "Your bloke—Beri. He. Is. Bloody. Brilliant."

"He's so kind to let Cor have another chance tonight," Hazel said. "Especially after Cor annoyed him. I admit I'm often not as forgiving." She rolled her eyes.

Cor lightly punched her arm. "Again, sorry for being an ass."

Beri *was* great, Fern thought. But you'd never know that from talking to him. Sheesh. *This is his thing, not school or grades. I will never pester him again about homework or missing class or taking a* rumspringa *break. He needs to be here, doing this.*

"Ready," Beri called.

Six wizards flew up, Dad among them. They grasped the perimeter of the cloud and began flying the energy down. As they did, those along the rip sprang into action. The yellow energy peeled back, the ice-blue stacked over it. Within the exposed hollow lay a boiling pit of blue-green Pines energy. The new cloud lowered to it, Beri guiding it.

"This is certainly more than we need to finish the seal," Lady Mimosa called. "Yet this has been a stubborn rip, so we'll use it all. Hold the edges close while he releases it, then keep a grip on them after it's in, until we complete the seal."

So this was like healing over a cut? Well, this was one massive bandage to do it.

At Lady Mimosa's wave, Beri fluttered down and laid a hand on the energy. It rippled, and the disturbance moved downward until, at the bottom, a gap opened. Energy poured out. Some spilled across the ground. The kids ran squealing to chase it back—and Fern's palms itched to join them. Problem was, no one had invited her…and her parents worked too far off to ask.

Most of the energy flowed into the rip. The hollow filled. The jutting boulders settled into their places. The torrent of water slowed into a smooth stream, and the Streams wizards shoved their energy over the water. A mirrorlike, blue surface formed in places, but still pockets of Pines energy still winked along the rip. Right behind them, Mimosa, Ash, Willow, Raven, Gran, Mom and others swept the Forests' yellow energy forward. It moved faster than fog, swirling as it surrounded the blue-green.

Still, the rip burbled and splashed energy. People yelled back and forth, using their own energies to push the Forests' energy. A geyser of blue-green erupted—feet from where Fern stood with Cor and Hazel.

"Catch it," Lady Mimosa shouted.

She was looking at them.

Wings unfurling, Cor leaped forward, hands dripping with honey energy to dam over an escaping flow. With only a second's hesitation, Hazel ran and swung her arms, hands together as if holding a golf club. A shaft of gold sprang from her underhanded swing to smash back another rivulet.

Fern ran, too, a massive ball of her energy forming… But should she toss it? Touch the other energy? Protect herself in some way?

No one has told me how to do this!

Think of a way to block it, Beri said. *Touch it only with your energy.*

The image of dense, strangling vines popped into her head—and her energy splintered. Dozens of vines cascaded from her hands and streamed across the ground, flushing new leaves. She threw it at the bubbling geyser—half wishing it would get sucked in and disappear. It landed over the hole like a medusa head and stoppered it.

People craned to see what had happened, still swooshing the yellow energy over the rip. Her circling plant collected mist, too, squeezing up the yellow energy between its bright green leaves and arm-sized vines. The vegetation forced the rip edges together—and several wizards jumped the streambanks to get out of the way.

Fern had stuttered to a standstill, her fear that any second someone would ream her out warring with pride at what she'd done.

Beri glided over the mirrorlike water, landed and threw an arm around her shoulders. "You can direct it to hold still now."

She did, still expecting Lady Roda to yell and desperately glad Beri was beside her. Amid the flurry of activity that closed off the one remaining section of the rip, Lady Mimosa and a Streams wizard flew overhead. They cast shots of magic onto the banks and water, making them shimmer.

"Withdraw your energies," Lady Mimosa called, and Beri gestured to a vine.

Stomach flipping, Fern stepped forward with a dozen others and touched a finger to her magic. It retreated with a thought, thank goodness.

Beneath the disappearing energies, the ground looked normal. Sir Humus strode up and down it, as did Lady Mimosa and the Streams wizard. They put their heads together for a quick discussion, then Sir Humus announced, "The rip is sealed!"

Everyone whooped and congratulated each other. Fern weathered a few comments that sounded like congratulations, but were more like, "Didn't realize you had other skills." Duh, did they not see that hers was still plant magic? Then she was ready to go. Cor and Hazel had been hanging back, but clearly waiting for her.

She edged to Beri's side. "I need to pereport Cor and Hazel home. Can you help me?"

He rubbed the back of his neck. "Unfortunately, that truly is a skill better left to your mother."

34

BLOODY BEST ENERGY EVER

Bonterra City

Late Monday evening, Cor returned to the conservatory after dinner. He plucked dead leaves off the plants and, for something to do, brought out the hose. Hazel had left for her art program. Aunt Syl had gone to bed, and he thought Master Harold had, too. He'd taken a long flight over the grounds with Toots swooping circles around him until she'd left to hunt.

He was bored. After the past two weeks, who wouldn't be?

With a sigh, he stuck the hose nozzle into the pot of a foot-high tamarack larch he'd ordered from Canada. Master Harold had found and watered many of his seedlings, but this one was high on a sunny support beam and well hidden from the main path's sight.

He turned the tree. It looked terrible, branches on the window side losing their narrow leaves and a flush of energy showing the cambium had nearly cut off those spurs. He flicked off the faucet with a shot of magic and headed for the green-house to get it a dose of worm tea then settle it under a mister.

The door reopened behind him. "Cor?" asked Master Harold. "Barnaby says you have visitors at the gate."

His energy leaped. "Me?"

"Lady Pina and Lady Mimosa, Fern, Beri and…Oyster?" Master Harold's gaze dropped to the tree, and he reached for it. "Best give me that."

Cor looked down and winced. The tufts of foliage shone the gold of his magic rather than their normal blue-green. He shoved the pot into his boss' hands. "So…I'll be going down to meet them." He hurried for the door.

Why were they here? Was it a social call, or something more? Bloody freakin' spells, he hoped it was something more. Why else would the ladies come all this way? Oh. It could be about his Energy Song recordings. But at night and with Oyster? At the door, he turned back. "You think—would it be all right if I bring them around to the conservatory?"

Harold joined him, and they walked out. "They're here for a tour? This late at night?"

"I don't know. Aunt Syl has gone to bed, so I hate to take them to the cottage."

Master Harold patted Cor's back. "Take them into the house, m'boy. I'll put the kettle on. The parlor?"

That was so…formal. *He* wasn't comfortable in there. "The breakfast nook."

"I'll call Syl."

"I'm not sure…can we just wait until I find out what they've come for?"

His flight to the gate was the longest ever in his head… Would he be accused of something? Asked to return? If they wanted him to return, why wasn't the head bloke here? And why was *Oyster* here?

In reality, the flight was quick. Nerves made him flap hard. He swept beneath the arching rowans and landed near the entrance to the estate. He'd walk the last hundred feet to the gate. He wiped his brow, then his hands on his gym shorts—oh damn, he should have changed clothes.

Too late. Fern had spotted him over Barnaby's shoulder and waved.

Everyone else turned.

What should he say?

Nothing, for spells' sake! Safer to say nothing. Invite them in, that was it. *They* had come to talk to him.

He hoped.

Barnaby had already signed in everyone, but had him verify he knew these wizards before opening the gate and ushering them through. The ladies wore their long dresses, Beri and Oy trousers and homespun shirts, Oy's tucked in and more trim looking with a belt. Cor refused to look at himself... Gray T-shirt and shorts. *Looking good, Cor.*

At least Fern was wearing jeans and a T-shirt.

She poked his shoulder. "You could look happier to see us."

"I am," he mumbled. "I just wasn't—surprised, that's all. Please, won't you come up to"—he gestured down the drive, realizing what he was saying—"the house?" He took a few steps and checked if they were coming.

Oyster's gaze was fixed far beyond, on a long garden view that Cor knew well, one in shadows now, but still leading to a castlelike building. His eyes widened. "You live there?"

"Not exact—sort of." He drew a breath. The truth. "My parents own the Gruen Estate, but we don't live here full time. And not in the estate house." He began walking.

Fern blocked his way. "Your parents aren't dead?"

"No?"

"You cut me off when I asked about them, and every other time it was, 'My aunt this and my aunt that.' I assumed your parents were gone."

"Aunt Syl is in charge right now. Hazel and I are staying with her while our parents travel for the foundation."

"Are you rich, then?" Fern asked bluntly.

"It's all tied up in the foundation, and Dad has never allowed us to get things based on the family name. We have to earn everything ourselves. That's why I never said anything. He'd make me start again. Somewhere else."

They were all staring at him.

He started to cross his arms—no, too much attitude. "Does my family matter?" He sidestepped Fern and gestured in his tour docent manner again, but this time Lady Pina put up a hand.

"Do your parents know you came to the Isle of Giuthas?"

"Yes. Getting their permission was nearly as difficult as..." He'd been about to say *getting yours*.

Lady Mimosa's hand slid over his shoulder and rubbed his back. "Thank you for being truthful. Didn't you invite us in?" she asked. "I should like to be able to see everyone for this conversation. And perhaps sit?"

He nodded. How could he not? Her motherly touch reassured him as much as her hint that this was something he'd want to hear.

Cor led the way up the drive, in an awkward silence that, as host, should have been his job to diffuse. "Clarence planted these rowans back in the 1800s when the belief was that they provided protection against intruders." He winced. That bit from the tour had popped out automatically.

"Two hundred years and counting," Beri said softly. "That's very good care."

Beyond the rowans, Lady Mimosa commented on the silver birch, and Cor wasn't able to stop himself. He babbled facts about them, the oaks, sycamores and yews.

"No common hazel?" Lady Pina asked.

"Of course," he answered. "A copse shelters the cottages. Would you like to see them?"

"Yes," she said, but Lady Mimosa took her arm.

She nodded toward the house. "Discussion first."

"Very well, but I wish to see the stand because it's quite curious that both children would be named for the same species."

Cor laughed. She had caught on to their names as bloody few others did. "That's the van Gruen tradition for each generation. My dad is Pinus. Aunt Syl is Sylvestris, and their brother is Scot, all representing the Scots pine. Do you understand now why I'm so keen to work with your trees?"

As they arrived at the front, the inside guard opened both front doors, and Cor's nervousness crept back.

"Tea… Would you like tea?" he clarified. "Let's go to the kitchen."

Clamping his lips closed on bits of the house tour, he led them straight back. Harold had left the teapot brewing on the breakfast nook table with mugs. Cor served, got sugar and cream and found a box of biscuits in the cupboard, along with a stack of paper napkins that didn't seem overly fancy. Still, he couldn't meet Oy's gaze and found himself tugging at the diamond stud he'd put back in his left ear this morning. Damn. He dropped his hand back to his mug.

Well, they'd had plenty of chances to see it and to comment.

Fern finished a biscuit and pushed back her untouched tea. "Could we get on with this offer for Cor?"

An offer? No one else had mentioned that.

She flashed him a smile. "No offense, but I have homework tonight, and you look like you need to know what's going on."

He reached for his ear again, then dropped his hands to grip the edge of the table. "Right, I was wondering."

Lady Mimosa sighed and lowered her mug. "This is a good blend. But yes, of course." She looked at Lady Pina.

Setting her own mug aside, Lady Pina cleared her throat. "You worked hard to master my lessons. Using your technology to record my songs was a technique I never considered using in training. A good lesson for an old-fashioned lady."

Cor smiled. She hadn't considered it blasphemous.

"Last night, your confidence in stepping up to complete the ceremony demonstrated the type of spiritual steadiness I am looking for in an apprentice. I wish to offer you an apprenticeship with the Pines. This is not a guarantee of permanent acceptance onto the Isle of Giuthas, but a one-year trial to train with me, at the end of which your work will be assessed by the council."

Beri leaned in to face him. "'Tis how all apprenticeships run."

"You might not achieve the level required in that year," Lady Mimosa added, "but if you show adequate progress, the trial will be extended. I also would like to offer you a position teaching my son Kory. We can't pay you in trade credit, but we can pay you in food stores and a weekly invitation to dinner with the family."

Lady Pina tapped the table. "You would have to live in the main grove to properly bond with the habitat. None of this flying in from another part of the island."

Cor nodded. It'd be freakin' brilliant to wake up every morning with a view of the sea from a Scots pine.

Lady Pina nodded back. "There are two rooms separate from the rest of the dwelling at the end of my log home. They've been used for storage since my bachelor uncle passed when I was a child. It's quite rustic, but if you decide to take the position…" She looked at him expectantly.

Had he not answered? Everyone was looking at him. "Yes," he said quickly. "I accept. Both positions. Whatever the arrangements are."

Fern snickered. "No doubt in my mind he'd do it."

"You're sixteenth year," Lady Mimosa said. "Will your parents agree?"

"They know how much I want an apprenticeship in a forest, but they will want to review my living arrangements, who's supervising me and so forth."

"We can certainly review everything with them," Lady Pina said.

The nervous energy of the last fifteen minutes and the disappointment of the last two days peaked like Vivaldi's crescendo in his head. He'd done it. He, Corylus Avellana van Gruen, had landed the job of a lifetime. Well, almost. But he would. He could feel it in his magic. And his head was clearing enough that he realized he was sharing a silly grin with Oyster.

Oh. That sobered him. "These offers for food and a place to live will reassure them," he said while thinking quickly.

"In a few days, I'll have things sorted and would welcome a visit from your parents," Lady Pina said.

"Meantime," Beri said, "I'll let you use the hollow."

"Right, I, uh…" Cor tugged at his earring. Blast, this might be the freakin' bloody end of her brilliant offer, but after this weekend, he knew his magic wouldn't work right it if he wasn't truthful about this to everyone. "Another thing for you to consider." His gaze met Lady Pina's. "I'm gay. I told Oyster Saturday. If I return to Giuthas with you, Oyster and I will be seeing each other. I hope you don't have a problem with that."

"Well. That explains his insistence on accompanying us. I thought he was concerned for my safety." Lady Pina looked down her nose at Cor. "Yes, that will be a problem—one I will put to Oyster to remedy. I cannot stand Sedge's current grousing about the lad's future, and with this addition, she will be unbearable." She pointed at Oyster. "Tell her I have offered to let you move into the Pines."

He grinned. "Have you?"

Was this some sort of running joke? Cor held to the table, waiting for them to withdraw the apprenticeship offer or make it contingent on keeping it secret he was gay.

"You will have to build a shelter. That means you will have no time for your Estuary duties this autumn, perhaps through the winter." Lady Pina patted her lips with her napkin and then folded her hands over it on the table, her lips twitching.

"Spells, Mother will be beside herself."

"The only thing I can think of that will get her to agree to keep her mouth closed on the subject."

"Excellent." Oyster was still grinning, and then, with a twinkle in her eye, Lady Pina was, too.

Cor looked from one to the other. "I don't get it. Or maybe I do. You don't care that I'm gay, just that Oy's mother quits harping on it?"

"Correct," Lady Pina said.

He turned to Lady Mimosa. "Do you still want me to teach Kory?"

She smiled with tears in her eyes. "More than anything."

Lady Pina stretched out a hand and covered Fern's. "Do we have time for a quick look at this hazel copse?"

She shrugged. "Fifteen minutes?"

"It's just out back." Cor jumped up and keyed in the code to release the alarm as they got to their feet. When he opened the door, a brown shadow swept inside.

Fern ducked. "Ohmigod. An owl!"

Cor pursed his lips and whistled. Toots zeroed in on him and landed on his outstretched arm. "This is Toots. She's a tawny owl born on the estate this spring."

"Is she your pet?" Fern asked.

"She isn't exactly, but I didn't realize until I returned how attached she's become to me. She hatched last, and I fed her extra so she'd make it." He eyed Lady Pina. She didn't seem flustered by Toots' appearance. "Would you...might I bring her with me to the isle? Bonterra is getting crowded with owls."

She turned to Beri. "Is there space?"

He cocked his head while his eyes flicked like he was listening… "Aye, Merlin says another owl would help with the rabbit issue in Upper Meadows, if she can be convinced to hunt there."

Cor fist-bumped with Beri. "Thanks, mate."

After admiring Toots, Lady Pina and Lady Mimosa headed down the path. Fern and Beri followed, holding hands. Oyster lingered outside the door, while Cor turned out the lights and reset the keypad.

Could he put his arm around Oy? Or maybe hold hands with him like Fern and Beri were? The alarm began flashing. Spells, he'd fumbled the code. He pushed the buttons again, slowly, and huffed when the green light flashed.

He turned. "I tell you, technology—"

Oy bent and kissed him. It was a light brush of lips, then he stepped back. His eyes searched Cor's.

"I, uh…" Cor swallowed, staring at the tumble of curls backlit into a halo over Oyster's head. "That's a brilliant welcome."

Oy smiled hesitantly. "I'd like to make it better, but…that was my first time kissing anyone."

"Mine, too." His fingers twitched, because all he had to do was reach up and he'd learn if Oy's wayward hair was as soft as it looked. Instead, he smiled and knocked his knuckles to Oyster's hand, opening his own. Oy glanced down and threaded their fingers together.

Gold and pink glows blossomed from their hands, swirling up their forearms. Oyster laughed, and Cor tugged him through the garden. "Plenty of time now to learn everything."

AUTHOR'S NOTE

The Scots pine, *Pinus sylvestris*, is a real tree species. It is the national tree of Scotland, a long-lived and tall tree species that has only survived in small numbers across its original range. In Gaelic, it is known as *giuthas*.

Many plants and animals are associated with Scots pine forests. When I noted specific ones in the story, they were correct. Beyond that, I have taken many fantastical liberties with the Scots pine. In 2009, I visited the redwoods and had the first seed of an idea for this story. In 2016, I visited the sequoias and knew I had to finish it. Then I read *The Wild Trees*, in which Richard Preston described the Scots pine as one of the taller, 300-year-old species he had climbed during his research adventures. I knew I had found the basis for my trees in the UK setting of my Windborne series.

The island became the Isle of Giuthas, the Isle of Pines, for the special groves growing there. In my mind, these trees had to be as tall as redwoods and as broad as sequoias to house my characters, and their magic massive enough to inspire even wizards. It wasn't long before Cor came along and insisted he must have a place among these ancient pines.

Thank you, Richard Preston, for your inspiration.

ACKNOWLEDGMENTS

I wanted to write more about Fern and Beri but had hesitated until Clarissa asked me what happened to them next. Thank you so much, sweetie!

Thank you to the best big-picture beta reader ever, Allison! You have made this story flow so much better.

My life is enriched with diverse friends and family, but for the first time I've written a main character far afield from my background. My grateful thanks go to my sensitivity readers, Rashad and Kamari. Any remaining mistakes are my own.

The odds and ends of blurbs and covers are always a trial. My thanks to Leeyanne, Karen, Em, Julie, Jessica, Jen and Andy for bearing through revisions. Thank you, Nancy and Lucy, for beta reads, and Joyce, for your stellar editing.

I couldn't survive any of this without the support of my dear husband, Bill. Love you always!

ABOUT THE AUTHOR

Before kids, Laurel Wanrow studied and worked as a naturalist —someone who leads wildflower walks and answers calls about the snake that wandered into your garage. During a stint of homeschooling, she turned her writing skills to fiction to share her love of the land, magical characters and fantastical settings.

She's the author of *The Luminated Threads* series, a Victorian historical fantasy mixing witches, shapeshifters and a sweet romance in a secret corner of England, and *The Windborne*, a nature-focused YA fantasy series set in our world.

When not living in her fantasy worlds, Laurel camps, hunts fossils, and argues with her husband and two new adult kids over whose turn it is to clean house. Though they live on the East Coast, a cherished family cabin in the Colorado Rockies holds Laurel's heart.

Visit her website at www.laurelwanrow.com.

facebook.com/laurelwanrowauthor

twitter.com/laurelwanrow

instagram.com/laurelwanrowauthor

bookbub.com/authors/laurel-wanrow

pinterest.com/laurelwanrow